Murder in the Hollows

A Jake Cashen Novel

32P2YM

Declan James

ONE

One of Judge Sampson Rand's bad habits would kill him tonight. But not the obvious ones. Not the pipe he smoked that caused a malignant spot on his lung he didn't yet know was there. Not the artery-clogging poutine and burgers he secretly binged four nights a week even though he swore to everyone else he'd gone vegan. No. Tonight, his death would come because of his Friday evening habit of listening to Puccini at a deafening decibel level, oblivious to the world as he sat in his recliner, sipping a martini, and smoking his pipe, puffing perfect rings into the air.

Judge Rand didn't hear the front door open. The one he kept unlocked because no one, not even the delivery drivers, could easily find him at the end of his half-mile, winding driveway through the hundred-year oaks.

The man came quietly through the front door. Knowing it wouldn't be locked. Knowing the rising strains of an Italian opera from the man-cave at the back of the brick ranch house meant the judge had just finished his first martini. He would not get to have a second.

He stepped softly, careful not to let his wet shoes squeak on the tile kitchen floor, not that the judge would even hear it. The judge sat with his back to him in his leather recliner, his hands poised above him as he waited for the next aria to begin. He would wave his arms like a conductor, his eyes closed, murmuring as if he truly understood the words.

The man raised his Colt .45, aiming it at the back of the judge's head. That would be easy. One shot. Judge Rand would never feel it. He would just be gone. Clean. Instantly fatal. Merciful.

But that's not why the man was here.

He slowed his breathing, quieting the adrenaline rush he knew should come. Judge Rand began to sing off-key. He stared straight ahead, admiring the wooded landscape that was his backyard in peak, Southern Ohio fall.

The man waited. Stepping slowly until he stood no more than ten feet from the judge. If Rand had even the slightest situational awareness, he should have sensed the looming figure beside him.

He didn't.

The man pulled the hammer back, letting the unmistakable echo of it send a signal to the judge. But not even that drew the judge's attention. He stayed oblivious.

Typical, the man thought. Judge Rand surrounded himself with the trappings of a man who loved the outdoors. A floor-to-ceiling, built-in glass cabinet housed his shotguns. The centerpiece of his wall decor was the head of a trophy 10-point whitetail buck. Rumor was the judge shot the thing on a fenced-in hunt. He had pheasant, duck, and turkey mounts nestled between the ebony-bound, gold-trimmed law books and a golden gavel he'd gotten to commemorate his investiture on the Worthington County Common Pleas Court bench.

Look at me, you idiot, the man thought. But the crescendo of the chorus and Italian singer's clear tenor held the judge entranced.

The man cleared his throat with disgust. The click of his hammer apparently meant nothing to this man who bragged about the guns he owned and his prowess with the game he'd shot in little more than petting zoos.

The judge's eyes snapped open. He turned. Finally, he turned.

A beat passed. Judge Rand's face split into a strange smile. "What are you doing here?" he asked. It was as if his brain refused to process the gun pointed straight at him or the man holding it.

The man held it steady. He would never waver. Not once. He answered the judge's question, watching his words register in the judge's eyes.

The judge put his hands on the armrests of his chair and started to rise.

The man kept his aim leveled at center mass. He squeezed the trigger, hitting Judge Rand just to the left of his heart on purpose. Let him feel it. Let him truly understand.

Judge Rand jerked backward, then sideways as the iron tang of blood and gunpowder hit the man's nose. Rand clutched his chest then drew his hand away. He stared at it for a moment, transfixed by his own blood. He leaned sideways, grabbing perhaps for the cell phone he'd rested on the end table. He missed, knocking over his martini glass. It shattered as it hit the floor.

"Stop," he whispered. "Please." His eyes widened. His pupils grew. His gray eyes turned paler, somehow.

Breathe in. Breathe out. The man took two steps toward the judge, adjusting his aim as he pulled the trigger once more.

The next shot went right through the judge's left eye, blowing it out, exiting out the back of his head in a splatter of gore against the oak paneling behind him. A kill shot.

The man could afford to take his time after that. Carefully retracing his steps, he went out to his pickup truck and brought in the supplies he kept for the occasion.

A blue tarp. Duct tape. Bleach.

Pavarotti or whatever Italian tenor the judge chose launched into something the man recognized but could not name. He would learn it later. Tosca. He taped the gun to Judge Rand's chest, rolled him into the tarp, and tied it shut around him, closing the ends like a murder burrito. He hauled the judge out the side door.

It was then he let the adrenaline fuel him. Sweating, he heaved the judge into the bed of his truck, climbed in, then dragged the dead man the rest of the way in by his feet. Rain pelted over the tarp in echoing, staccato beats. It made the job harder, but would wash away his path. He'd been counting on that. He'd watched the weather all week.

He went back into the house one last time with the bottle of bleach and a sponge.

They called it the Devil's Eye. The gateway to hell. Nestled deep in Shepherd's Hollow at the core of Ohio's Blackhand Hills, an ancient waterfall had carved a perfect circle through the sandstone cliff.

Only the most rugged hikers ventured up this way anymore. It wasn't even part of the ranger's designated trails. Too many people had nearly broken their necks trying to traverse the steep embankments on the north face of Shepherd's Hollow. Several had died.

Danger signs pointed the way.

Now, at pitch-black midnight with the rain still hammering down, the man knew he was utterly alone. He took his time, dragging the judge's body like so many deer he'd harvested from the state hunting lands below.

Though he'd left the judge's house hours ago, he could still hear Puccini's opera blaring in his head. Maybe he always would.

Thunder cracked. Lightning showed him the way along with the headlamp he wore. There was no danger of anyone seeing it this time of night. He was well protected by the sandstone walls as he ascended.

He reached the edge of the hole. Though the storm masked it, on a quiet night, you could hear the wind echoing through the gorge. It produced a wailing sound that some said emanated from the spirits trapped down in the Devil's Eye. Or maybe it was the devil himself.

The man wasn't sure he believed in that stuff. He wasn't sure if he believed in anything anymore. Except for this.

He shined his light down the hole. He couldn't see anything. Just a black expanse into nothingness. No one had ever found the bottom. Many had tried. Along with the ghosts said to haunt this place, rumor had it a pair of stagecoach bandits had tried to hide their treasure on a rocky ledge off the Devil's Eye.

No one ever found it. At least a dozen people had fallen to their deaths trying, their bodies never found. Now, they haunted the place too.

If you believed in that sort of thing.

The man made sure his tape job held. He could feel the hard outline of his .45 on the judge's chest. Even with the pelting rain, he could smell that unmistakable metallic, iron scent of blood.

He dragged the judge up that last few feet. He rolled the judge's body until it was perched at the edge of the hole.

Should he say a prayer? Ask for forgiveness? The man knew he was long past that. He rose, his clothes soaked completely through now. It was getting cold.

He took a last, deep breath, then kicked the judge's body over the ledge and watched it slide down the jagged sides of the hole and disappear.

Judge Rand would join the other ghosts now. His body, like theirs, would never be found. The man straightened and turned his back on the Devil's Eye, satisfied that he'd just sent Judge Sampson Rand through the gates of hell.

Two

Sinking ankle deep in mud and dog shit was only the third worst thing that happened to Deputy Jake Cashen on Monday morning. He steeled himself as he heard shouting from inside the rickety double-wide just outside the town of Maudeville, the furthest point west in Worthington County.

Jake scraped his shoe on one of the cement blocks littering the front lawn, then approached the door. He heard someone moving around inside. The whole trailer shook. Jake took a slightly bladed stance from the front door, away from the window, and unsnapped his gun.

He knocked on the door. "Ma'am," he said. "You called for the Sheriff's Office? Can you please come to the front door? You and anyone else in there."

Something crashed to the floor inside.

"Ma'am!" he shouted. "I'm gonna need you to open this door."

From inside, a woman's voice let loose a stream of obscenities. One more thud as something heavy hit the ground and the whole trailer shook even harder. Finally, the front door opened and a greasy-haired woman wearing a pale pink robe, fuzzy slippers, and not much else stood glaring at him.

"Are you Mrs. Bloom?" Cashen asked. "You called in a domestic disturbance. I need ..."

"Took you long enough!" she shouted. "You better get on in here. I *told* you, you better watch yourself!"

Cashen realized the last bit was for somebody else. He peered round the woman's shoulder and saw a small figure sitting on a torn orange couch.

"Well, get on in here," she said to Cashen, opening the door wider.

"Why don't you step outside with me here for a minute and we'll talk," he said.

Mrs. Bloom scowled at him. She at least pulled her robe closed. He'd seen enough. The woman was wearing nothing more than a sports bra and some sort of granny panties. She pushed the door open and stepped out onto the porch with him.

"He don't listen," she said, brushing a stringy lock of hair behind her ear. She gestured wildly toward the house. "Can't get him to do one damn thing I ask him."

"Who we talking about here?" Cashen asked.

"Him!" Mrs. Bloom said, swinging her arm wide back toward the living room.

"Wants to sit there with his face on a screen all the time. You think I could even get him to take out the garbage?"

"Is that your son in there?" Cashen asked, his anger rising.

"Yesss," she said. "You slow or something?"

He clenched a fist and tried to do a quick ten-count.

"Ma'am," he said. "Are you in danger? You called 9-1-1 and told the dispatcher your son was abusing you. Is that him sitting on the couch?"

"Yes," she said, exasperated. "Go talk to him."

"And what, tell him to do his chores? Lady, we're not a babysitting service."

"He's abusive," she said. "That's what I said."

Cashen could see this was going nowhere fast. He had half a mind to just leave the woman standing there swearing at him. But he caught the eye of the little boy sitting inside and something made him pause.

"Fine," he said. "I'll go talk to him. But before I do, is there anyone else in the house?"

She shook her head. "Just my Brady. Oh, and Corky's in the kitchen eating breakfast. But he won't bother you none."

"Great," Cashen said. He stepped around the woman and went inside. Taking a quick look to the left, toward the kitchen, he got ready to walk right back out.

A big, fat, black-eyed raccoon sat on the kitchen table nibbling what looked like Fruit Loops from a pink plastic bowl.

Cashen looked over his shoulder. "Corky?"

"Yeah," the woman said. "I told you. He won't bother you."

"Of course not," Cashen said. He avoided the kitchen and went left to the orange couch and the brooding, scabby-kneed six-year-old sitting there.

Cashen squatted down in front of him. "Hey, little man," he said. "How's it going?"

"See?" Mrs. Bloom said. "I told you. You don't pick up your room, they'll come and take you to kid jail. Today's the day!"

"Enough," Cashen said. "I'm not here to take you to jail, Brady. You doing okay?"

Brady's lip quivered. Two fat tears threatened to spill down his cheeks.

Cashen looked the kid over. He could use a haircut and his tee-shirt was two sizes too big, but he could see no cuts, bruises, or any other outward signs of abuse.

"You promise?" Brady asked Cashen, meeting his eyes.

"I promise. I'm not taking you to jail. But maybe keep your room clean and take out the garbage when you're told, okay?"

Brady nodded forcefully. Cashen had the urge to pick him up. He reached over and tousled the kid's already tragic head of hair.

"Keep your nose clean, kiddo," he said. "You'll be fine." From the corner of his eye, he saw Corky the raccoon rise up on his hind legs. He took it as a sign to go.

He crooked his finger and gestured for Mrs. Bloom to meet him back outside.

"Good," she said. "That ought to scare him."

"No good," Cashen said. "You call 9-1-1 or the Sheriff's Department at all for crap like this, I'm going to write you up for misuse of 911."

She dropped her jaw. "You have no right to talk to me that way. I know who you are. Surprised they gave you a gun. How do I know you're not a psycho like your old man?" She spun an index finger around her head, bugging her eyes and sticking out her tongue. Then she turned her finger into a gun and simulated pulling the trigger.

He felt heat rising up the back of his neck. Cashen took a breath and stepped back. Right into a pile of raccoon shit.

Cashen was still swearing under his breath as he pulled out of the trailer park. His shoulder radio squawked.

"Central Dispatch to Unit 10. Can you take a disorderly conduct at the Dollar Kart?"

Jake didn't answer right away.

"Unit 10? Jake? You free?"

"Just heading out of Galway Park, Darcy," Cashen said.

"I got a call about, um ... a disturbance at the Dollar Kart on County 11."

Cashen gripped the wheel, feeling the tension through his right shoulder. "Darcy, that's clear down in Poznan Township. There's gotta be somebody closer you can call."

"I think you should go," Darcy said.

Cashen was none too pleased, considering Darcy had just sent him to the Bloom residence for nanny duty.

"Darcy," he said more forcefully. "I'm still in Maudeville. It's gonna take me twenty minutes to—"

"Jake," she barked. "I said I think you're gonna want to handle this one. The call came in as an elderly male wearing jeans, a Carhartt jacket, and a John Deere cap."

Jake laughed. "You just described two thirds of the old men in the county, Darcy."

"Jake," she said. "It's Max causing the disturbance, okay? The manager at the store is a friend of mine. She said one of the cashiers already called Gemma and ..."

"Shit," Cashen muttered. "I'll make it in fifteen." He floored the gas and headed east, straight into the second worst thing that would happen to him that Monday morning.

THREE

Cashen drove Code 2, rolling through all eight west to east stop signs in Worthington County on the way to Poznan Township.

Worthington County encompassed three hundred and eighty square miles in Southern Ohio. Blackhand Hills, the hollows, and the surrounding state forest made up most of its northern section with the county seat of Stanley smack in the middle. Furthest east was Carlow Township and Hart Lake, where anyone *with* money lived. There weren't many of them. Furthest south was Poznan and Lublin Townships and the tiny town of Ardenville where everyone *without* any money used to live. Primarily a ghost town now, its inhabitants had long since migrated to points west. In the post-war era, the townships of Navan, Arch Hill, Brown Creek, Galway, and Duris were "built up" with a smattering of subdivisions, trailer parks, and the mostly unfulfilled promise of a better life.

County Road 11 ran straight through the deepest valley in the Blackhand Hills. The giant jagged sandstone cliff faces whizzed past Jake as he tried to get his sister, Gemma, on the phone. It went straight to voicemail. Which meant she was ignoring him completely, or had already beaten him to the Dollar Kart.

"Shit!" Cashen shouted. He smacked a hand against the steering wheel. Fifteen minutes later, he screeched his cruiser to a halt right behind Gemma's blue F-350. He would have rather dealt with a hundred cereal-eating raccoons than walk into that store.

Cashen slammed his car door shut and straightened his back before he walked inside. He heard the old man before he spotted him.

"Crooks!" Grandpa Max shouted. "You're all crooks!"

"Mr. Cashen." The store manager held her hands up. She stood between the old man and the teenage cashier with a yellow ponytail and fear in her eyes. She clutched a wad of dollar bills in her hand. Twice, the old man tried to reach over and grab it from her.

"Grandpa!" Gemma shouted. She stood at the old man's shoulder. His sister was five foot three, but today she wore a pair of red velvet boots with four-inch heels. It brought her almost nose to nose with their grandfather.

"You're a bully!" Gemma shouted. She jabbed a finger into Grandpa Max's chest. "Misty is just trying to do her job. Go back to the car and let me take care of this."

"You're another one!" Grandpa Max shouted. "Always waiting back there like a spider. Trying to wrap those spindly little tentacles around my money."

"Spiders don't have tentacles and you don't *have* any money," Gemma said. "And I said that's enough out of you."

"Everybody just calm down," Cashen said. Gemma jerked her head toward him. His sister was beautiful in a trashy sort of way she played up when it suited her. Today she had on a tight black-and-white polka-dot dress that showed every curve. If he mentioned it, she'd probably brain him with her high-heeled red boot and maybe he'd deserve it.

"Finally," Grandpa Max said. "These women are all crazy. And they're liars."

"What's going on?" Cashen asked. He wasn't sure who to even direct the question to.

The manager's shoulders sagged with relief. "I'm willing to go with a misunderstanding," she said. Cashen called her over to him, leaving his hot-headed sister and grandfather squared off with each other.

"What happened?" Cashen asked.

"I'm not exactly sure," the manager whispered. She was a middle-aged woman in black polyester pants, sensible shoes, and a red golf shirt with the Dollar Kart logo emblazoned over her heart. Her nametag read Diane.

"My cashier tried to give him back his change and the old guy accused her of stealing. He went completely psycho. He grabbed her wrist and tried to take the money from her hand."

It was then she read Cashen's silver name plate. "Oh," she said. "I'm sorry. You're ..."

"His grandson," Cashen said.

"I'm really, really sorry," she said. "That was insensitive of me. I didn't mean psycho, I meant ..."

Cashen smiled. "It's okay. We're used to it."

"Look," she said. "He grabbed that girl. Misty's like ninety pounds soaking wet and it's her second day. Do you know how hard a time I'm having getting kids to work? He assaulted her."

"Is she hurt?" Cashen asked. "Does she want to press charges?"

Diane opened and closed her mouth. "We have a zero-tolerance policy. I have to protect my employees."

"I understand that."

"I'll tell you exactly where you can stick that!" The shout came from Grandpa Max. He had his own finger jabbed in Gemma's shoulder.

"She made it worse," Diane said, gesturing with her chin toward Gemma. "It's like a bomb went off when he saw her."

"Yeah," Cashen said. "You don't know the half of it."

Diane smiled. "Believe me, I've got plenty of family drama of my own. It's just ... this has to be a safe space for my workers. You understand."

"I do," Cashen said. "Look, if I get the old man to agree never to shop here again, will you let me just take him home?"

Diane looked from Grandpa Max back to Jake. "Um ... I think I can work with that. I feel terrible. He comes in here at least once a week. I know he just lives up the hill. We ..."

"It's okay," Cashen said. "He can shop somewhere else. I really appreciate it. You call me on my cell phone if there's any other trouble."

Cashen wrote his number on the back of a generic sheriff's deputy business card. His own cards hadn't come in yet. He hadn't even been on the job for a full month.

"I'll point wherever I damn well please!" Gemma shot back. Grandpa snarled, reminding Jake of a bull getting ready to charge.

"Oh boy," Diane said. "Good luck with all that. But he's gotta go. Um ... they both do."

"On it," Cashen said. He shook the manager's hand and went over to his sister and grandfather.

"Get him in the car," Jake said to Gemma through gritted teeth. "And Grandpa, you're going to let Gemma drive you home."

"She took my money!" Grandpa shouted toward the terrified cashier. Jake reached into his pocket and pulled out a twenty.

"Here," he said. "You're square. Take the things in your cart and go on home."

Grandpa growled, but grabbed his three plastic grocery bags out of the cart near the cash register.

"Finally," Grandpa said. "Somebody who can talk some reason into all these crazy women."

"Enough," Jake said. He looped an arm under his grandfather's and ushered him out the front door. Gemma followed in a cloud of fury and bleach-blonde hair.

Jake scanned the parking lot. Grandpa's vintage red F-150 wasn't in the parking lot, which meant he'd walked. That was a fight for another day. He was still muttering obscenities as he climbed into the cab of his sister's truck. Jake said a silent prayer Gemma could drive him the half a mile home without the two of them killing each other.

"Can you handle this?" Jake asked her.

She was fuming still, her face red. Her green eyes smoldering.

"You gonna take his side, little brother?" she asked.

Jake let out a breath. "Just get him home. You don't have to talk to him. You don't have to help him. Just get him back up the hill. I'll try to talk to him later tonight."

"You gonna break it to him? He can't set foot in here again."

"I'll handle it!" Jake said.

Gemma took a step back, shaking her head. "Right. Of course you will. You're back in town for what, three weeks now? Sure. You've got it all figured out."

"Gemma," he said. "Not now."

Jake's shoulder radio squealed. He pleaded at Gemma with his eyes. She threw her hands up. "By all means."

"I'm at work!" Jake protested. He turned away from his sister and answered his radio. "Go ahead, Darcy."

"Hey, Jake," Darcy said, her tone heavy. Jake braced himself. "I'm gonna need you to call me."

"What now?" Jake sighed. Pursing his lips, he took a few steps away, pulled out his cell phone, and called into dispatch. Darcy answered immediately.

"I'm sorry," Darcy said. "But Sheriff Landry wants you back at the station."

"I'm still out in Poznan ... where *you* sent me."

"I know," she said. "If you're finished there, I think you better hurry though."

"What's the matter now?" Jake asked.

"I don't know," Darcy said. "I don't know Landry well enough to get a good read on her. Nobody does. But she sounded sort of pissed. I think you better get here."

"Darcy," Jake said. "I'm beginning to really hate these little chats of ours."

"Yeah. I get that," Darcy said.

Jake clicked off and turned to his sister. "You got this? I've gotta go."

Gemma squeezed her eyes shut. Jake realized she was having a pretty crappy day of her own. "Yeah," she said. "Go do what you gotta do."

Jake pursed his lips. He touched his sister's arm. Then he climbed back into his cruiser, headed for the worst thing that would happen to him that day.

Four

J ake Cashen was never supposed to have much to do with Meg Landry. That wasn't the deal. A few weeks ago, when he first clipped on his deputy badge, Landry was serving as undersheriff. A glorified pencil pusher for Sheriff Greg O'Neal.

O'Neal was a cop's cop. A man of his word. He'd known Jake since he was just a kid. Their grandfathers had worked side by side at the Arden Clay Mill until old man O'Neal dropped dead of a heart attack right next to him. Jake called in a family favor when he walked back into town a month ago and asked O'Neal for a job.

Barely a week later, it turned out Greg had inherited the family bum ticker. He died of a massive heart attack while sitting behind the wheel of his cruiser at the bridge on County Road 12.

The Worthington County Sheriff's Department was situated smack-dab in the middle of the county seat of Stanley, Ohio, a two-story brick, federalist-style building right next to one of the state's oldest barber shops. The county courthouse sat on the other side of it. Newly minted Sheriff Meg Landry's office was located at the end of the hall on the second floor.

She was waiting for Cashen, pacing in front of her desk. Actually, it was still Greg O'Neal's desk. She hadn't yet had the time or inclination to take Greg's family pictures off the wall or the framed, folded American flag he displayed in a prominent position on the credenza behind the huge oak desk. O'Neal had been a Marine before he was a cop. Cashen heard Landry was an accountant. O'Neal plucked her out of the Administrative Services Bureau for the Dayton PD.

"Close the door," Sheriff Landry said. She stood with her arms folded. Her wiry brown hair was pulled back into a bun but her curls threatened to revolt. She had a healthy amount of gray sprinkled throughout and wide-set eyes with dark circles beneath them.

"Something wrong, Sheriff?" Cashen asked. He stood at attention by the door. "I was just about to clock out."

"I'll approve the overtime," she said. "Have a seat. I don't think either of us is going anywhere anytime soon."

Darcy's read was right. Landry was pissed about something. Even as he took a seat like she asked him, Meg Landry kept pacing. She was short, five one at best, but trim and tightly wound.

"This hasn't gotten out yet," Landry said. "But Judge Rand has gone missing. No one's seen him since he left his chambers Friday afternoon. He didn't show up for his docket today."

"Okay," Cashen said. Sampson Rand came from a long line of judicial nepotism. His father held his seat on the bench for thirty years before Sampson came along. Though Cashen had yet to appear in front of him, he knew cops generally liked him. He'd served as a prosecutor before being elected to the Worthington County Court of Common Pleas.

"Who reported him missing?" Cashen asked, still wondering what any of this had to do with him.

"His clerk," Landry said. She walked over to her desk and pulled a thin file off the top of it. Then she perched herself on the edge of the desk right in front of Cashen.

Though she hadn't touched any of Greg O'Neal's things, he noticed she had added a few of her own. Cashen spotted a single family photo on the credenza next to O'Neal's flag. It was one of those awkward ones taken at a Sears or a JCPenney. Landry herself, maybe ten years younger, with brighter eyes and a little less gray. Laughing with light in her brown eyes. Her husband sat beside her wearing an unfortunate maroon sweater with a collar and tie underneath. He was pudgy around the middle and had thinning blond hair. A little girl, about five years old, with a mass of unruly brown ringlet curls framing her face beamed at the camera with a gap-toothed smile. She was cute. They looked happy.

"I've looked into you," Landry said.

Cashen's eyes snapped back to hers. He said nothing.

"Couple years with Chicago PD before the Feds snapped you up out of the Violent Crimes, Gang Task Force," she said, her eyes scanning the file she held.

Still, Cashen said nothing. He gripped the arms of the chair and tried to keep his face neutral.

"Pretty impressive, from what it says in here." She waved the folder in front of him. "Operation Black Box. You took down the Blood Money Kings. Helluva notch on your belt, Cashen.

Some of their crap filtered down to Dayton. I know their organization was responsible for most of the heroin and coke coming into Chicago for more than a decade. They were supposed to be untouchable. But you got them from the top down. I'd love to hear that story if you care to share."

He didn't. Not even a little bit.

Landry waited for him to say something. He didn't.

"But you left the Bureau right after," Landry said. "Why?"

"It was time to come home," Jake answered through tight lips.

Landry studied him. She raised a brow but didn't ask another question. For now.

"Judge Rand has never missed a docket," she said. "Not in the seven years since he took the bench. Never so much as called in sick, I'm told. He's got no immediate family. No wife. No kids. Nobody to report him missing until this morning."

Cashen looked at her.

"I'd like your take on it," Landry said, finally getting to the point of why she asked him up here.

"My take? Wouldn't this be Ed Zender's job?" Cashen said. Ed Zender was one of only two detectives in the Worthington County Sheriff's Department. Ed handled crimes against persons, Gary Majewski handled property crimes.

"I think maybe Ed could use some help from somebody like you," she said.

Cashen raised a brow. "Someone like me?"

Landry took a breath as if she were going to answer him, but swallowed it. She put his file back on her desk.

"I can't figure you out," she said.

"Why are you trying?" Cashen asked.

"From the looks of your resume, you lit out of Stanley pretty much right after you walked across the auditorium stage with your high school diploma. State champion wrestler with a scholarship to Northern Illinois. You were an all-star. Hall of Famer. I looked. They've got your picture up on the wall at Stanley High. I've seen the trophy case. Over a decade with the FBI Chicago Field Office after the Chicago PD. Cashen, that's about as big as it gets. But then you came back here. That had to have been a pretty jarring re-entry."

Cashen stared straight ahead. He felt his shoulder muscles turning to granite. "I told you," he said. "It was just time to come home."

"I asked around," she said. "In all these eighteen years you've been gone, you barely made it home for Christmas. You dropped off the face of the earth as far as everyone around here is concerned."

He wanted to grill her why she was asking. What right did she have to poke around into his personal life?

"I was ready for a change," he said. "Something simpler."

She nodded. "Oh, I get that. That's the pitch Greg O'Neal sold me on, too. People don't generally come to Stanley."

"You did," Jake said.

She didn't respond. She took a breath. "Homegrown boys though. They're either stuck here or they get out as fast as they can. Just like you."

Jake clamped his mouth shut. She was baiting him. He wouldn't bite.

"And that's all fine and good," she said. "You wanting something slower-paced? Doesn't get much slower than Worthington County. Only you haven't exactly acted like someone who wants to live the quiet life."

"What are you talking about?"

"You've been here what, three weeks? Both Majewski and Zender have cleared more cases in those three weeks than they have in five years combined. Did you know that?"

Cashen didn't answer.

"You were on scene with Gary after Nick Holt's store got robbed. I heard you took control of it. Collared a guy off of fingerprints on the cash register."

"It was Majewski's case," Cashen said.

"Right. And I know Gary Majewski's fingerprint kit was probably sitting under the passenger seat of his cruiser covered in cobwebs, Jake."

"Look," he said, rising from the chair. "This isn't my problem. If I've done something wrong, write me up. I need to get home."

"I need you on Judge Rand's case," she said.

"That's not my job," Cashen said.

"Your job is what I tell you it is."

"I was clear with Sheriff O'Neal. I'm not interested in detective work."

"I thought I was pretty clear with you. You haven't been acting like someone who just wants to collect a paycheck," she said.

He gripped the back of the chair.

"Look," she said. "I don't know what your deal is and at the moment I don't care. I've got a missing judge and the county commissioners are breathing down my neck already. You don't work for Greg O'Neal anymore as much as you wish you still did. As much as I wish I still did. I didn't sign up for this gig either, Jake. I was supposed to be dealing with grants, contract negotiations, and budgets. All the stuff Greg hated. Well, my deal with Sheriff O'Neal died when he did. So did yours. I need you. I'm not asking you to sell me your firstborn child. I'm asking you to head out to the judge's house with me and tell me what you see. That's all."

Jake let out a breath. "If I refuse?"

"I'm giving you a direct order," she said. "Come on, Jake. Help me out. It's an hour of your time."

"You think Ed Zender's going to see it that way?" Cashen asked.

"Ed Zender is my problem, not yours," she said. "You'd be doing me a favor. That might not mean a whole lot to you yet, but I can assure you. I'm someone you want in your corner. Greg O'Neal understood that. That's why I'm here. And if he were here, he'd tell you to get your ass in the car and follow me out to the judge's place."

Cashen had to suppress a smirk. He could almost hear Sheriff O'Neal's voice as she said it. Dammit all to hell if she wasn't right.

"Come on," Landry said. She went to the door and held it open for him. "One hour. Check out the scene with me. That's it."

Cashen grumbled, but followed her out the door knowing full well this was a bad idea for him all the way around.

FIVE

Judge Rand lived on a thirty-acre plot of wooded land bordering the Arch Hill nature preserve. After forty-odd years of wrangling with the township planning commission, a developer had finally gotten the green light to put in luxury homes in the northwest corner, overlooking the Blackhand Hills.

Cashen had Sheriff Landry follow him down Grace Church Road. He knew she'd have missed the turn for sure if he hadn't signaled as he came up to the unmarked road. Rand's home was nestled way back, almost at the edge of the property line up an asphalt-paved driveway. This was prime deer country. As such, Cashen couldn't figure why Rand wouldn't have built the place closer to the road.

Angling his vehicle next to Landry's, Cashen got out and waited for Landry to join him. There were three other vehicles parked out front. A patrol car, an unmarked cruiser identical to Landry's, and a black Acura with vanity plates reading LGLEGL. Cashen bristled. He had a good guess who might own it. If he was right, they had no business here.

"What do you want from me?" he asked Landry, feeling the tension creep into his shoulders.

"Take a look," she said, gesturing toward the marked patrol car. Deputy Chris Denning leaned against the hood of it, staring at his phone.

Gritting his teeth, Cashen walked up to him. Denning graduated about three years after Cashen did. His older brother had briefly dated Gemma.

"Hey, Chris," Cashen said. "You got the crime scene log?"

Denning looked up from his phone and furrowed his brow. He seemed confused. Cashen felt his anger rising even higher.

"Never mind," he said. "Were you first on scene?"

"Uh, yeah."

"Well, let's have it."

Denning looked back toward the house. When he looked back, he finally noticed Sheriff Landry waiting by her car. She gave him a wave and a pointed stare.

"I, uh, I ran through all this with Zender," Denning said.

"Well, now she wants you to run it through with me."

"Got it," Denning said. "Well, when I got here the front door was unlocked. Same with the side door running through the garage. No signs of forced entry. Me and Lloyd, er, Deputy Kenner cleared the house. No sign of the judge. But the den was kinda messed up so I called Zender."

"Who's inside?" Cashen asked.

"That'd be Zender, Lieutenant Beverly, and Brouchard, um, the prosecutor."

The prosecutor, Jake thought, fuming. Mr. LGLEGL himself. "You let the prosecutor in there?" Cashen asked. He tried not to let his anger show. Denning had always been skittish. He'd tried out for the wrestling team when Jake was a senior and hadn't made it past the first week.

"Yeah," Denning said. "I think Zender called him. You know. Just to be on the safe side."

"The safe side of what?" Cashen muttered. He let it go for now.

"All right," he said. "Just stay here and don't let anyone else in besides me unless the judge himself rolls up. Not even her. Got it?" He gestured back toward Landry. She gave him a quick nod of approval.

Cashen went back to his car and grabbed a pair of latex gloves and booties. He prayed that Denning and Kenner had done the same before they went inside, but didn't want to ask. Yet.

Cashen walked in the front door. It opened up to Rand's living room. Directly beyond that was the kitchen. Lieutenant John Beverly and Tim Brouchard, the county prosecutor, were standing smack in the middle of it with no gloves or booties on.

"Unbelievable," Cashen muttered. The pair turned and waved but looked confused by Jake's presence. Before Jake could respond, Ed Zender came down the hallway to his left where he presumed the bedrooms were.

Ed was a beefy, barrel-chested guy with thinning gray hair and a bulbous nose. He had a booming voice that vibrated through you when he shouted. Which was often.

"Hey, there, Jake," Zender said. He walked up to Cashen and slapped him on the back with his meaty hand. He took a wide stance, hands on his hips, splaying his jacket wide. The buttons on his dress shirt strained over his belly. No gloves. No booties. No brains, apparently.

"Landry thought you could use an extra set of eyes," Cashen said, hating it. He tried to keep his tone light.

"Oh sure, sure," Zender said. "Not much to see. Looking like a burglary gone south. Judge has a lot of shit to steal. I'd been telling him for years to put an alarm system in. Offered to install it myself. He figures the woods are all he needs."

"You care if I look around?" Cashen asked.

"You bet," Zender said. "Good experience for you. Hey, Tim, Lou? You don't mind if Cashen shadows me, do you?"

Lieutenant Beverly and Tim Brouchard walked over to him. Beverly was huge, six five, with baseball mitts for hands. Lieutenant Beverly held a paper coffee cup in one of them and extended the other to shake Jake's. "Your gramps has been bragging you up for years. Wasn't surprised to hear you got sick of pushing paper with the Feds," Beverly said.

"Good to meet you, Jake," Brouchard said. He had a slick look about him with a tanning-booth complexion and a flashy gold watch. "We want to make sure nothing gets missed out here. I know Sam. This just isn't like him to up and disappear."

"Right," Cashen said, scanning the living room. Nothing looked out of place. There were perfect carpet vacuuming lines in front of all the leather furniture to the right of them. Cashen walked down the hallway where Zender had just come from. Three bedrooms total. The judge had converted one into a home office. His oak desk was neat and tidy. All the drawers were closed. His MacBook lay closed on top of it.

In the judge's bedroom, the bed was still made. Jake spotted a large safe in one corner. It was closed. There just didn't seem to be a single thing out of place.

"Does he have a housekeeper?" Cashen asked, pointing to the vacuum lines across the hall in the guest bedroom carpet.

"Not sure," Zender said. "I'm looking into it."

Zender followed him into the kitchen. Cashen did another quick hello to Beverly and Brouchard, but cared more about the state of the room. Again, nothing was out of place. Not even so much as a dirty dish in the sink. Meanwhile, Beverly and Brouchard sat at the judge's kitchen island, drinking their coffees as if they were in a Starbucks, not a potential crime scene.

Jake made his way to the den off the kitchen. The judge had a giant flat screen TV mounted to one wall. A leather recliner pointed toward a large floor-to-ceiling window. It showcased a breathtaking view of the woods.

It was here Cashen noticed the only thing remarkable. The judge's cell phone sat on the side table next to the leather recliner. On the floor beside it lay a pipe and a cracked cocktail glass. There was a dark stain on the floor beside that.

"Might be blood," Zender said. "The judge also used to have a dog. A Husky. Damn thing was never housebroken so he got rid of it maybe six months ago."

With the pristine condition of the rest of the house, Cashen doubted the judge would have left a pet stain untreated for that long. He said nothing.

On another wall, the judge had a glass built-in gun case. He walked up to it. Cashen counted at least three Benelli over/under shotguns. "Those things are worth at least six grand each," he said. Zender grunted his approval at Cashen's estimate. There were also several other high-end rifles and antique shotguns.

"He was a collector," Zender said. "Used to bug us to take him out to the range all the time. Fancied himself a hunter. Sweet old guy, but the judge couldn't hit the side of a barn at ten feet. We were more worried he was going to shoot his own foot off."

"You smell that?" Cashen asked. He stood behind the recliner.

"Cherry pipe tobacco," Zender said. "Doc McGann was on him to quit. He likes that aromatic crap. Buys it in bulk."

Cashen nodded, but that wasn't what he meant. He smelled bleach. Cashen turned and faced the wall behind the recliner. The judge had a mahogany sideboard against the wall. He was using it as a liquor cabinet. There were a few stapled pieces of paper on top of it. Cashen picked them up.

"Brought home some light reading," Zender said. "He's in trial on Buddy Grant's case. A home invasion out in Galway Township. Perp scared Buddy into a heart attack. The defense is arguing his dirtbag client shouldn't be held culpable for that. Can you believe it?"

Cashen cocked his head to the side. There were some tiny dark specks in the corner of one of the court briefs. He put them back on the sideboard.

"Looks like dull reading." Cashen smiled. He'd seen enough.

"You learn anything?" Zender asked.

"A few things, Ed," he said. But he was already on his way out the front door, headed for Landry.

She was pacing in front of her vehicle. Her face was red. Cashen waited until the front door closed; he was reasonably sure he was out of Ed Zender's earshot.

"Well?" she asked.

"This is a shit show," he said, trying to keep his temper in check.

Her shoulders fell. "Give it to me."

"You want the short version or the long version?"

"Just tell me what you think, Cashen," she said. "Is he dead?"

"I don't know," he said. "With what's going on in there, we might never know. Christ. There's no crime scene log. I walk in there and the damn prosecutor is standing in the kitchen. In the kitchen! Shooting the breeze. If the judge is dead, good luck ever getting a conviction if Zender is lucky enough to figure out who did it. It would take even a shitty defense lawyer about two seconds to figure out how to tear Zender up for not doing the bare minimum, crime scene 101 out here."

"What's the worst of it?" she asked.

"We drove right up? There should be a patrol car at the end of that drive by the road. Denning should be logging anyone who comes and goes. How the hell Tim Brouchard thinks he's going to prosecute this case if the judge is dead is beyond me. By even being here, he makes himself a witness."

"Zender thinks it was a burglary," she said.

"That's bullshit," Cashen said. "There's no forced entry. Just by my eyes, there's at least thirty grand worth of shit worth stealing out in the open in there."

"What would you do differently?" she asked.

"Everything."

"I was hoping you'd say that," she said.

"No," Cashen said. "No way. This thing's too far gone."

"He's missing," Landry said. "Sampson Rand is a crime victim. Maybe dead. We need to find out what happened. I need *you* to find out what happened. And you want to. I can practically smell it on you. You didn't take too much convincing to come out here. You could have said no."

"Really? I distinctly remember you telling me I couldn't."

"Look at yourself," she said. "Your blood's racing. You want this case. Badly. You're ready to rip Ed Zender, a new asshole. I *read* your file, Jake. I know your record. Greg had newspaper clippings in his desk about you. All your accolades with the Bureau. I'm not an investigator like you. I'm an administrator. But even I know what it had to take to bring down the Blood Money Kings. It takes a master interrogator, coordination with CIs, and snitches. Years of laying the groundwork. And your stuff was tight enough to get thousands of guns and millions of dollars of dope off the street. You took out the entire command structure. Life sentences. I've read it all, Jake. This case? Judge Rand? Even this is beneath you. But here you are. You really want me to believe you want to spend the next fifteen years kicking down trailer doors?"

"I don't care what you believe," he said.

"Tell me what you need. I'll let you run this thing top down. I'll see to it you won't get micromanaged by command. Including me. If you need to work OT, work it. If you need stuff run down by patrol, I'll make sure Beverly's aware and you *will* get it. Equipment? Whatever I can get my hands on, you'll have. I will take care of the county politics and the media. They will not have direct contact with you. I won't get in your way. That's a promise. How often did your bosses at the Bureau give you that? That's why you left, isn't it?"

He paused. That's the one answer he wasn't willing to give her or anyone else yet. Dammit if she wasn't right about the rest of it though. He was jazzed. Adrenaline coursed through him.

"Why?" he asked. "What's the catch, Landry?"

"No catch," she said. "I need this case solved and quickly by someone who knows what he's doing. That's the catch."

"What about Zender?" he asked.

"You let me worry about Ed. That's my job. I'll get you what you need. I swear it. You just have to tell me what that is."

"Well, BCI for starters. This scene is nowhere close to being properly protected. Ed should already have an APB out on the judge. Phone subpoenas. The judge's credit cards. I want his car GPS. Search warrants on the house and property. If Tim Brouchard truly wants to make himself useful, that's the first thing. And Ed, he's done enough damage. He needs to be gone."

"Done," she said.

"He's not going to like this," Cashen said. "Ed's gonna make trouble."

"I told you. That'll be my problem."

He walked away from her and started pacing. He felt like running. He felt like smashing in a wall. Something. Anything to keep feeling the rush. He heard laughter coming from inside the house. Zender, Brouchard, and Beverly were all still bullshitting with each other in the kitchen.

She said all the right things. Even the bit about kicking down trailer doors. It occurred to Jake that Landry might even have been the one behind sending him to the Bloom trailer this morning. The instant he thought it, he knew he was right.

Landry was playing him. She may not be an investigator, but even she had to know what was wrong out here. That was the catch. She needed him, sure. But maybe she also needed him to deal with her bigger problem. Ed Zender. How many other cases had he bungled out of the gate like this?

He came back to Landry and stared her down. Her face betrayed nothing. Her eyes though. He knew he'd hit on it. She was playing some chess game.

"What's your end game?" he asked.

"My end game?"

"All this," he said. "I think you already had a pretty good idea the kind of shit show we'd find out here. This is a carrot you're dangling. What's the stick?"

"No stick," she said. "But this case … this victim, if that's what he is, matters. He's one of us, Jake. Judge Rand. If something really bad happened to him, I need to know if it's part of something bigger."

Jake wondered too. His brain hummed with scenarios. Questions. Motives. He wanted to find Judge Rand.

"If I agree to this, you'll give me anything I need?" he asked Landry.

"You name it," she said.

"In return for what?" he asked.

"Do you still own a suit?" she asked.

"One or two," he answered.

"Good," she said. "Plan on wearing one tomorrow."

Landry walked up to him. She was holding something in the palm of her hand. She extended it as if she wanted to shake his. He acted on reflex and took her hand. She pressed something cold and metallic into it. He looked down. It was a detective's badge. Jake closed his eyes and sighed. She might as well have yelled checkmate.

SIX

Cashen tried not to take the shattered glass around his feet as an omen. He held the coffeepot handle in one hand. The pot itself hit the floor two seconds ago after he accidentally knocked it against the granite countertop.

"Shit," he muttered. It was six thirty. His head was already pounding from lack of caffeine. Pulling the dustpan and brush off a hook under the cupboard, he made quick work of the mess.

He grabbed his keys off the little bistro table in the kitchen and carried the pan outside. Two tiny beads of glass stuck to his tie. He shook them out along with the rest of the glass in the pan.

Cashen's cabin sat nestled at the bottom of the hill toward the road. Grandpa Max owned the property. Two hundred prime wooded acres rising up the hill. The tall oaks obscured the main trail leading up to Grandpa's place. Cashen checked his watch. There wouldn't be enough time to head up and grab coffee with the old man. Besides, he'd see the suit and start asking questions Jake wasn't ready to answer yet. Not even for himself.

Tonight, he swore he'd make time to head up the hill and bring dinner. Maybe by then he could cook up a good story for why, after all the promises he made when he came back to town, he hadn't just handed the detective badge back to Meg Landry.

As it was, Cashen clipped it to his belt and climbed into the cab of his truck. There'd be just enough time to stop at Papa's Diner downtown and grab a coffee and maybe a slice of apple pie.

Cashen turned onto Grace Church Road heading north. If there were a different route into Stanley, he would have taken it. But unless he wanted to go a half hour out of his way outside the county and back around, there was no way to get from Grandpa's property to the county seat without heading right past the one place that still twisted his heart.

Ardenville. Just one square mile, the place had once been the second-oldest company town in the State of Ohio. The clay mill where Grandpa Max and three generations of Cashens had worked still operated. Still owned by the Ardens, the same family who had established the town one hundred and fifty years ago.

Grace Church Road had winding, hairpin curves and eventually became Ardenville's main street. The identical rowhouses on either side of the street were constructed from the same dark-red brick pulled from the blast furnaces by the miners who built this town. Now designated as historically significant, it was more historically dilapidated as far as Jake was concerned. The church for which the road was named had long since burned to the ground. Only the cemetery remained. It was there that an ornate, out-of-place modern quartz monolith rose against the backdrop of crooked, century-old tombstones. It drew Jake's eye every day even though he tried not to look. Gemma always said the monument reminded her of a middle finger. She would give one right back. It was the shrine itself that made her angry, not the woman buried beneath it.

Jake kept his hands gripped tightly at ten and two as he passed by the cemetery this morning. He did not need the reminder today of all days. He kept his gaze on the freshly painted yellow center line as he passed that shrine ... the one that marked his mother's grave.

He headed north, out of Ardenville and across the town line into Stanley. Downtown Stanley boasted just three traffic lights. Papa's Diner was at the corner of First Street and County Road 9. Jake pulled into a metered spot right in front. Those were new, the meters. They'd been installed well after Jake left for college, much to the uproar of the entire town.

Smoothing his tie, Jake headed into the diner, his head pounding. The strong scent of Tessa's special brew beckoned. He took a seat at the counter. Behind it, Tessa's husband, Spiros, hummed as he worked the grill.

Over the last quarter century, Tessa and Spiros Papatonis had become a town fixture as much as the streetlights. They'd emigrated from Greece and bought the property across from the courthouse. It had been a retail no man's land until the Papatonis had opened their kitchen. Their young daughter Nina's picture hung on the wall just above Spiros's head. A shrine of sorts, not unlike the one to Jake's mother that he'd passed on the way into town. Today, Spiros spoke to his daughter's picture in Greek as he flipped crepes. Something awful had happened to Nina Papatonis sometime after Jake left town. Raised around his own family tragedy and gossip, Jake felt it was none of his business to find out more. It was enough that he recognized the haunted way both Spiros and Tessa smiled, the light never quite reaching their eyes. His own grandmother had the same look until the day she died.

"Jake!" Tessa sang out as she saw him come in. "Two times, one week? You come every day now." Jake wasn't sure if that was a question or a command. Either way, it felt welcoming.

Tessa already had the coffee pot in her hand and grabbed an empty cup off the shelf beside her. "One cream?"

"Two eggs, toast almost burnt?" Spiros called out behind her, his accent just as heavy. That, too, had been his order from the day before.

"Yes," Jake said to both of them.

"Sit," Tessa said, setting the cup in front of him. She poured it for him and finished it off with a quick dash of cream from the carafe on the counter. Jake didn't much care if he burned off the roof of his mouth. He needed a jolt of caffeine so badly.

"Nice suit," Tessa said. Spiros turned and eyed him. He gave Jake an approving nod, then turned back to the griddle.

"Thanks," he said. "Still not sure I like the fit."

Tessa took a step back. She was what you'd call a handsome woman. She had a broad face with dark eyes and deep lines across her forehead. She had toned, muscular arms from decades of carrying heavy trays of food.

"Looks good on you," she said. Tessa reached across the counter and took the liberty of straightening Jake's tie. "You could use a haircut. Stop by Gunther's. He probably get you in on your lunch hour. He asks about you."

Jake smiled. Gunther Redmond was one of the "wrestling dads." His son Paul had been the 103 pounder Jake's senior year.

"I'll try to remember," Jake said.

"So how's Max?" Tessa said, her expression turning serious. "Trouble at the Dollar Kart, we heard. Kicked over a soup display?"

"What? No." Jake pursed his lips. The Worthington County rumor mill had a life of its own. If it was canned soup in the morning, by the afternoon, they'd be saying Gramps gunned down Aisle 5 with an AR.

"It was just a misunderstanding. The kid working the register couldn't count change. Typical millennial," Jake lied. But it was the kind of thing Tessa might eat up and far closer to the truth.

"Oh sure," she said. "Well, good then. I worry. He don't come in enough. You tell him."

"I make him poached eggs," Spiros called out. "Only guy I make poached eggs for. Where's he been?"

"Maybe it's the food!" a rowdy shout came from a booth far in the back. Jake couldn't see who it was from where he sat at the front of the diner. But he vaguely recognized the voice.

"You, you shut your pie face back there," Tessa gave it back. "Or maybe better. I'll give Jake your breakfast instead."

She was met with raucous laughter.

"Is that Frank Borowski?" Jake asked.

"Yes," Tessa answered, exasperated.

"Is that Jake?" Borowski called out. Jake turned on his stool.

"Oh boy," Tessa said. "Maybe run. Last chance before they get their hooks into you."

Frank Borowski came into view. Jake felt a little twist in his heart. Frank had been Worthington County's homicide detective before Ed Zender. Though Jake knew him best as

Coach Frank. For thirty years, he had moonlighted as Stanley High School's head wrestling coach. He was Jake's coach. A man he'd spent more time with than his own father. He was one of the reasons Jake had gone into law enforcement in the first place.

Jake rose. Tessa topped off his coffee. He thanked her and grabbed it as he walked back to meet Coach Frank and the others.

Frank came from the only table in the place big enough to seat twelve people. Tessa jokingly referred to the far end of the diner as her banquet hall.

Besides Frank, Jake recognized a few other retired cops. There was Bill Nutter, the property crimes detective who Gary Majewski replaced. Chuck Thompson, an old shift lieutenant, Jake heard was a detective before that. Virgil Adamski, who'd worked the property room. The rumor was, Adamski had been forced down there after too many excessive force complaints. The rest, Jake didn't know.

"I heard you died," Jake said to Thompson, genuinely surprised.

"We heard that too," Frank said, slapping Jake on the back. "Come on back and join us, kid. It's just our weekly meeting of the Wise Men."

"You mean Wise Asses!" Tessa shot back. "Better fit."

"Wise Men?" Jake asked.

"Bunch of us retired guys get together every Tuesday morning when we can swing it."

"Right," Tessa cracked. "They got nothing better to do."

"Oh pipe down, Tessa," Frank said. "If it weren't for us, you'd have no business at all today."

Tessa scowled at him, but it was all in good fun.

"Good to see you, Jake," Adamski said, rising. He shook the other men's hands in turn. Then Frank shook his hand. Seeing him took Jake off guard. He found himself a little choked up.

Jake got a good look at Coach Frank. He was beefier than he remembered. He'd put on a few pounds around the middle. The man liked his kapusta and kielbasa. He had thinning gray hair and sharp blue eyes. He was solid, like a tree trunk. Jake flinched on instinct as Coach pulled him into a proper over-and-under bear hug. An old wrestler's muscle memory took over and Jake broke the grip, raking his knuckles across Frank's ribs. Laughing through a grunt, Frank let go.

"You look good, Coach," Jake said. "You look tan!"

Jake couldn't ever remember Frank with a suntan.

"Don't let him fool you," Adamski said. "Asshole probably hasn't taken a bath in a week."

"Zip it," Frank said. "I just got back from my Fort Myers trip. Grouper and Snapper."

Nutter laughed and said, "Translation, he went out to the Tiki bars and pickled his liver."

"You still use Captain Russ?" Jake asked. Years ago, on Jake's spring break before leaving for college, Frank had taken him along on his annual Florida charter fishing excursion. It had been the only vacation Jake ever went on growing up.

"Sure do," Frank said. "He's just as ornery as ever. You should come next time."

"I'd like that," Jake said.

"Sit down," Frank said. "It's damn good to see you, kid. We, uh, heard about your promotion."

Jake was about to ask him how, but remembered this was Worthington County. Tessa's was probably ground zero for the rumor mill.

"Congratulations," Bill Nutter said. "How'd Zender take it?"

"Not sure he knows yet," Jake said.

"You looking into Judge Rand's disappearance?" Chuck Thompson asked.

"You know about that too?" Jake asked.

The group of men exchanged glances. Jake realized the judge's fate had likely been the main topic of this week's meeting of the Wise Men.

"Word's getting around," Frank said. "Landry giving the case to you?"

Jake didn't want to answer. He wasn't sure whether Landry had officially informed Ed Zender yet.

"You'll have to ask her," Jake demurred, sipping his coffee.

"Gotcha," Nutter said. "Yeah. I'd avoid the office this morning too if I were you. You heading over to the courthouse?"

Jake smiled. He realized the collective knowledge these men shared might actually help him with this case. But until he and Zender had words, it was probably better to wait. Besides, if he knew Frank and Nutter, they probably already had their own theory of the case. He didn't want to risk letting their opinions cloud his objectivity this early in the investigation. So, he took the wiser course and simply finished his coffee.

"Did Judge Rand take breakfast here very often?" Jake asked.

"Nope," Tessa answered. She reappeared to refill the men's coffee.

"He turned into a health nut over the last year," Adamski explained. "Dropped thirty pounds and started some ridiculous plant-based diet. Can you believe that? Plant-based. What does that even mean?"

Tessa thrust a piece of apple pie under Jake's nose. "See that?" she said. "Apples. Flour. Sugar. You know what that comes from? Plants. Judge started going to that vegan place two blocks over."

"There's a vegan place?" Jake asked, nearly choking down his last sip of coffee. "Here? In Stanley?"

"You've been gone a while," Frank said. "The place is going to hell. I think your Grandpa Max has the right idea. Hardly ever comes down that hill anymore. I've been meaning to pay him a visit."

"He'd like that," Jake said. "So would I."

Frank's eyes shone. It really had been too long since he'd seen Borowski. During wrestling season, Jake had always had Sunday dinners at Coach's house. His grandmother had never understood cutting weight and tried to bribe him with the most deliciously fattening Irish meals. Coach Frank would simply make him a salad and they'd watch old movies together.

"So how's Landry doing?" Frank asked. "It was a hell of a shock losing Greg O'Neal last month. He didn't tell me he was bringing you on. Man, I wished I could have seen him one more time. I didn't find out he died until I got back from Florida. They really aren't having a service?"

"Greg didn't want one," Nutter said. "He'd have hated it."

"Yeah," Jake said. He avoided answering the question on Landry. He didn't have one just yet.

"Well," Coach Borowski said. "I'd say giving you that shield is the first smart thing Landry's done. She's gonna have a tough time getting the rank and file to respect her. I hate to say it, but you might want to watch your back for a while. Zender might not take any of this lying down. I'll deny ever saying this, but Ed should have retired years ago."

Jake once again, chose diplomatic silence.

"It's good seeing all of you," he said. "But unlike you, I still have to work for a living."

After another round of good-natured ribbing, Jake rose to leave. He knew Frank Borowski and the others were right about Zender. He left a twenty on the counter for Tessa and headed across the street to the courthouse. Sampson Rand's clerk would be his first interview.

SEVEN

Deputy Court Clerk Tony Byers's voice echoed through the marble halls as he hailed Cashen. Cashen didn't know him well. Byers graduated at least a dozen years before he had and attended Worthington County's only private high school, St. Isidore's.

Despite the unfamiliarity, Cashen sensed Byers's distress. The man bounced on his heels, panting like he'd just run a hundred-meter dash.

"We can talk in here," Byers said, opening the door to the only jury room in the entire courthouse. Judge Rand and his Municipal Court counterpart Judge Finneas Cardwell shared it, staggering their trial schedule when needed.

Byers carried a weathered briefcase, which he lobbed on the oval mahogany conference table. He pulled out one of the twelve wooden chairs and sat, quickly clasping his hands together.

Cashen pulled out his notepad. "Thanks for meeting with me. I know this has to be a tough one."

Byers nodded. "It's been awful. Everyone around here is scared to death."

"When did you last speak to Judge Rand?" Cashen asked.

"Friday when we left the courthouse. Six o'clock. We park in the county lot. We usually walk there together."

"Six o'clock on a Friday? Does the judge usually stay that late?"

Byers nodded. "It's not unusual. He's got a felony murder trial coming at the end of next week. Some eleventh-hour evidentiary motions came in. We were reviewing the briefs."

Cashen made a note of it. Byers's story tracked with what he'd already observed at the scene. Rand's copies of those briefs were on his liquor cabinet.

"How did he seem?"

"The judge? He was fine. His normal self. He was eager for the trial to start. He always is. He had a few questions he wanted answered before Monday morning so I had my marching orders for the weekend."

"Did he mention any plans he had? Anyone he was meeting with over the weekend?"

Byers shook his head. "Not that I recall. I knew he was going to be available though. I knew I could always text him if I had questions or wanted to pick his brain on whatever he had me working on."

"Did you?"

"Yes. I texted the judge on Saturday afternoon. There was a case I wanted him to take a look at. I sent him a link. He never answered that text."

"Was that out of character for him?"

"Very much so," Byers said. "Judge always has his cell phone on him. It's not unusual for us to text each other ten, twenty times a day during the weekend. He'll even text me from my office to his office, just a wall away. I mean, it's constant. But I hadn't heard from him since that Friday night after we left."

"You tried to call him?" Cashen asked. He was still waiting on the report from Rand's cell phone.

"Oh yes," Byers said. "I called him three or four times. On Saturday and on Sunday. It kept going straight to voicemail."

"Had that ever happened before?" Cashen asked. "Where he went radio silent on you like that?"

"Not often," Byers said. "Maybe once or twice. Once I didn't realize he'd gone on a spur-of-the-moment trip down south. Bad cell reception, so he didn't get my messages. But we're talking a couple of hours. Not days."

"Did you go out to the house?" Cashen asked.

"I mean, I thought it was odd," Byers said. "Him not responding. But I wasn't worried like anything happened to him. Not until yesterday morning when he didn't show up here. Sampson Rand hasn't missed a day of court in the seven years he's been here. I worked for him at the prosecutor's office too for ten years before that. Twenty years I've been his clerk. I think I can count on one hand the times he's called in sick."

At the last, Byers's voice cracked. "He's like a father to me," Byers said. "He was on me for years to go to law school. Once he got elected judge, we both knew he'd need me too much until he got acclimated. Then seven years went by and here we are. There's something wrong. I feel it in my gut. Tell me. Did you find anything? Do you know anything?"

"It's early," Cashen said. "I'm afraid there's not much I can share."

Byers nodded, but worry lined his face.

"Who else was the judge close with?" Cashen asked. "I know his folks passed some time ago. I'm not aware of any other family he had in town."

"He didn't," Byers confirmed. "He had a sister but she moved down to the Louisville area. She passed away. Breast cancer. It's been seven or eight years. I think he had a niece by her, but they weren't close. The judge never goes out there. They never came to visit. We were his family. Those of us working in the court system with him."

"He was never married," Cashen said.

Byers shook his head. "He kept that part of his life super private."

"But do you know whether he was seeing anyone?"

It was then Byers shifted in his seat. His eyes darted to the side.

"Tony," Cashen said. "If you know, you need to tell me."

Tony met his gaze again. "Something bad happened. I know it."

"Let's not get ahead of ourselves. As of right now, Sampson Rand is a missing person. But you knew him about as well as anyone, I'm gathering. If there was a girlfriend, a significant other, I need to know."

"He never talked about it openly," Byers said. "But yes. I believe the judge was seeing someone."

"Her name? His name?"

Byers started to sweat. Cashen put his pen down. Byers reached across and picked it up. He wrote down a single name.

"You cannot let anyone know I'm the one who told you this. And it's a rumor, nothing more. I hate myself for even giving life to it. It feels ... it feels like I'm violating the judge's trust."

"You're helping me try to figure out where he is, Tony," Cashen said. He looked at the name scrawled on his notepad. Mandy Lovett. He didn't recognize it.

"She works in Judge Cardwell's court," Byers explained. "His court reporter. And I don't know for sure. I swear to God. I've never seen her with the judge. Never heard her talk about him. Never heard him talk about her. Not once. But a lot of people in this building think they know the judge's business. It's an ugly rumor."

"Why ugly?" Cashen asked, though he could pretty much guess.

"Mandy is married," Byers said, confirming his suspicion.

"I don't think any of it's true," Byers said. "At least, I don't want it to be. Mandy is a great girl. Don't get me wrong. But she's drama."

"How so?"

"Just a complainer. And probably one of the biggest gossips in the courthouse. Which is the only reason I'd think there's truth to the rumor about her and the judge. Because I've never heard her spreading that particular one."

"It would make sense," Cashen said. "If she's at the center of it."

"Exactly," Byers said. "But please, please, don't tell anyone I'm the one who gave you her name. I just know that nobody else here will. Mandy is pretty well liked around here. I'm not."

"Why is that?" Cashen asked.

"Because I don't hang out with the rest of them socially. I'm here to do my job. Serve the judge. That's it. I've got a life of my own. A family of my own."

He choked up again. He pulled out his phone and showed Cashen a picture. He was driving a pontoon boat. Behind him sat a pretty red-haired woman. Judge Rand sat beside her, holding a maybe three-year-old red-headed girl on his lap.

"That's my wife Lucy. My daughter Matilda. She calls him Judge Grandpa."

Cashen slid the phone back to him. "Thank you," he said.

"We were his family," Byers repeated. A dark thought entered Cashen's mind. If Rand had no family and Byers were telling the truth about how close they are, Rand's estate plan could provide a motive. Perhaps Byers himself stood to gain from Rand's death.

"So you've worked with Judge Rand since he was a prosecutor? What about death threats?" Jake asked.

"Oh, he's had them," Byers said. "I can't recall anything recently. But you're always going to encounter a few crackpots with the kind of career Judge Rand had."

"I would expect," Cashen said. "It would really help me if you could make a list of his most recent cases. If there are any litigants who made threats, I need to know it."

Byers reached into his beat-up briefcase. He pulled out a green file folder and slid it across to Cashen.

"Here's what I came up with so far," he said.

Cashen opened the flap and glanced at the top page inside. There were names, dates, case numbers, and a brief summary of the facts of each case.

"I started this last night," Byers explained. "I get what you're saying. About this only being a missing persons case. But Detective Cashen, I know. I just know."

Byers's words chilled him. Both the content of them and how he'd addressed him. Detective Cashen. It would take getting used to, but dammit if he didn't like it.

"I tried to tell all this to Ed Zender. I don't think he really understands how big a deal this is. Something bad has happened to the judge. I can just feel it."

"This is great, Tony," Cashen said, picking up the file folder.

The two men rose and Cashen extended his hand to shake Byers's. They walked out of the room together. Byers walked Cashen to the second-floor elevator and waited as Cashen stepped on.

"I'll let you know if I have any other questions," Cashen said. "But again. Thanks for this. This will save me hours of work."

Byers got a quizzical look on his face as Cashen pressed the first-floor button.

"Don't thank me yet. You haven't read all the names in there. You might not like what you find," Byers said just as the elevator doors closed.

Eight

Sergeant Jeff Hammer had one of those naturally turned-up mouths and constantly flushed cheeks that made Cashen think he was always happy. For the most part, he was. Cashen knew he'd graduated with his dad and that they'd been friends once upon a time. But like everyone else in Stanley, Hammer knew not to ever bring it up.

"We've got you set up over here," Jeff said. He gave Jake a good-natured slap on the back as he walked him into the office tucked at the end of the hall on the second floor. "Welcome to the Detective Bureau!"

The term Bureau was loose. Until last night, Worthington County had only ever had a maximum of two detectives at a time. The room, however, was the most coveted space in the building. Ed Zender and Gary Majewski enjoyed their own break table and coffee station. The rest of the department would find excuses to come up here and shoot the breeze until Ed or Gary would shoo them out.

"Right here," Jeff said. "Maintenance brought a desk and chair up from the basement. Your computer is hooked up already. If you don't like the configuration, we can deal with that."

Cashen thanked him, trying to swallow the irritated growl rising up. He preferred setting up his own computers. He knew it meant he could look forward to half a day unsnarling whatever set-up they'd done.

"Looks good, Jeff," Jake said. "I really appreciate you getting this done for me on such short notice."

So far, Ed and Gary hadn't come in. Cashen tried not to look at that as a bad omen. As if they couldn't be bothered to welcome Jake personally.

He turned to Hammer. "Look, I know this is a little awkward. You can cut the shit. Be honest. Ed's pissed. I wouldn't mind a heads-up on that. Or if you've got any advice for how to handle him."

Jeff shrugged. "Aw, Ed's all right. He's just set in his ways."

Cashen nodded. That was exactly the problem. "But he's a good guy at heart. He really has been grumbling about his workload for years. I'd been on Sheriff O'Neal trying to get approval for a second guy in crimes to persons. He'd have gotten to it eventually."

"Gotcha," Cashen said. Hammer hadn't really answered his question but he figured that was the best he'd get.

"Anything you need though," Hammer repeated. "We need a win on Judge Rand."

"Did you know him well?" Cashen asked.

"I knew him. We weren't exactly fishing buddies or anything."

"There was a rumor he was seeing his court reporter on the side. Have you heard that?"

Hammer sucked a breath in through his teeth. "Sticky, that one. I don't like to be the one spreading rumors."

"We're beyond that, Jeff," Cashen said, irritated. He had the sense that Hammer might be protecting Ed's turf despite everything he'd just said.

"Yeah. I guess so. Yeah. I'd heard that rumor. But there was no substance to it as far as I know. Nobody ever said anything concrete. Just a wink-and-a-nudge kind of thing."

"Well, thanks," Cashen said. "Any idea where Ed is now?"

"No, actually. He's usually up here by now. He had Brouchard running a few warrants for him. The judge's cell phone, his safe, his computer, all that stuff."

Cashen bristled. Those were his instructions to Tim Brouchard. Sheriff Landry had made it clear Judge Rand's case was his and his alone. The last thing he needed was a butthurt Ed Zender muddying the waters. He and Zender were going to have to have an uncomfortable conversation sooner rather than later.

"Well, tell him I need to talk to him if you see him?" Cashen said. "I should probably dive into the leads I do have."

"Sure, sure," Hammer said, looking relieved for the out. "I'll let you get to it. Anything though. Anything at all. I'm just on the other side of this wall."

Jake thanked him again and waited for Hammer to disappear down the hall. He took his suit coat off and hung it over the back of the chair. The thing immediately began to list to the side under the weight of the coat.

"Great," Cashen muttered. The chair obviously came from the bowels of the basement after countless other cops cast it aside.

When he tried to boot up his computer, it hung up on endless updates he never would have opted for. He'd be lucky if he got a welcome screen before lunch. He clicked off the monitor and pulled the beginnings of his file out of his bag.

There wasn't much yet. Not until his warrants were in place. For now, he had Tony Byers's notes and the most basic cell phone records for Judge Rand. Cashen looked at those first.

He saw multiple incoming calls from Tony's cell phone number to the judge, just like Tony had said. He at least had one witness who had so far told the truth. The timing of the call matched Tony's story as well.

The case files were going to take far longer to get through. Cashen grabbed the desk phone and made a call down to the Probate Court Clerk's office. There was one other thing he could check without needing a warrant.

"Worthington County Probate Clerk," a chipper voice answered.

"Hey, Em. Jake Cashen. How are you doing today?"

"Jake!" Emily Kennedy gushed. "I'm good! What can I do for you?"

Emily was good people. Two grades below him, she'd served as a trainer for the wrestling team. Jake had spent plenty of time with Emily as she wrapped his knee. He'd heard she married, divorced, and was now raising six kids all on her own.

"Well," he said. "This is a strange request, maybe. But I suppose you've heard about Judge Rand."

"Of course," she said, her voice lowering. "And I heard Sheriff Landry has you looking into it."

Jake shook his head. There probably wasn't a single soul in the county who didn't know he came to work in a suit this morning. "This is a stab in the dark. But can you check whether Sampson Rand has already filed a will or anything in probate court?"

Jake knew many estate planning lawyers would file their clients' wills with the court as standard practice for safekeeping, long before they died. It didn't mean he'd be able to see the contents of it yet, but it would help to at least know it was there. Plus he might be able to quickly find out which lawyer Judge Rand had handling his affairs.

"Gimme one sec," Emily said. He could hear her fast fingers typing away at her keyboard.

There were people out in the hallway. Jake looked over his shoulder. He recognized Ed Zender's voice. He was shouting at someone further down the hall.

"Mmmm," Em said. "I don't see a will on file. But there's a trust. It was filed two years ago. He used some lawyer who practices out of Cincinnati. You want his contact information? It's right here in the filing."

"You're a gem," Jake said. He grabbed a pen and wrote down the lawyer's information.

"Do you think he's dead though?" Emily asked.

"He's just missing at this point," Jake said. "I'm just getting my ducks in a row."

"Sure," Emily said. "What a welcome back to Stanley, huh? You know everybody still asks about you. Gemma gets bombarded with questions all the time. We missed you around here."

"Thanks," Jake laughed. The shouting in the hallway got louder. Gary Majewski walked into the office. Jake waved as he cradled the phone between his ear and shoulder. Gary waved back but cast a furtive glance back into the hallway. Clearly neither he nor Zender realized he was already here.

"Don't be a stranger, okay?" Emily said. "A group of us get together over at Blackhand Hills Lanes during season. We bowl a few games after the home meets and tournaments. You should come. Everyone expects great things from your nephew Ryan this year. I'll bet he's loving getting some pointers from his Uncle Jake."

"Sure," Jake said, distracted by the shouting. Zender threw an F bomb or two. "I'll try and make it. It's good talking to you, Em. And thanks. You've been a big help."

"Anytime. Have a good day, okay, Jake?"

"Will do," Jake said and hung up.

"You wanna clue me in?" Jake said to Gary, pointing toward the hallway.

Gary gave him a dismissive wave. "I wouldn't worry about it. Did you make the coffee yet?"

"Uh ... sorry. I just got here."

Gary scowled. "Well, for the future. First man in."

"Next time," Jake said, rising. He heard Landry's voice. He couldn't make out what she said, but now Jake knew who Zender was swearing at.

He poked his head out in the hallway. Two uniformed deputies scurried past him, anxious to get as far away from the altercation brewing near the stairwell.

"Complete bullshit," Zender shouted. Jake could only see his back. But the back of Ed's neck was purple. He was shaking his finger in the air.

"Get over it, Zender," Landry said. "Not everything's about you." Lord. Zender had her practically pinned against the wall. Every muscle in Jake's body tensed.

"O'Neal never would have approved of this. This is not how he does things."

"It's how I do things," she said. "If you don't like it, you're back in field ops, Ed. The words you want here are thank you." Jake was on the move. Zender towered over Meg Landry. He was twice her size. He put a big, beefy hand on her shoulder.

"Yeah, thanks for nothing, bitch," he said.

Jake Cashen moved with the force of an avalanche fueled by rage and adrenaline. He plowed into Ed Zender, shoving an arm under the larger man's chin. He lifted with such force, Zender flew off his feet before Jake put him into the wall and held him there.

"You got a problem?" Jake said.

"Jake!" Landry shouted.

Zender held his hands out wide. "Get your hands off me!"

"Not until you apologize," he said.

"Jake!" Landry stepped forward. She gripped Jake's arm and pulled at him, hard.

"Cool off, Ed," Jake said. He let go of Zender. Zender jerked his shoulders, straightening his suit coat. His face had gone pure white. He eyed Landry.

"Don't look at her!" Jake said.

"That's enough, Detective!" Landry shouted. "Ed, I'm sure you've got plenty to do in your office. Go there!"

Ed sneered at Landry, but he seemed grateful for the chance to make a getaway. He stormed past Jake and slammed the office door behind him. There were now about a half a dozen uniformed deputies and a couple of civilian clerks poking out of various doorways to catch a glimpse of the drama.

Meg Landry still had her hand on Jake's arm. She pulled him into the stairwell.

"You okay?" he asked her.

"Am I okay?" Her eyes bulged. The woman was pure, coiled fury. "Yes, Jake. I'm okay. What the hell was that?"

"I was trying to help you out," Jake answered, incredulous at Landry's anger.

"I don't need your help."

"He called you a ..."

"I'm aware of what he called me. You think I haven't been called worse? Christ, Jake. I've been a female cop for twenty-five years. I've faced down way bigger than Ed Zender."

"I was trying to help," Jake insisted.

"Please don't," she said. "While I appreciate that there's still some chivalry left in the world, I sure as hell don't need it. Not here. This is my house now."

Jake put his hands up in surrender. He backed away from Landry.

"Like it or not, you have to work with Ed Zender. You think you can manage that?"

Jake nodded. "I'll deal with Zender."

"Good," Meg said. "Do it quickly. We have a missing judge to find. Come find me at the end of your shift."

With that, she turned on her high heel and clacked down the stairs in a flurry of curly hair.

Jake let out a breath and closed his eyes, steeling himself for his walk back into the Detective Bureau.

By the time he got there, Zender was gone again. Gary tried to look busy at his desk, barely acknowledging Jake's presence.

"Fine," Jake muttered. He hunkered down on his crooked chair and grabbed the file Tony Byers made for him. He'd listed any cases or litigants that had gone on record with a beef against Sampson Rand.

He got three pages into it and his stomach dropped. A single name stared back at him.

"Shit," Jake muttered. Through gritted teeth, he picked up his cell phone and punched in his sister's number.

"Gemma," he said, barely waiting for her to answer. "Whatever you're doing, cancel it. Meet me at your house in an hour."

NINE

Jake Cashen knew that look. Gemma stared ice lasers at him, hands on her hips as he stepped out of his car. She was about to try "big sistering" him like she'd done a thousand times growing up.

"What in the hell, Jake?" she said as he slammed his car door. "I had to push back a showing. I've got a listing in Carlow Township. Just off Grace Church Road in Ardenville. Hart Lake lakefront. Do you know how long I've been trying to get those people to take a chance on me up there?"

"I don't even know why you keep trying," he said. And he didn't. But that was one major difference between Jake and his sister. She still craved acceptance from their mother's family. Acceptance she'd never get as long as their father's blood flowed through her veins, too. As far as the Ardens were concerned, Jake and Gemma might as well be spawned by Satan himself.

"Because it'll make my year," she said. "Because I've got two boys who enjoy getting new clothes every once in a while. And, oh, I don't know. Maybe a college education like their famous Uncle Jake."

If he stood there and took it, Gemma might wind herself up into a real thunder.

"We need to talk," he cut her off. "Not out here."

He strode right past her and let himself into Gemma's front door. She lived on the very edge of Poznan township, two miles from Grandpa's place. This had been their parents' property. They'd torn the old house down years ago and rebuilt Gemma a small, but sturdy three-bedroom brick ranch. She'd redone it all in the farmhouse style made popular on every home remodeling show from the last decade. Barn doors everywhere. Giant wooden signs designating every room for what you're supposed to do in it. Jake didn't get it. Why in the hell do you need a sign telling people to "EAT" when you were clearly in the damn kitchen?

"This will be quick," he said to Gemma as she stormed in behind him.

"Sit," he said, pointing to her living room couch. She did. Seeing something in his eyes, maybe, that told her he wasn't screwing around.

"Nice suit," she said.

"Dickie," Jake said.

Gemma furrowed her brow. "Okay?"

Jake towered over his sister. She looked small on that couch as he began his interrogation.

"You know what I'm doing," he said, putting his hands on his hips so his jacket spread and she could see the badge. "The whole town knows I'm investigating Judge Rand's disappearance. Don't try to pretend you didn't know."

"I knew," she said, swallowing hard. All her bravado was gone. Gemma was every bit as sharp as Jake was. More so. Of course, she knew he'd come asking these very questions.

"I asked his clerk for a list of people on record threatening the judge. You wanna tell me why your ex was at the top of it?"

Gemma let out a hard breath. "Rand handled our divorce," she said. "He handles everyone's divorce. Things were going along fine for a while. But last year, Dickie got a burr up his ass and sued me for full custody of Aiden. It went nowhere. With his track record, that was a no-brainer for Judge Rand. Dickie didn't take it well. When Rand issued his final ruling denying Dickie's motion, he kind of lost it."

"Kind of?" Jake said. "Gemma, he threatened to kill Rand. In open court. On the record."

"I know, Jake, I was there."

"You should have told me," he said.

"I'm telling you now," she said.

There was something in her eyes. Gemma wasn't a crier. God knew she had reason to be. But not even when she put her firstborn in the ground five minutes after she was born had Gemma shed a tear. She was one of the mentally toughest people Jake knew. She'd had to be.

Now, though, it was just an instant. A quick flutter of lashes, and Jake realized his sister damn near broke down right in front of him.

He sat on the couch beside her. Just like that, the moment passed. Gemma squared her shoulders and met her brother's eye.

"Gemma," he said. "What else haven't you told me?"

"You know what you need to know, Jake. We're fine. We're all fine."

"How'd Aiden take all of it?" Jake asked. "The custody crap."

Gemma shrugged. "He's six. Dickie and I have been divorced for as long as he remembers. Dickie pays attention to him when he feels like it. Aiden's learned not to depend on his dad for anything. I kept the court stuff away from him. Figured if by some long shot Rand granted Dickie more visitation, I'd cross that bridge when we came to it. We never came to it. Dickie can say all he wants to about being a changed man. But then he goes and threatens the judge. So he's down to limited, supervised visitation. He barely even asks for it. Aiden hasn't seen him since the summer."

"So why was he trying to sue you for full custody?" Jake asked.

"It was never about Aiden. Dickie was trying to get me to pay attention to him. To see him. He knew I'd have to go to court and be in the same room with him. He still thinks there's a chance I'll take him back. He's never really had the slightest interest in being a dad to Aiden."

"Gemma," Jake said. "If Judge Rand ends up dead. Or hurt. Dickie's a suspect. I'm going to have to get into it. I need you to tell me right now what I'm going to find in that court file."

A slow, sad smile spread across Gemma's face. "What do you want me to say, Jake?"

"The truth."

She looked skyward. "I don't know what I was thinking with that one. I mean, I should know better. The entire Gerald clan is messed up. I know their reputation. I don't know. Seven years ago, when I was pushing my mid-thirties, it just hit me. I wasn't feeling too great about myself. Like, what did I have to show for it? Two failed marriages already. Ryan was nine years old at the time and I was still smarting from my divorce with *his* dad even though it had been a couple of years. And then Dickie came along. Twenty-eight he was. Looking like Brad Pitt."

Jake wrinkled his nose. He'd never thought of Dickie Gerald as anything other than a greasy, scrawny redneck.

Gemma saw his expression. "Yeah, well. I thought I was getting *Legends of the Fall* Brad Pitt. Turns out Dickie was more *Twelve Monkeys*."

"Gemma ..."

"He hit me, okay?" she blurted.

Every muscle in Jake's body went rigid. He had to remind himself to breathe.

"How bad? When?"

"Does it matter?" she asked. "It was just the once. I packed his things and threw them all out on the lawn the next morning while he was at work. I called Grandpa. When Dickie came back, Gramps was sitting on a lawn chair with a shotgun. Dickie was smart enough to know Gramps is crazy enough to actually blow a hole into him. That was that."

"Why didn't you tell me?" Jake asked.

"And then what? You'd have grabbed another lawn chair?"

"Don't," he said.

"No, I mean it, Jake. What? You were going to drop everything? Leave Chicago? Hightail it out here and beat the crap out of Dickie? You know the Geralds' reputation too. They would have made trouble for you. You'd have done something stupid and got yourself kicked out of the FBI."

"You're blaming me?" he said.

"I'm protecting you," she said. "From yourself. And we handled it."

"Gemma," he said. "You call me."

"I was embarrassed, okay?" she said. "I knew what you'd think. What everyone thought. There goes Gemma Cashen again. The town tragedy. One more bad decision coming back to bite her in the ass."

"Dickie hit you," Jake said. "That's not your fault."

"Sure," she said.

"And he's still trouble," Jake said.

"Don't do anything stupid now, Jake," she said. "Not again."

He bristled. "Meaning what?"

"I know you," she said. "You came back. Here. Something happened with the Bureau you're not telling us. I haven't asked you. I won't. But I know you. You let your temper get the best of you or something. Or you broke some rule and the Bureau bounced you. Admit it."

"I resigned," he said through gritted teeth.

"Fine," she said.

"You should have told me," he said. "You're my sister. Ryan and Aiden are my nephews."

She didn't answer.

"I'm going to have a talk with Dickie," he said.

"Jake ..."

"I'm investigating a missing judge," Jake said. "A man Dickie Gerald threatened to kill. I'm going to have a talk with him. And good for the old man, by the way. You should cut him some slack."

Gemma shot to her feet. Her face turned purple. "Slack? Jake, you need to be careful. You've been gone a long time."

"And I'm here now," he said. "The way the two of you go at it ..."

"Stop," she said. "Just stop. You have no idea what you're talking about. He puts on a show for you. You don't know what he's really like."

"He's stubborn," Jake said. "Just like you. And he knows you're trying to get him to sell the land."

"I'm trying to do something that will benefit the entire family. Me. You. My boys."

"It's his land," Jake said. "He worked for it. Fought for it. And it's his decision."

"I'm not trying to get him to sell it, you idiot," she said. "I'm trying to get him to let me build another cabin or two up by the road. Let me turn them into rentals. Do you have any idea how much money we can make? He doesn't have to do a thing. Doesn't have to even see the people in those cabins. Jake, Blackhand Hills is turning. City people are paying hundreds of dollars a night to rent cabins in the Hollows. I could make us close to a quarter of a million a year."

"You wanna turn Grandpa's land into a tourist attraction?" he said. "I live in one of those cabins, Gemma."

"For how long?" Her words were a whip-crack.

"What?"

"For how long? You don't have to admit what really happened with you and the FBI. I already know."

"You don't know anything, Gemma," he muttered.

"I know you! This is a pit stop for you. You've been trying to escape Blackhand Hills your whole life."

"You wanted me to!" he snapped back. "You begged me to go when I got that scholarship."

"I know," she said, softer. "I know. And I'm glad you did. But this? This isn't for you anymore. Even now. When you came back, you said you just wanted the quiet. You wanted to be left alone. No drama. No excitement. And here you are, not a month into it and you're investigating Judge Rand's disappearance. If he's dead, it's going to be one of the biggest scandals to hit this town since ..."

"Don't," he said.

"Since Mom and Dad died," she finished. "With you, right at the center of it. Pretty soon, that won't be enough. You'll want more. You were born for wanting more."

"You want to turn the family land into an Airbnb!" he countered.

"Jake, come on," she said.

"I can't do this right now," he said, rising. "I've got to get back to work."

Gemma nodded. He hated the pain in her eyes. Guilt washed through him. Men had hurt his sister. He never wanted to be one of them.

"I talked to Emily Kennedy," he said, abruptly changing the subject.

"Oh?" Gemma said, brightening.

"She said Ryan's been looking really good on the mat."

Just like that, her face darkened a bit. "He's got potential," she said. "But he's wild. Just like ... well, you were."

Jake smiled. He couldn't fault her observation. If it weren't for Frank Borowski, Jake likely never would have learned the discipline it took to make it to the state tournament, let alone win the whole thing.

And just like that, he understood his sister's tone. Jake had Frank. Who did his sixteen-year-old nephew have?

"I'd like to watch a match," Jake said.

Gemma nodded. "There's a pre-season dual next week."

"I'll be there." Jake smiled. He hoped Gemma took the weight of his words.

She turned toward the window, denying his ability to read her face. He supposed that was answer enough.

He might have said more but a text came through from Sheriff Landry. The warrants were signed. The Ohio Bureau of Criminal Investigations wanted him to meet them at the judge's house first thing in the morning.

TEN

Agent Mark Ramirez had a face that was hard to read. He stared at Cashen down a long nose through readers perched at the end. Cashen shook his hand.

"Thanks for getting out here so quick," Jake said. Ramirez worked out of the Bureau of Criminal Investigation's Richland, Ohio office. The second he had his warrants secured, Ramirez moved Judge Rand's house to the top of his list.

It had been five days now since anyone had seen or heard from Sampson Rand.

"Glad to do it," Ramirez said. "I knew Rand. Good judge."

It wasn't lost on Jake that Ramirez had just used the past tense.

"I'll cut to it," Ramirez said. "You're not looking at a burglary, Detective."

Cashen's pulse quickened. Of course he'd known it. His gut told him as much the second he stepped foot in Rand's house the first time. Still, he'd hoped his instincts were wrong. They rarely were.

"Come on," Ramirez said, pulling the crime scene tape leading to the front door. "I'll walk you through it."

Jake followed him into the living room. Ramirez had three other agents still dusting for prints and bagging evidence. Jake walked only where Ramirez did. He turned left down the hallway and led Jake into the judge's master bedroom. He had the large fire safe opened.

"Everything's inventoried," Ramirez said. "Judge kept his personal papers in here. He had a few handguns, ammo, gold coins. A few rare ones. Some cash and jewelry."

"I didn't find anything out of order in the rest of the house," Jake said. "Didn't look like the safe had been touched."

"We lifted only one set of prints off the safe," Ramirez said. "There's a partial handprint on the top. I should have that run through by tomorrow afternoon."

Ramirez had the judge's papers in a clear plastic bag.

"You mind?" Jake asked.

Ramirez handed Jake the tablet he'd been holding. "Everything's already scanned in," he said. "I figured you'd want to see."

Jake thanked him and took the tablet. He scrolled through the scanned images of the papers contained in the bag. The judge had a will and a trust set up. He'd left everything to the niece who lived in Louisville. Same with the life insurance policy. If the judge's clerk Tony Byers was right, the girl hadn't spoken to her uncle in years. Jake was happy he could at least check Tony Byers off his list of people with a possible motive to hurt Rand.

"Desk was locked too," Ramirez said. "More work and personal documents. He had a .38 Smith and Wesson snub nose revolver in the top drawer. The thing was fully loaded."

"Interesting," Jake said.

"The interesting bits are in the den," Ramirez said. Jake handed him back his tablet and walked with him back to the den.

Jake already knew the judge's wallet and phone had been on the side table next to his leather recliner.

"What'd you find in his wallet?" Jake asked.

"Nothing unusual," Ramirez answered. "He had three hundred and twenty bucks in it. Fifties and twenties. A couple of credit cards, driver's license, his hunting and fishing licenses, a concealed carry permit. We had the locksmiths come out and open up the gun cases over there. I've got them all cataloged and in custody for safekeeping. Same with the .38 we found in his desk."

"Did you find any signs of forced entry anywhere?" Jake asked.

"Nothing," Ramirez said. "Not a one. No pry marks on the safe, the desk drawers. Nothing. We lifted a few more prints out here in the den. Got the ones on the martini glass found on the floor. The ones on the desk. We'll of course compare everything to Rand's prints on file with the county."

"Appreciate it," Jake said. "The man had a lot of valuable property in the house."

"Yeah," Ramirez agreed. "You knew this wasn't a burglary already though, right?"

"Yeah," Jake said. "I could smell it."

"So did I," Ramirez said. "Bleach. It was faint. But there's no mistaking it. I'll get to that. There were a couple of other things though. Those papers he had on the credenza behind the chair. You saw them?"

"I did," Jake said. "Powder burns?"

"You got it in one," Ramirez said. "Duffy, can you catch the lights?"

One of Ramirez's men came forward and pulled the blinds to the sliding door on the other side of the room, darkening it. Then he flipped the light switch on the wall. Ramirez held a blue light and switched it on. Jake immediately saw the ghostly, glowing blue splatter patterns on the corner of the credenza on the floor from the luminol sprayed earlier.

"And here," Ramirez said, moving the light up the wall. Another splatter pattern. There wasn't a large amount of blood in either spot. The judge could have been shot. It still didn't mean he was dead.

Ramirez squatted down behind the recliner. He brought the light to the floor and pointed. "Here," he said. "It's tough to make out. But we've got suspected blood between the wood planks. I think this is where your suspect tried to clean up. The bleach smell is strongest here. They did a good job of it. Just not good enough."

"You think this is enough blood to presume somebody was killed here?"

Ramirez rose to his feet and handed the black light back to Duffy. Duffy opened the blinds and turned on the room lights. "I don't like to presume. But I don't think we really have to in this case." He jerked his chin toward Duffy. The younger man handed Ramirez a clear vial. Ramirez placed it in Jake's hand.

Jake held the vial up to the light. A large chunk of pink tissue floated in liquid.

"I mean," Ramirez started. "You know as well as I do that any decent defense attorney would argue no body, no murder. But it's gonna be kind of hard to sell that argument when you can hold up a chunk of your victim's frontal lobe."

Jake raised a brow and handed the vial back to Ramirez.

"Found it in that potted plant against the wall," Ramirez explained.

"That'll do it," Jake said. "Good catch."

"We've got the judge's toothbrush. I'll have the lab do a rush on the blood samples and that bit of brain. The prints. I should have your phone forensics report for you in a couple of days. We're pretty backed up but I'll see what we can do."

"I really appreciate it, Mark," Jake said. He scanned the room, letting his mind's eye take in everything Ramirez had confirmed.

"Shooter stood here, you think?" Jake asked. He walked to the front of the recliner. "What's your guess? He shoots him no more than ten feet away?"

"I'd say you're spot on," Ramirez said. "I mean, the man could have been asleep. Who knows? But I'd say the judge was looking right at the guy."

"He didn't shoot him from behind," Jake said. "He could have." Jake walked around so he faced the back of the recliner. He brought his hand up, simulating a gun and pulling a phantom trigger.

"He wanted to see his face," Jake said. "Know who he was."

"Or she," Ramirez said.

"Or she."

"I'll get a hold of you when my full report is done. But with the amount of suspected blood we found and this"—Ramirez held up the vial with the brain tissue—"I'd say you've got yourself a homicide."

Jake nodded.

"For what it's worth," Ramirez said. "It's good you're here." He emphasized the word "you're."

"Thanks," Jake said.

"How much shit did Zender give you when your sheriff pulled you into this?"

Jake chewed his lip. He didn't know Ramirez well. He already knew he could trust him to run a crime scene. But so far, that trust couldn't extend beyond that.

"We're, uh, still working out the kinks."

Ramirez laughed. It was the first emotion the man had expressed. "Kinks. I'll bet."

"You got a read on Zender?" Jake asked.

"Well," Ramirez said. "Zender tends not to call me in when he should. And he tends not to listen to me when he does. Between you and me, it will not at all surprise me if that partial we found on the top of the safe belongs to Ed. He's a menace at crime scenes. I can think of at least a half dozen cases that never made it past the grand jury because Ed blundered the chain of custody or traipsed through my scene like it was a playground. I'm hoping ... praying ... I don't find anything more of his than that partial. But if you ask me, and I know you haven't yet, but if you did. Don't let Ed Zender anywhere near this one again."

"I appreciate that, Mark," Jake said. "And I'll keep it in mind."

"Make sure you do," Ramirez said. "Sam Rand was one of the good ones. Treated law enforcement with respect. This is a real loss to the bench down here. If these are his brains I'm holding, that is. They don't make 'em like Rand anymore."

"So I hear," Jake said. He shook Ramirez's hand as the two of them walked back out of the house.

"I'll be in touch," Ramirez said.

Jake climbed behind the wheel of his cruiser and pulled out his cell phone. He texted Sheriff Landry as he'd promised to do the second he got in the car.

"Will need final confirmation from the lab. BCI will have it by tomorrow. So no press conference yet. But the judge is dead. Can confirm."

He watched three blinking dots for a moment. Then Meg Landry answered with the single word that summed up the day.

"Shit."

Eleven

Dickie Gerald lived in Maudeville not too far from Corky the raccoon. He and his brothers ran the family business, Gerald Auto. Jake had always heard they had low level connections to the Hilltop Boys, Southern Ohio's most notorious organized crime syndicate. They ran everything from drugs to guns, and had a hand in the casinos along the Kentucky border. Dickie's father Jerry got popped for armed robbery about a decade ago and was serving federal time.

The girl at the counter shouted at Jake as he blew past her. "You can't go back there!" Jake clocked just one security camera in the right corner of the ceiling, but nowhere else.

He found Dickie sitting on a stool at the workbench in the back. He was texting someone. Another mechanic had his head under the hood of a Chevy Cavalier. A kid about fifteen leaned on a push broom near the back.

"Out," Jake shouted, showing his badge as he spread his suit jacket, hands on his hips.

Dickie looked up from his phone. Gemma's words echoed in Jake's mind. The only similarity he could see between Dickie and Brad Pitt was his stick-straight, shaggy blond hair, and the fact both men had arms and legs.

"Prodigal brother." Dickie smiled. "I heard you were back in town." He gestured to the two other men, giving them permission to do as Jake asked.

"Go on, Syl," Dickie shouted over Jake's shoulder. The counter girl backed out of the room too.

"What do I owe the pleasure?" Dickie asked. He wiped his hands on a greasy towel and tossed it back on the workbench. Jake kept his arms at his sides when Dickie offered to shake hands.

"I've got a few questions for you," Jake said. "Your answers to them are gonna dictate the rest of your day."

Dickie smiled. He was younger than Jake by about five years. Which put him a decade younger than Gemma. He was Gemma's mid-life-crisis marriage.

"You gonna arrest me, brother?" Dickie said.

"I need you to think back, Dickie. Think hard. Where were you last weekend? Start with Friday night."

Dickie jerked his head back, surprised by the question. "Whatever that crazy sister of yours told you, I'm not ..."

"Dickie, you're gonna need to come up with an answer to my question."

Dickie scratched his chin. "Well, lemme see. You're talking this past weekend?"

"That's what I said."

"That was the night of the McBain fight. UFC. He wiped the floor with that Spanish kid. Broke his jaw, they're saying. Snap. Pow! That kid's so dumb he just kept on coming."

"You've just told me where Ewan McBain was. I asked you where you were."

"Watching. The. Fight," Dickie said.

"Where?"

"My brother Jordy's. You know Jordy. I think he graduated with you."

Jordy Gerald had been a Grade A bullying asshole, if Jake's memory served.

"Right," Jake said. "And I'm sure Jordy's going to confirm this."

"Of course he will. I ain't lying. We watched the fight. Jordy's got a trailer out on County Road 14. Better internet than I get out here."

"Who else was there?" Jake asked.

"Jordy's girlfriend, Stacy Mays. She didn't stay for the whole night. They got into a fight. She kept at him about something or another. You know how they get."

Jake wasn't sure if he meant Jordy and Stacy specifically, or women in general. Either way, the urge to punch him in the throat poured through Jake.

"What about the rest of the weekend?" Jake asked.

"I stayed over," Dickie asked. "We got to drinking. I passed out on the couch. Came back here to the shop around dinnertime the next day. See that pretty little Mustang over there?"

Jake looked over his shoulder. Dickie had a lime-green '71 Mustang Mach 1 up on blocks.

"I'm rebuilding the engine. It's going to purr when I'm finished. Anyway, a part I'd been waiting for came in Saturday afternoon. You can see the package for it right here."

Dickie waved an empty brown shipping box at Jake. "I wanted to get started right away. Worked all through Saturday night and Sunday."

"Who else was here?"

"Sylvia came in Sunday morning. My boy Trace, the one you just kicked out. He'll tell you. He's the one who called me to tell me the part came in. What's this all about? I asked you once. What the hell's Gemma been telling you? I haven't seen her for weeks. Not my boy either."

"About that," Jake said. "You got yourself in a little trouble a few months ago, didn't you? Rumor is you don't really care for Judge Sampson Rand."

Dickie's face changed. Gone was the shit-eating grin and bravado. For the first time since Jake walked in, Dickie slid off his stool and stood up straight.

"What's she been saying?" he asked. "Gemma's the one keeping me from seeing that boy. She tell you that?"

"I'm not here about Gemma," Jake said. "I asked you about Judge Rand. You're on record threatening to kill him in open court. You pay attention to the local news at all?"

Dickie looked utterly mystified. His eyes darted back and forth, as if he were expecting someone to swoop in and save him.

"Yeah, I said some stuff," Dickie admitted. "Your sister likes to spread lies about me."

"I feel I need to strongly recommend you stop mentioning my sister's name to me," Jake said. "You got any guns registered in your name, Dickie?"

Dickie's face turned sheet white. "Now hold on. What the hell's this all about?"

"Answer the question."

Dickie started to sweat. "Yeah," he said. "I got two shotguns and a muzzle loader. I hunt. You know that. Everybody hunts. They're locked up at the house. You can check for yourself. I got nothing to hide, man."

"Maybe I will," Jake said. "In the meantime, don't get any crazy ideas, Dickie. Stick around."

"Look," Dickie said. He stopped pacing. "Whatever she said, it's bullshit. That girl's been trying to turn my head around for years. Posting those pictures online with her tits hanging out. She knows I'm gonna see it. Wrapping herself around any guy that'll look at her. It's sad. She's old and sad."

Jake shot an arm out. Quick as a snake, he had Dickie's right cheek smashed against the workbench, one arm bent backward, high in the middle of his back. Dickie's breath came hard with his nose squished against the wood.

"First and last warning, Dickie. You go near my sister, you so much as look at her or mention her name, I'll end you. We clear?"

"You're just as crazy as she is," Dickie snorted. He kicked backward, hitting air as Jake stood with a wide stance.

"Wrong answer, Dickie," Jake said. "The words you're looking for are yes, sir."

"I'll kill you, man," Dickie said. "You're a psycho. Just like she is. Just like your old man. Batshit crazy. All three of you."

"Shut up, Dickie," Jake said, his anger turning white hot.

"I know what you are," Dickie said, snorting against the plywood. "My old man said your pop came in here one day ranting about aliens and the government putting sensors in his brain." Dickie broke out in a high-pitched laugh. Jake squeezed his neck.

"You got his blood," Dickie cried out. "Does it scare you? I bet it scares you. We all know what you are. My dad knew the coroner. You wanna know what he said? He told me your dad ate your mama's brains after he blew them out. You're next, you piece of shit."

"I really wish you hadn't said that, Dickie," Jake said. He could barely see straight. It had been the likes of Dickie Gerald who had spread the worst of the rumors about his parents all over town. "You're getting close to hurting my feelings, Dickie."

"Go to hell," Dickie said. "You got no idea who you're messing with."

"Oh, I think I do."

"Stupid bitch," he said.

Molten rage poured through Jake. He eased up, letting Dickie raise his head far enough so Jake could smash it right back down to the table.

Jake let him go. Dickie cried out and held his nose as blood gushed out of it. He retreated to the corner, crying. Jake turned on his heel and walked away.

TWELVE

By the end of the week, the whole world would find out Judge Sampson Rand was dead. Sheriff Landry would handle the press conference right alongside the prosecutor, Tim Brouchard, on the courthouse steps. Jake chose to stay far clear of it, ducking into Papa's Diner on his way into the office.

Like before, Tessa and Spiros had his order down pat. Coffee with cream, no sugar, and toast just shy of burnt slathered with melted butter. As Jake handed Tessa a ten-dollar bill, he heard familiar laughter from the back.

"Oh, they've been waiting for you today," Tessa said. "Wise asses are in rare form. Go on. Let them dazzle you with war stories and tell you how to do your job!" Tessa raised her voice to a shout at the end of her sentence so the men at the round table could hear.

"Thanks for the warning," Jake said, taking a bite out of his toast. Spiros worked magic with a griddle. The bread was toasted to perfection. Crunchy on the outside, but soft in the middle.

Jake wolfed it down and walked to the back of the diner, intending only to say hello.

It didn't work out that way. Within five minutes, Frank Borowski had him seated right next to him.

"What can you tell us?" Frank asked. It was a smaller group today. Only Bill Nutter and Virgil Adamski joined Frank. Frank gestured for Tessa to bring a fresh pot of coffee for the group.

"Not a lot," Jake said. "I had BCI out to the judge's house. I should have lab results back by the end of the week. Somebody died out there. Odds are it was Rand. I can tell you that much."

"How's Ed handling it?" Nutter asked. "I saw him over at the hardware store the other day. Wasn't too chipper, that one."

"He'll get over it," Frank interjected. "Landry was right to bench him on this one. With Jake on it, there's a good chance this thing might actually get solved."

"I appreciate the vote of confidence," Jake said. "I actually wouldn't mind picking your brain on a few things. Ed's been less than … um … collegial."

"You want me to have a talk with him?" Frank asked. "Ed's a good guy deep down. He might listen to me. You know it's my spot he took when I retired."

"Yeah," Adamski said. "Frank taught him everything he knows."

The men laughed. It wasn't a compliment. Jake stayed diplomatically neutral.

"I think that might do more harm than good," Jake said. "Ed and I will figure it out. Like you said. He's probably a good guy deep down. And I know he wants to find who killed the judge as much as I do."

He got a round of begrudging assent around the table. Tessa came with the fresh coffee. Before Jake knew it, he was on his third cup.

"I do have a few questions," Jake said. "I've been gone for a while. Some of the players aren't as familiar to me as they used to be. If any of you were me, who's the first person you'd want to talk to?"

The men talked over each other for a moment. Finally, they quieted down and let Frank have the floor.

"Sampson's been around forever. You know he was a prosecutor for maybe a decade before they handed him a gavel. There are any number of criminal lowlifes who wouldn't lose sleep if he dropped off the planet."

"Not losing sleep and actually doing something to make him disappear are two pretty different things though," Jake said. "I've got a couple of leads from people close to him. I just wondered if there's anything big that pops in your heads. Anything obvious I might be overlooking on account of me not having my thumb on the pulse of Worthington County lately?"

"Judge wasn't close to many people," Nutter said. "He was a bullshitter. Good guy. Don't get me wrong. But a poser. If he was talking, he was bragging. Used to spend a stupid amount of money on all these collector's guns. He'd go on those canned hunts. The ones where it's pretty much like shooting into a buck petting zoo."

"He used to try worming his way onto the range with us," Adamski said. "Guy was a menace. Almost shot off Chuck Thompson's foot once. There was an unspoken rule among cops. Don't be the asshole that lets Rand onto the range."

This got a good laugh out of the whole table. It led to another round of unrelated war stories.

"What are *you* thinking, Jake?" Frank asked. "I see your wheels turning already. I know that look."

"Well," Jake said. "What's the lay of the land with the Hilltop Boys these days?"

Nutter reached over and grabbed the creamer from the center of the table. "You think it was a hit? What's the prosecutor, Brouchard, say about that?"

"We haven't talked much," Jake said through tight lips. "But he was out at the damn crime scene day one."

"Zender's idea?" Frank said. "Christ. The hell was he thinking?"

"I don't know," Nutter said. "You think the Hilltop Boys had something to do with Rand's murder? That'd be a pretty bold move on King Rex's part. I've never known Rex Bardo or his family to go after judges. How much do you know about him, Jake?"

"Not a lot," Jake answered. "When I was working organized crime for the Feds, his name would come up from time to time. But Chicago and Worthington County are two different worlds. Whatever Rex Bardo was into, he didn't step on any toes in my neck of the woods. They wouldn't have let him survive it."

"Nah," Frank agreed. "Rex Bardo isn't stupid. I'd say he's running a tighter ship down here with his boys than before he went in the joint. He's better protected, for one thing."

"Taking out a county judge isn't his style," Nutter agreed. "Too much heat for that."

"But Rand's put Hilltop Boys affiliates away, hasn't he?" Adamski said. "There was one last year. I can't remember the guy's name, but it was for sure one of Bardo's crew. Drug trafficking. Rand put him away for something like ten years. You remember, Frank?"

Frank shrugged. "I think it was Bobby Lang. But Rand put plenty of Bardo's people away over the years."

"Cost of doing business," Jake said. "I'll look into it. But as far as you all know, Rex is still running the operation from prison?"

"That he is," Frank answered.

"You thinking Rand's murder could be some kind of power play? Now that there's a new sheriff in town?" Adamski asked.

"I think that's what the new sheriff is worried about," Jake answered. "I think that's why she wanted me for this case. Look, I know you're all out now. But I'd appreciate it if you kept your ears to the ground. You hear anything that makes you think there's a shakeup within the Hilltop Boys organization, give me a heads-up. Whether it's related to Rand's death or not, that's a thing I'd like to know."

The men agreed. Jake checked his phone. It was past nine already. More than safe to head back to the office. He had one more question though.

"Dickie Gerald," he said. "It came to my attention that he threatened the judge on the record a few months back. Any of you have a read on how capable he might have been on making good on that?"

Frank and Nutter passed a look. It seemed like they were mentally flipping coins to see who wanted to answer first. Finally, Nutter did.

"The Geralds are tricky," he said. "You know they've got at least a tenuous connection to the Hilltop Boys. Word was when their old man, Jerry Gerald, tried to rob that Brinks truck, he was trying to prove something to King Rex. Not that he did it on Rex's behest or direct order. But he was trying to show what he was capable of."

"Didn't work out too good," Frank said, pouring a packet of Splenda into his coffee. "I can't say I've heard Dickie himself has gotten his hands dirty with the Boys. King Rex would be too smart to trust him with anything big. I think they sometimes use the body shop as a meeting place. Nothing outright illegal."

"So," Adamski said. "I heard a rumor that you and Dickie already had words. I picked up my daughter's Chevy last night. Dickie's nose was looking more crooked than usual. That you?"

Jake sipped his coffee. "Gemma told me some things," Jake said. "Some things I couldn't let slide."

Frank sat straighter in his seat. Jake watched a tremor go through him. His face turned a dark shade of red. Jake knew Frank's looks too. This was pure rage.

"She didn't tell me. Dammit, Jake. She never said. I would have killed him," Frank said. "I want you to know, I told Gemma after you left. If she needed anything. Anything at all, all she had to do was call. I should have talked some sense into her when she started hanging around Dickie. By the time I heard about it, I'm sorry, Jake, she was already knocked up."

"I appreciate it, Coach," Jake said. "More than you know."

"Real glad to have you back, kid," Frank said. "Real glad." The men grew quiet. Frank didn't often show emotion. His eyes glistened. He patted Jake on the back.

"You heading to the high school later?" Frank asked, breaking the tension. "Everyone's saying your nephew Ryan's a real beast. Haven't had much chance to watch the team recently. Coach

Purcell's doing a great job with them. A lot of his assistants were my boys though. It's better if I just keep my fat face out of his for a while yet."

"I don't know. If he's a good coach, I think Brian Purcell would appreciate having you there every once in a while," Jake said. He downed the last of his coffee and put another ten on the table. "I'll try to head over. I know it'll make my sister happy."

He rose to leave. "She's a good kid too," Frank said. "Just has lousy taste in men. Got some good kids out of the deal though."

Jake nodded. He raised a flat hand, giving them all a quick wave. He answered the coach as he turned to leave.

"Yeah. I don't know what she ever saw in Dickie Gerald." It was a throwaway comment. Not one he expected them to answer. But the whole group broke into raucous laughter once more. Bill Nutter practically spit coffee out of his nose.

"You mean you don't know?" Adamski answered for him. "I hate to tell ya, son. But Dickie's just a nickname. That kid's real name is Steve."

It took a beat for the probable meaning of Dickie's nickname to sink in. When it did, Jake could only hang his head and absorb the laughter as he went out the front door.

THIRTEEN

Still wearing his suit and badge having come straight from the office, Jake sat in the parking lot of Stanley High School, hands white-knuckling his steering wheel. He'd cut the ignition minutes ago. He just couldn't seem to compel himself to get out of the car.

The place looked the same. Smelled the same. That pungent scent of sweat, metal, and fear wafted from the wrestling room on the north side of the building. The current class had painted runny silver graffiti over the class rock in the center of the parking lot. Silver and blue painted paw prints led visitors to the gymnasium door. Jake hadn't expected the memories to hit him so hard. He hadn't expected to care. Maybe he had Dickie Gerald to thank for that. Dickie had reminded him of the biggest reason why he'd left home in the first place. And the reason he might not stay.

If he closed his eyes, Jake could still hear the wall of sound. A thousand voices screaming his name. Pain shot through his right shoulder, an old injury that flared every time it rained.

"Jake?" A familiar voice pulled Jake out of his head. His whole body tensed and his hand went to his weapon on instinct as someone tapped on his passenger-side window.

"Holy crap!" the familiar voice said. Jake broke into a smile as he finally opened the door and got out of the car.

Ben Wayne barreled into him, damn near lifting Jake's feet off the ground.

"I can't believe it," Ben said. "I can't believe you're here!"

Ben let go and stepped back, looking Jake up and down. "You got old!"

"Speak for yourself," Jake said. It was a lie. But for a few extra lines at the corner of his eyes and a head shaved bald, Ben looked exactly the same. Tall, reedy, and bird-like, Ben looked more like a basketball player than a wrestler. All legs, his opponents could always take him down easily, but struggled with what to do with him when they got him there. Ben didn't look muscular, but he was bull-strong and just as stubborn.

"We heard you were back in town," Ben said, slapping Jake on the back as the two of them headed for the gym entrance. "Why didn't you call?"

"It's been a crazy few weeks," Jake answered. Which was true, but not the real reason he hadn't called. The Dickie Geralds of the world were the problem. For every guy like him who spouted off the worst rumors about his family, there were a dozen more who silently judged. Ben Wayne had never been one of them, of course. Which was why Jake knew he'd owe him the truth to the one question the people who cared about him wanted answered. Was he here for good? The trouble was, he didn't have an answer for Ben or anyone else. Only now that Ben was here, Jake was glad.

"You're with the sheriffs?" Ben asked.

"So far," Jake answered. They walked through the gym doors. Jake handed the teenage girl at the ticket table ten dollars for two tickets. Thunder came from the gym itself as hundreds of pairs of feet stomped on the bleachers in unison. They were just starting to introduce the varsity line-up.

Ben and Jake passed by a row of old senior pictures. Fresh, shiny faces with bad haircuts from decades past. The hall of famers. Jake's picture was there right beside Ben's. It felt like a hundred years ago. It felt like just last week.

As they walked into the gym, Jake spotted a giant blue and silver banner hanging on the far wall.

"That's new," he said to Ben.

Ben laughed. "Banner's been up there for eight years, Jake. There was a ceremony. They inducted the whole team into the Alumni Hall of Fame. It felt pretty empty without you here. Gemma said you were working a case and couldn't break away."

Jake stopped, staring at the banner commemorating the 2000 State Championship team. It meant more to Jake than his individual title. The year Stanley High School finally broke through and ushered in the powerhouse it remained for more than a decade. There'd been a parade through town in their honor. They were interviewed on the local news. He, Ben, and Lance Harvey were given keys to the city.

"Something like that," Jake said. "I'm sorry I missed it." He caught Ben's far-off expression. Just a subtle flicker in his eyes. Something no one else would have caught, but once upon a time, Jake knew Ben better than anyone. He recognized his grief when he saw it.

"I'm sorry I missed a lot of things, Ben," he said. "I wished I could have been here for Abby's funeral."

Ben shrugged it off and replaced the sadness with a goofy grin. "Don't worry about it. Abby would have hated you seeing her like that anyway. She got so sick toward the end."

They walked up the bleachers together. Gemma stood, waving both arms in the air, as if there were a chance Jake would have missed her. His youngest nephew, six-year-old Aiden, stood on the seat beside her, hopping up and down. Gemma had put her purse and two sweatshirts on the seats above her. Lucky she had. The place was packed.

Jake and Ben excused themselves down the row and took the two seats Gemma had saved. Before Jake could fully sit, Aiden launched himself at him. Jake got his arms up just in time to catch the kid. His lower back cried out in protest as Jake held the wriggly six-year-old, then gently set him down. He was a sweet little kid. No thanks to Dickie, his loser father.

"Hey, turbo, your mom let you have a Mountain Dew and Pixie Sticks or something?" Jake asked.

Gemma scowled at him. "I'd call it lucky if the squirt would eat that much. Pickiest damn eater ever. Don't let him bamboozle you into getting him nachos or cotton candy at the concession stand. Not until he eats a balanced meal."

"Hot dog and Doritos?" Ben offered.

"Damn straight," Gemma joked back. She pulled a beef stick out of her purse and waved it at Aiden. "Get some protein in that skinny little body of yours at least. You're going to turn into a puppet."

"What does that even mean?" Ben asked.

"No idea," Jake said. "It's what Gramps always says. Makes no ever-loving sense."

"He coming?" Ben asked.

This time, it was Gemma's subtle expression Jake read. "Next time," she answered quickly. "He doesn't like crowds anymore."

"My dad says he misses seeing him down at the Lodge," Ben said. This was news to Jake. Gramps used to practically live down at the Elks Lodge growing up. He shot Gemma a look. She waved a hand, dismissing him.

"How's Grassley looking this year?" Jake asked. Grassley High had never been much competition for Stanley's team. Two counties over, the two schools had a tradition of hosting the pre-season scrimmage dual meet for each other. Ben had actually taken a lot of heat for dating a girl from Grassley their sophomore year. He was serious about her for a while until Abby Clinton moved to town. Ben was done for the moment he met her. They'd been inseparable for fifteen years, marrying their senior year in college when Abby got pregnant. Five years ago, after Jake lost touch, he heard Abby succumbed to leukemia just after her thirtieth birthday.

"They're not too bad," Ben answered. "Since they built that Amazon warehouse there a few years ago, a bunch of people have moved in. Shot some life into their athletic programs. I wish something like that would come to Worthington County. Don't get me wrong, the Stanley boys are hard workers. They're just a lot softer than we were. Ever since Coach Frank retired, it's just not the same."

"Blah blah blah," Gemma teased. "You sound eighty, Ben. Frank Borowski is even worse. Back in my day ..." She stretched her lips over her teeth, mimicking an old lady.

"You beat a monster!" Aiden said, hopping up and down on the seat beside his mother. "He was two hundred pounds!"

Jake caught Aiden around the waist just as he was about to tumble down the riser.

"On your bottom," Gemma said. "Or I'm going to make you sit in the car."

"Come here, buddy," Jake said. He cleared a space next to him and helped Aiden up. Aiden squeezed himself in, practically carving his body into Jake's. Jake put his arm around him.

"Settle down and watch," he said. "The match is about to start."

Ben's son Travis came bounding out to the center of the mat under the spotlight. Wrestling at 106 pounds, he was painfully skinny for his tall frame, just like his dad had been.

Jake found it was more entertaining to watch Ben watching Travis than it was to actually watch Travis. Ben bobbed and weaved, then rose to his feet shouting as Travis got the first take down. His opponent was in trouble pretty quickly after that. Travis wrapped his bird legs around him and twisted. The kid was tiny. Didn't look much older than Aiden even though he had to be at least fourteen.

"Go, Travis!" Aiden screamed, reaching a pitch that cleared Jake's sinuses. Thirty seconds later, Travis Wayne got the pin. The roar went up and Ben pumped his fist in the air.

"He looks strong," Jake said.

"He's gonna hit a growth spurt though," Ben said. "Next year's gonna be a whole different world for him. Coach has an eye on him to fill the 113 spot after Landon Burgess graduates. They've got a beast at that weight at St. Isadore. Two-time state champion."

"He'll be ready," Jake said. Ben didn't look too sure. Jake could tell there was something else on his mind about it, but he wouldn't say anything with so many other ears around.

"Jake Cashen?" someone said behind him. "I'll be damned. Good to see you, kid."

Jake turned. It was Mitch Harvey. Mitch's son, Lance, had been another teammate. Jake shook his hand and the two exchanged the usual banter.

"We still talk about the two thousand team," Mitch said.

"Match of the century!" Aiden offered, standing on the riser again. "That's my Uncle Jake. Dexter Oaks was a state champ THREE times! He was two hundred pounds and seven feet tall!"

"Aiden," Jake said.

Mitch Harvey kept a straight face, but barely. Aiden went on, regaling anyone who would listen.

"They called him Oak Tree!" Aiden said. That part was true. "Uncle Jake was losing by four whole points. He pinned him with fifteen seconds to go! My great-grandpa showed me the tape. They gave him a medal!"

"They gave everybody medals, Aiden. Sit down. Ryan's the next match. Plus, Mr. Harvey knows all about it. He was there," Jake said.

Aiden's eyes got big. Then Aiden barreled into Jake's side again, hugging his uncle for all his little body was worth.

Jake caught Gemma's eyes. She covered quickly, but he could have sworn he saw the makings of a tear in the corner of her eye.

A few matches later, Ryan Stark, Gemma's oldest son, took the mat.

"He's another one who's got a beast in his weight class at St. Iz," Ben explained. He spoke low in Jake's ear so Gemma couldn't hear.

Jake watched as Ryan shook hands with his opponent and waited for the ref to blow the start whistle. The kid was coiled strength, bobbing on his back foot, ready to explode. Jake's whole body went rigid. His hands involuntarily clenched. He felt ready to erupt right along with Ryan.

"This kid's All-State," Ben explained. Just as he said it, Ryan shot forward toward the kid's midsection. He rolled him, earning the first takedown and two points on the board. Ryan followed that up with two more takedowns to open up a six-point lead heading into the second period.

"He looks good," Jake said.

"Go, Ryan!" Aiden screamed, blowing Jake's hair back.

"He's fantastic on his feet," Ben said. "He's a takedown machine. Watch this."

Sure enough, Ryan exploded with ferocity as the period opened. He did it again, letting his opponent up each time when he couldn't quite get him into pinning position.

"He's got no bottom game," Jake observed.

"No top game either," Ben said. "Remind you of anyone?"

Ben shot Jake a wry smile. "He wrestles just like you did. Hell, he looks just like you. Lot of people ask me if he's your kid, actually. Lucky Borowski got a hold of you when he did. Made you go to that Gene Mills camp and you became a pinning animal."

"An animal!" Aiden repeated, his voice little more than a growl.

Ryan had a 16–8 lead at the start of the third period. Jake could see his nephew was running out of gas. His movements were more sluggish. His chest nearly hollowed out each time he drew a breath. He got called for stalling. Ryan's eyes narrowed in fury as the ref put a hand on his shoulder. Ryan jerked away too quickly, hot-tempered.

"Watch it," Jake said.

Ryan circled his opponent, but the fight was nearly out of him. He looked almost drunk. He got called for stalling again. He threw his arms around his opponent and the pair of them staggered left and right until the buzzer finally went off.

Aiden jumped up, raising his arm just as the ref raised his brother's.

"That was sloppy as hell," Jake observed. "He'll get killed against anyone worth anything."

"That's what I'm saying," Ben said.

But Ryan wasn't finished. Jake watched in horror as his nephew bolted toward the other team's bench and started pointing fingers.

"Ryan!" Gemma shouted. She was on her feet.

The ref ran forward and grabbed Ryan by the shoulder. Brian Purcell, the Stanley coach, rushed to them, but it was too late. The ref went to the scorekeepers. He instructed a full team point be taken away for Ryan's unsportsmanlike conduct.

Gemma was practically purple. "He doesn't listen," she said. "He thinks he knows everything. He's going to ruin it all, Jake. He's too young and too stubborn to realize it. He has a future if he doesn't get in his own way. He's got all the talent in the world but he doesn't know what he's doing, Jake."

Aiden was still wrapped around Jake's waist. "Coach Purcell is a good guy," Ben said. "But he's too touchy-feely. If you'd have pulled that crap, Frank Borowski would have had you running the Gulag right after the meet."

"He won't listen to anybody," Gemma said. She gave him a pointed stare and Jake knew exactly what she wanted to say.

Maybe Ryan would listen to Jake. Gemma's gaze shifted to her younger son. Aiden was still wrapped around Jake's waist, clinging to him as if he knew Jake might disappear.

Fourteen

Wednesday morning, BCI and Mark Ramirez came through in a big way. Jake had their full report sitting on his desk.

The office was empty. Detective Gary Majewski had come and gone already, dealing with a convenience store robbery out in Navan Township. Ed went with him as the store owner got pistol-whipped in the exchange. It left Jake with a quiet stretch of time to try to make sense of everything in Ramirez's report.

The minute he dove into it, Sheriff Landry appeared in the door frame, hands on her hips, barely able to contain her agitation.

Jake flipped through the pages, looking for the answer to the biggest question of all. He ran his index finger down the columns of scientific data.

"Well?" Landry said, walking fully into the room.

"He's definitively dead," Jake said, tapping the page. DNA on the judge's toothbrush matched the gray matter they found in the plant.

Landry went a little gray herself. It was news they expected.

"I don't know whether that's better or worse," she said. "Judge Rand was either going to be the victim or possibly a killer."

"We've got to inform his next of kin," Jake said. "There's just the niece in Kentucky. I'll call her later today."

"I want to be on that call," Landry said. "You'll take the lead, of course. But she's going to need to hear from me that we're prioritizing this case. I don't need her talking to the press without that reassurance."

"I don't want her talking to the press at all," Jake said.

"We'll try to impress that upon her as well," she said. "But they're going to come calling. I don't see how this story isn't picked up by national news outlets."

"Which means I've got a pretty short window of time to try to make headway."

Jake dove back into the report. BCI had found no unidentifiable prints or DNA anywhere in the home. They'd found only one set of prints that didn't belong to the judge.

"Son of a ..." Jake started as he read the results of the partial handprint found on the top of the judge's bedroom safe.

"What is it?" Landry asked.

"A problem," he said. "Potentially a big one." He tilted the page so Landry could read it. She squinted to make out the tiny type.

"Zender rested his hand on the top of the safe without gloves," Jake said. "He contaminated the damn scene. I knew it."

"It's one partial print," she said. "It's not the end of the world."

"It's an opening," Jake said. "Any half-wit defense lawyer will make hay out of it."

"We'll cross that bridge when we get there," she said. "You took control of that scene quickly, Jake. We can manage this."

Jake was already deeper into the report. The cell phone forensics painted a different picture, one that matched what Tony Byers, the judge's clerk, had told him. The judge's phone pinged the cell tower closest to his home just after six o'clock on Friday the 1st. It never moved again. If Rand had left the house, he hadn't taken his phone with him. Jake saw the series of calls and texts Byers made throughout the weekend. They went unanswered.

"No security cameras?" Landry asked. "Not even a Ring?"

"No," Jake said. "He lived tucked so far back in the woods, maybe he didn't think he needed it. Nobody'd be going back there unless they meant to."

"Ed said the address doesn't even show up the right way on most GPS apps. He said he'd heard the judge complain about delivery drivers screwing it up all the time."

"This wasn't a burglary," Jake said. "No forced entry. Not a single valuable missing. This was an execution. The splatter patterns we found extended from behind the judge's recliner. The killer was facing him when he or she pulled the trigger."

"Not from the back?" Landry asked.

"It means the killer wanted Rand to know what was about to happen to him. Ramirez is theorizing there were two shots fired. One hit him maybe in the arm or the chest. He leaned over, tried to grab his phone, shattered the martini glass sitting on the table. Then the killer made the kill shot to the judge's head."

"How'd he get the body out? There was no blood anywhere else in the house? Just in that den?"

"That's all they found," Jake confirmed as he skimmed through the rest of the report.

"So the killer wrapped him up in something before he took him from the house?" Landry said. "What about tire tracks?"

"It was raining that night," Jake answered as he read. "Judge has a blacktop driveway. There likely wouldn't have been any tire marks at all and if there were, any trace would have been washed away."

"You're sure he died Friday night?"

"Most likely," Jake said as he popped a thumb drive into his computer. The full cell phone forensics report displayed. "Tony Byers said the judge was pretty good about answering his texts. They were gearing up for Buddy Grant's felony murder trial. He had Tony on some pretty hefty briefs that had been submitted. He said it wasn't like Rand to ghost him. Tony's first text came through at eight in the morning Saturday. I think it's a pretty safe bet the judge was killed sometime between say seven o'clock Friday night and eight o'clock Saturday morning."

"What's the rest of his phone look like?" Landry asked. She was antsy. Jake wanted to tell her he'd get through this quicker if he was left alone to do his job. It's what Landry promised him from the get-go.

Jake raised a sarcastic brow. "Sorry, boss, I looked for the *instant evidence* tab. There isn't one. This is gonna take a while."

"I'm sorry," Landry said, apparently reading his mind. "I need something. Anything. I'm going to have to go out there and hold a press conference. Any chance you'd want to do that with me?"

"I do not," Jake said. "And that's not our deal." He scanned Judge Rand's calls and texts. Nothing out of the ordinary popped out at him at first glance.

"There's not much here," he said. "Looks like he keeps in phone contact with four main people. Tony Byers. I knew they were tight. He's in a group text with Judge Cardwell, the county clerk, Tim Brouchard. Jesus. Looks like they're pretty much just sharing pictures of food. Then there's this."

Jake's pulse quickened. Rand had a lengthy text exchange with his plumber. More than forty texts in the week before he died. Multiple incoming and outgoing calls, the last one hitting the morning of his disappearance.

"What the hell?" Jake said. He started reading some of the messages. "What kind of plumbing emergency would this ..."

"What is it?"

Jake read a few excerpts. "Can't wait to see you next week. I've been dreaming about you. He responds back. When I walk in, I want you on the bed wearing nothing but your high heels."

"His plumber?" Landry asked.

"He's got the number listed as The Plumber. It's a local area code. And ... whoa, boy."

As Jake scrolled up, he got a good look at The Plumber's naked breasts covered in whipped cream.

"So not an actual plumber then," Landry said, looking over his shoulder.

"Byers said he suspected the judge was meeting with someone on the side. Not a girlfriend, but a hookup. Thought maybe it was Cardwell's court reporter but he had no proof of it. He said there was a lot of innuendo on the judge's part. He didn't pry.

Rand liked to compartmentalize his life. I'd ask you if you recognized her but, uh, there aren't any pictures of her face on here."

"What's the number again?" Landry asked.

Jake wrote it down for her. Landry picked it up and stared at it.

"Let me get this to Darcy. She's a Lexis/Nexis ninja. You mind if I put her on a reverse look-up for you?"

"By all means," Jake said. "The sooner we find his, er … plumber … the better."

Landry was already starting to walk out of the room. She nearly ran smack into Ed Zender as he came in from the hall.

"Ed," Landry said. She slipped the piece of paper in her pocket and eyed Jake. Ed grumbled something, but held his tongue.

"I'll call you as soon as I have anything," Sheriff Landry said, then disappeared out the door.

Every muscle in Ed Zender's body seemed tense. Jake figured it was better to get this over with sooner rather than later. He rose.

"Hey, Ed," he said. "I've been meaning to talk to you. About the other day. About all of this. Do we have a problem?"

"Don't know what you're talking about," Ed said, brushing past Jake's shoulder with his own as he made his way to his desk.

"Listen," Jake said. "We are going to have to work together out of this same 12 x 12 space. As far as I'm concerned, we need to do that. Work together. You need anything. All you gotta do is ask."

"Doesn't seem like I have much of a choice," Ed said.

Not the answer Jake was looking for.

"So I'm asking you," Jake said. "Again. Do we have a problem?"

Ed narrowed his eyes at Jake. Sized him up. Jake watched something go through his face. He settled, relaxing his shoulders. Jake wondered if it finally dawned on Ed there was no real point puffing his chest out. What was he going to do? Take a swing?

"Fine," Ed finally said. "We can work together."

"You sure?" Jake asked.

"You going to leave? Turn down that shield?" Ed asked.

Jake locked eyes with him. "No, Ed. I'm not going to do that."

"So then I guess I have no choice."

"We can actually help each other, Ed. I think that was the whole point of Landry bringing me on. She said you'd been asking O'Neal for some help for years. Well, I'm it. I don't know what else you had in mind."

Ed gripped the back of his chair. "I just don't like how she went about it."

"I gotta be honest," Jake said. "I wasn't a fan of it either. But she's learning. She's trying. And as much as we can help each other, I think Meg Landry is going to need the most help of all. Our success is her success. It goes both ways."

Jake reached over, extending a hand to shake Ed's. The older man hesitated, but finally took it.

A tenuous detente, maybe, but Jake would call it a win. He went back to his report.

"How'd it go over Navan Township?" Jake asked.

"Already have a suspect in custody," Ed answered. "Low level dirtbag trying to score points with the Hilltop Boys. It'll be interesting to see how that works out. Knocking over convenience stores isn't their usual style."

"I wouldn't think," Jake said. "You know, if you can think of anyone who might have had a beef with Sampson Rand, I sure would appreciate your insight."

Ed nodded as he turned on his computer. "I'll think on it," he said.

The two men worked in companionable silence for the next hour. Jake was about to ask him if he could treat Ed to lunch when his cell phone rang. It was Landry.

"We got a bingo on your plumber," she said. "It's a cell phone number belonging to Amanda Lovett."

"Tony Byers's tip was right," Jake said. "Mandy Lovett is Judge Cardwell's court reporter. She works one office over from Rand."

"Yep. How the hell'd he managed to keep that quiet?" Landry said. "Jake, Mandy Lovett is extremely married."

Jake sat back hard in his seat. He picked up the cell phone report again. Amanda Lovett's whipped cream bra stared back at him. "Roger that," he muttered. He stuffed the records in his leather bag and headed for the courthouse.

FIFTEEN

J ake knew he'd have to get Mandy Lovett away from the courthouse to get anything useful out of her. He checked Judge Finneas Cardwell's docket. He wasn't on the record again until later in the afternoon. He found Mandy in the second-floor break room chatting with Emily Kennedy, his old trainer from high school.

"Hey, Jake!" Emily said. She looked exactly the same as she had almost twenty years ago. A round, pleasing face framed by white-blonde hair. She wore purple glasses and bright colors.

"Hey, Emily," Jake said, accepting it when Emily met him with a hug.

"I've got a bone to pick with you," she said. "You were at the dual the other night. I told you, we hang out at Blackhand Lanes after. Everyone missed you."

"Next time," Jake said. "I promise."

"Ryan looked pretty good," Emily said. "But he needs the crap kicked out of him. He's a lot like you before Coach Borowski got a hold of you."

It was the second time he'd heard that. "'Yeah," he answered as Mandy Lovett rose from the table.

"I'll let you two catch up," she said, smiling.

"Hang on a second, Mandy," Jake said. "I was actually hoping I could talk to you."

Emily looked puzzled. "I didn't know you knew each other," she said.

"We don't," Jake said. "Not officially."

"Well," Emily said, brightening. "Jake Cashen, Mandy Lovett. Watch out for this one, Mandy. He plays it tough, but he's got that lost puppy vibe that'll getcha."

"Lost puppy?" Jake said.

Emily winked at him and grabbed her coffee cup off the table. "I have to get back. Next home match though, Jake. It's in two weeks. You don't show up at the bowling alley, we're coming to find you with pitchforks and rope."

"Point well taken," Jake said. "I give up."

He turned back to Mandy as Emily left.

"I'm sorry," Mandy said. "Is there something I can help you with?"

"It might be better if we took a walk," he said. "You mind heading over to the Sheriff's Department with me?"

Mandy rose. She was pretty. Thin. A pile of dark hair she wore pulled back in a ponytail. Thick makeup and false eyelashes Jake didn't think she needed. When she stood, she teetered on heels so high they could double as weapons. But Mandy moved gracefully enough in them.

"Did I do something wrong? We heard you got promoted into Ed Zender's job. Is he retiring?"

"No," Jake said. "We work together."

"I don't have a lot of time," she said. "Can I just stop by your office after work?"

"I'd rather talk now," Jake said. He held the break room door for her. Mandy's face went blank. Her hand trembled as she brought it to her throat, fumbling at the ruffles on the white blouse she wore. She followed Jake across the street in an almost zombie fashion. By the time he got her into an interview room, Mandy was shaking from head to toe.

"First of all, thanks," Jake said as he sat down at the table opposite her. "I promise this won't take too long. Can I get you anything? Water, coffee?"

"What's going on?" she said.

"I'll get right to it. When was the last time you saw Judge Rand?"

Mandy folded her hands in front of her. "I don't work for him. I work for Judge Cardwell."

"I'm aware," he said. "But I need to know when you last saw Judge Rand."

"Am I in trouble? Is he okay? There are a lot of rumors going around. Nobody knows where he is."

"You're not in trouble," Jake said. He made copies of a few of the more problematic texts between Mandy and the judge. They were in a thin file folder on the table between them. Mandy's eyes kept flicking to it.

"Um, it's been a couple of weeks or so," she said. "Since I've seen Judge Rand."

"Where was that?"

"I'm not sure. At the courthouse, I think."

"How would you describe your relationship with the judge?"

Up until then, Mandy had been avoiding Jake's eyes. Now, she focused on him with a laser stare.

"Tell me what happened," she said.

Jake sat back. "I'm afraid Sampson Rand is dead."

Her eyelids fluttered. Every drop of color drained from her face for an instant, then red blotches appeared on her neck and slowly rose into her cheeks.

"How ... what ... he can't ... how?" Mandy clawed at the tabletop. She was hyperventilating.

"He was shot," Jake said.

"No. No. That doesn't make sense."

"Mandy," Jake said. "I really need you to tell me about your relationship with the judge."

She shook her head violently, biting her bottom lip. "No. God. No. This can't be happening. Sam can't be dead."

It was Sam now. Jake waited, letting Mandy catch her breath. Tears spilled down her cheeks.

"What do I do?" she asked. "How does this work?"

"I need you to tell me what you know," Jake said. "Starting with your relationship."

She nodded. "We were ... he is ... oh God. Was. I can't say this. I can't be here."

"But you are. And this is real, Mandy. The man is dead. I need your help."

She kept nodding. "Right. You know, don't you? You already know."

"Yes."

"I can't imagine what you must think of me."

"I don't think anything. I promise. I'm just trying to piece together what happened to the judge. That's all, Mandy."

"Okay," she said. "Right. He was, we were, we had a romantic relationship. It didn't start out that way, of course. He was a friend. Easy to talk to. He gave me good advice on everything. About money. Career stuff, you know, office politics, that kind of thing. He listened to me. Cared about me. He protected me. There's just a lot of crap that goes on in the county, you know?"

"I do," Jake said.

"Then, I don't know, I think a little over two years ago, things just changed. We were ... um ... compatible. You know, um ... physically. Um ... sexually."

"You've been in a physical relationship with Rand for two years?" Jake asked.

She nodded. "Something like that."

"I'll ask you again. When was the last time you saw him?" Jake asked.

"I've been so worried," she said, and just like that, Jake lost her again. "Everyone's been saying such awful things about what might have happened to him. I didn't know what to do. I didn't know who to ask!"

"Mandy," Jake said. "I need you to focus. You understand we have the judge's cell phone records."

It didn't seem to register with her. Talking to the woman was like trying to nail spaghetti to the wall.

"You last spoke when?" Jake asked.

"Oh ... um ... gosh. It's been almost two weeks. We really didn't talk at work. Rumors spread so fast in that building. We were very careful not to talk to each other at all unless we had to for work-related things."

"I take it your husband doesn't know about your relationship with Rand?"

The red blotches came back into her cheeks. "Oh God! You won't tell him. You can't tell him!"

"Judge Rand is dead. This is a homicide investigation, Mandy."

She scooted her chair backward away from the table. "He doesn't have anything to do with this. Neither of us do. Do I need a lawyer?"

"You're free to leave anytime you'd like," Jake said. "You're not under arrest, Mandy. It's like I said. I'm just trying to piece together what might have happened. You were close to the judge. Maybe closer than anyone else in his life. You can help me."

"I don't know what happened to him. Who might have done this? He was ... he was a Common Pleas Court judge. He put felons away. You make enemies doing that."

She snapped her fingers. "Oh ... Dickie Gerald. You have to talk to him. He threatened to kill him in open court last year."

"I'm aware," Jake said. "Mandy, where did you and Judge Rand meet? How often?"

She pulled her arms around herself. "I'm not some whore."

"I never said you were."

"We were good for each other. He helped me. There are things Doug, that's my husband ... we're so much better now. Sampson helped me. I'm a better wife because of Sam."

"You're saying Doug was aware of your relationship?"

"Oh no," Mandy said. "God no. He'd ..." Her eyes went wide. "No, no way!"

She leapt from her chair and started pacing. "You think Doug had something to do with this?"

"Do you?"

"No! Absolutely not. Doug won't even kill spiders when I find them in the house."

"Does Doug own a gun?" Jake asked.

"I know what you're doing. You couldn't be more wrong. This had nothing to do with Doug. I made sure of that. He was never going to find out about Sam and me. He doesn't know. This will kill him. Oh God. It's going to destroy him. He won't understand."

"Does he own a gun, Mandy?" Jake said. This interview was going nowhere fast.

"I don't think so. Some buddies of his roped him into taking this CCL class last year. It was stupid. So not Doug. He was going to buy a pistol but he chickened out. That's how much he hated those things."

"Okay, so tell me about how your relationship with the judge worked. How often did you meet? Where?"

Something about the question calmed her down. Mandy sat in the chair. "Once a month, usually," she said. "Doug is a sales rep for Mans Flooring. They're based in Fort Wayne. He goes up there for their corporate staff meeting the first Friday of every month. They fly him out on one of those puddle jumpers. I hate those things. Most of the time when you hear about plane crashes, it's those things."

"Where did you meet with Rand, Mandy?" Jake once again tried to refocus her.

"There's this motel," she said. "The Dreamfield Inn. It's right outside of Oakton over in Marvell County. He's got a standing room reservation. We'd meet there, usually. Never in Stanley. Never anywhere in Worthington County."

"What did you tell Doug you were doing?" Jake asked.

"I didn't," she said. "We'd go when Doug was out of town. I'm telling you, he doesn't know about any of this. If you think he wanted to hurt Sam, he had no reason to. None. Doug doesn't even know Sam personally. They've never met. You can't tell him."

"Mandy, this is a homicide investigation. You were having an affair with the victim. I'm going to need to ask Doug some questions. I'm afraid there's no way to avoid him finding out about you and Rand. I can be with you when you tell him, if you'd like."

She started to sob. "No. That will scare him to death. No. I have to do this in my own way."

"Do you have somewhere safe you can stay?" Jake asked. He pushed a box of tissues across the table to her.

"I don't need to stay anywhere. I told you, Doug isn't violent. This will break him. But he'll blame himself more than anyone else. You have to let me do this my way. I can handle him."

"All right," Jake said. "I'm afraid I have to ask you this. Can you tell me where you were the Friday before last?"

"What?" she said.

Jake waited, letting her absorb the question.

"You think I'd hurt Sam?" she said.

"I'm just asking where you were, if you remember. That would have been the first Friday of the month. And I know Rand wasn't at the Dreamfield Inn. Was he supposed to be?"

"No," she said. "I wasn't feeling well. I had a bout of the stomach flu. I stayed home. You can check. I had a doctor's appointment that day. I called in sick."

"And Doug was on the road?" Jake asked.

"Yes!" Mandy said. "He was in Fort Wayne until that Sunday morning. He and some of his work people took a long weekend. They went to some microbrewery, he said. He flew back Sunday morning. See? I told you. Doug didn't have anything to do with this."

"Okay, Mandy," Jake said. "But you understand I still need to talk to him. And soon. I can give you a day. But then Doug and I need to have a conversation."

She stared blankly at him. Jake sat back, letting her process it all for a moment.

"Mandy, do you know anyone else who might have wanted to hurt the judge? Specifically."

She shrugged, turning her palms up. "I mean ... like I said, he put criminals behind bars for a really long time. He handled divorce cases. Of course you're going to rack up enemies."

"Who else might he have been close with? I know he and Tony Byers, his clerk, were. But who were his best friends?"

"Sam's lifestyle was unique to him," she said. "He liked to keep things in neat little boxes. I don't think he ever told his family about us. I think he had a niece but he used to just send her money on her birthday. They didn't have a relationship. His parents were long gone. But honestly? He was liked more than he was hated. Ask anyone. Even cops were fond of him."

"I've heard that," Jake said.

"He's responsible for getting the Drug Court up and going. He helped so many people, Jake."

"Do you know if there was anyone new in his life? New friends? Were the two of you exclusive?"

"As far as I know, yes. Sam liked how things were with us. He never asked me to leave Doug and I never would. We weren't conventional, but it worked for us. Now everyone is going to say the worst things about me."

"Do you know where he liked to hang out outside of work?" Jake asked.

"He had lunch at the Vedge Wedge almost every day. He liked this vegan taco salad they make. He likes to sit at the booth near the register so he can see who's coming and going."

"Okay. That helps," Jake said.

"He went mostly vegan because of me. But he cheats. Cheated. He didn't think I knew. But Sam likes his barbecue. There's this roadside stand he'd go to when we were out in Oakton. I didn't mind. It made him so happy. I couldn't stand the smell of it. Did you know he had a heart attack three years ago?"

"No," Jake said. "I didn't know that."

"It's weird to say, but I think it saved his life. Made him realize what's important. We started ... the first time we ... our friendship went to the next level after that. I helped him get his diet under control. He lost fifty pounds. Started working out."

"At a gym?"

"At home," she said. "He had weights, I think."

"I see."

"Are we done here?" Mandy asked abruptly.

"For now," Jake said. Mandy looked ready to break down again. "Do you want me to call someone for you? I'm sure Emily would ..."

"No!" she shouted. "Emily Kennedy is the last person I want around me right now. She's the worst gossip of all."

Jake remembered Tony Byers had told him Mandy actually held that honor. "Okay," Jake said. "I just don't think I like the idea of you being by yourself."

"I won't be," she said. "I'm going back to work. If I don't, they'll gossip even worse."

He rose with her. As he opened the door, Sheriff Landry was standing just outside. She found a smile for Mandy. Mandy said a terse hello and practically sprinted down the hall.

"How'd that go?" Landry asked.

"About as awkward as you'd expect," Jake said. "So far I think she's telling the truth though. It's going to be a tough conversation with the husband."

"That's going to have to wait," Landry said. "I've got some news."

Jake raised a brow.

"I need you to hightail it over to Marvell County. There's been another murder."

"Since when do we have jurisdiction in Marvell County?" Jake asked. Though Mandy's words echoed. She and the judge had their trysts every month in Oakton, the county seat of Marvell County.

"We don't. The victim was Reese Sheldon. Does that ring a bell?"

"Not especially," Jake said.

"He was a defense attorney," she said. "He represented some real lowlifes. A few of them were connected to the Hilltop Boys."

"Christ," Jake said.

"Yep," she said. "I want you to talk to the detective out there and compare notes. It looks like it might be another hit, Jake."

"I'm on my way."

Sixteen

Oakton, Ohio, made Stanley look like a thriving metropolis. It was all farmland except for a one-traffic-light downtown area, a trailer park, and one high-end subdivision built over the objections of almost all of the ten thousand people who lived in the county up until that point.

The Sherwood Estate luxury homes were nestled in the foothills at the northeast corner of the county. A place so remote Jake's GPS would have had him driving smack into the middle of Lake Marvell if he didn't halfway know his way around these back roads.

As he turned left onto the only asphalt he'd seen for miles, Jake understood why the developer fought so hard to build here.

Each lot had at least two acres of pristine woods behind it, a stream running straight through the middle complete with a private park. The only thing to mar the tranquility of the place was Jake himself and the half dozen or so other police vehicles parked at haphazard angles in front of the two-story brick house at the far edge of the subdivision.

Jake got out and slipped on a pair of sunglasses. Mid-November, but late summer had one last, heroic warm front up its sleeve. The temperature would hit seventy again by late afternoon. They were calling for snow by late next week, just in time for Thanksgiving and deer gun season.

A uniformed deputy guarded the driveway. When Jake approached, he pulled out a tablet, ready to enter Jake's information into his crime log. Jake flashed his credentials.

"Your detective still on scene?" he asked.

The kid was young. Couldn't be more than a year out of the academy. But already, he was doing a better job of controlling the scene than what Jake saw at Rand's place that first day.

"That'd be Detective Yun," the kid said. "He's inside."

"Would you mind calling him down?" Jake asked. "I'm here from Worthington County."

"Oh, right," the kid said. "Dave's expecting you. He told me to send you right on up."

"Thanks," Jake said. He ducked under the crime scene tape and headed for the front door. It opened before he got there and a middle-aged, fit-looking detective emerged, his expression grim.

"Yun?" Jake said. "I'm Jake Cashen."

"That was fast," Dave Yun said. "Glad you could come out."

"What've you got?" Jake asked.

Yun took a breath. "Something godawful. Might as well show you rather than explain it all. I understand you're working a similar case."

Jake put on a pair of latex gloves and booties, and followed Dave Yun inside. They entered a long hallway with cathedral ceilings. Yun had crews dusting for prints and photographing in a study off the front foyer. Yun led him up a set of spiral stairs into the master bedroom.

"Coroner just left," Yun said. But Jake could already see the manner of death sprayed across the headboard.

"Victim was Reese Sheldon, forty-nine years old. He was here alone. His wife and two adult daughters were having a girls' weekend in Chicago."

"Lucky that," Jake said.

"Sheldon was shot once in the head, point blank. He was sitting up in bed, reading. Looks like the killer caught him by surprise. His phone's sitting on the charger right next to him."

The rest of the bedroom was in shambles. Dresser drawers half opened, clothes spilled out everywhere.

"Forced entry?" Jake asked.

"No, actually," Yun said. "The sliding door off the kitchen was unlocked. Looks like the perpetrator came through there. You can take a look around. I wouldn't mind a second set of eyes."

Jake went to the walk-in closet off the master bath suite. Sheldon's wife had custom shelving and built-in drawers. Every one of them lay open. Two of the smaller drawers were completely empty.

"The wife's pretty shook up, as you can imagine," Yun said. "She's on a train at the moment, heading back. The daughters are gonna stay with a friend. But I talked to the Sheldons' insurance agent. The missus had about thirty grand worth of jewelry in a drawer here. It's gone. There's a missing laptop down in the study."

"That's a left turn of an M.O. for what I've got over in Worthington," Jake said. "We haven't recovered Sampson Rand's body yet. Whoever shot him took him with him."

"I get that," Yun said. "And you don't have any signs of a burglary with your guy?"

"Nothing," Jake said. "Rand had thousands of dollars' worth of valuables. High-end guns. Cash. It's all still there."

"Huh," Yun said.

"But the way he died is pretty similar," Jake said. "Shot through the head at home. What do you know about Sheldon so far?"

"Local defense attorney," Yun said. "Not too popular with any of us around here. We checked with his office staff. Sheldon was in Judge Rand's courtroom as recently as last month. It's the first thing the wife said when I broke the news to her. She's the one who asked me if this had anything to do with Rand's disappearance."

"You mind giving me a second?" Jake said. Something had nagged at him since he walked in. He went back out to his car and grabbed his laptop out of its case in the trunk.

Yun followed him out. Jake put his laptop on the hood of his car and waited for it to boot up.

"What are you thinking?" Yun asked.

Jake had Tony Byers's file scanned in. He combed through the major cases Judge Rand had presided over in the last year. On three of them, Reese Sheldon appeared as the attorney of record. One of them brought up a name Jake had just heard from Frank and the rest of the Wise Men. Bobby Long.

"This," Jake said, turning the screen so Yun could see it. Yun squinted, holding his hand up to block the glare of sunlight.

"Yeah," Yun said. "Bobby Long. He was one of Sheldon's highest-profile cases. Drug dealer. I arrested that little puke at least twice."

"Why didn't it stick?"

Yun pointed back up toward the house. "You're looking at it. Long was connected to the Hilltop Boys. He was pushing meth for them down here. He did six months off of one of his charges, but went right back to it when he got out."

Jake checked the date on the sentencing order. Rand threw the literal book at him. Bobby Long went back in the system four weeks ago on another trafficking charge. With his priors, he wouldn't be eligible for parole again for at least a decade. Jake made a quick check online from his phone. Bobby Long had most definitely been incarcerated for at least a month.

"You think we're looking at the start of something?" Yun asked. "Rand sentences Long. Sheldon unsuccessfully defends him. They both end up dead of a gunshot wound to the head within a few weeks of each other. Looks to me like somebody's looking to settle some scores."

"Do you know anything about the facts of the case on Long this time?" Jake asked.

"Nope," Yun answered. "As far as I know, Long hasn't crossed county lines since his last conviction here. He got promoted to your neck of the woods."

"Right," Jake said. "But with two convictions, it doesn't look like he was too good at his job. Why the hell would the Hilltop Boys cause this much of a stink trying to get payback for him? I'm not sure that makes sense."

Jake pulled up the forensics report on Rand's cell phone. It was then he realized what had been nagging him about Reese Sheldon. Rand regularly engaged in a group text with six other people sharing food pictures.

"You run Sheldon's phone yet?" Jake asked.

"Still working on it," Yun said.

"Can you at least give me his cell phone number?"

"Sure," Yun said. He rattled off the series of numbers. Jake matched it with one of the members of the judge's group text.

It could mean something, it could mean nothing.

"What do you have?" Yun asked.

"I think your instincts might be right, Dave. There are a lot of things about your scene that just don't track with what I've got over in Worthington County. But there's a pretty solid connection between Sampson Rand and Reese Sheldon. I think we should keep sharing what we find."

"I'll give your contact information to the FBI field agent assigned to this one," Yun said.

Jake closed his laptop. "You'll what?"

"Here's the thing," Yun said. "It's like I said. Reese Sheldon and our department weren't on the best of terms. If I'm being totally honest, he's pretty uniformly hated around here. The dirtbags he represented were bad enough. But that? I get it's part of the system. Guys like Sheldon have to exist. But Sheldon's the reason Sherwood Estates is even here. His family owned most of the land you're standing on. He screwed everybody over and made a deal with the developers of this subdivision. It's a big mess. Lots of lawsuits. He's also got a few pending grievances against my office. Claimed our deputies were harassing him here at home."

Yun kept rambling. Jake's mind was already spinning out another possibility. He knew there was similar talk about developing the property surrounding Judge Rand's house.

"You think you could give me the name of that developer?" Jake said. "I'd like to talk to them."

"Sure," Yun said. "Anything I can do. Man, it's no secret I didn't like Sheldon. But he didn't deserve this. His wife Grace nor the girls either. My oldest goes to school with one of them. It's just godawful."

"I know," Jake said. "I'd better head back. If I think of anything you can use, I'll let you know."

"Right," Yun said. "But maybe you should just stick around a few minutes. Like I said, in light of everything I just told you, I'm calling in the Feds on this one. Special Agent Lilly from the Columbus Field Office is actually on his way now. I heard you used to work for the Bureau. Maybe you know him?"

"He's heading here?" Jake asked. "Right now?"

Yun looked puzzled. "Well, yeah? He just texted. Five minutes out."

"Then that's as good a reason as any for me to get the hell out of here," he said, leaving Detective Yun to wonder. But the last thing Jake needed was to lay eyes on anyone from the Bureau anytime soon.

SEVENTEEN

Two blocks from downtown Stanley sat a little cafe that shouldn't have thrived in Worthington County, but somehow did. For years, the two-story brownstone had been an ice cream parlor. Now, the brick was painted what Jake could only describe as "Easter Pink" with white trim and giant hanging baskets filled with silk lilacs hung from the outdoor patio that had been added on sometime in the last ten years. This was the Vedge Wedge. Worthington County's only restaurant specializing exclusively in vegan cuisine, Judge Sampson Rand's favorite lunchtime escape.

A bell over the door rang as Jake walked inside. Three of the cafe's dozen or so tables were occupied by young couples. Jake guessed they came from the neighboring Athens County, home to Ohio University. It would only have been about a twenty-minute drive for them and offered a quieter respite from that congested college town. A chalkboard sign told him to seat himself. Jake chose a table nearest the cash register and sat in the chair facing the door.

"Be right out!" a friendly voice called from deeper in the unseen kitchen. The menu was written in neon chalk on two large boards above the counter. Jake didn't understand half of what he read. He heard chatter and clatter in the kitchen as Van Morrison played softly from a Bluetooth speaker sitting beside the cash register.

Five minutes went by. Jake was about to get up and walk back to the kitchen. The door chimes rang again as two new patrons walked in. They stopped dead in their tracks as they immediately spotted Jake.

"You serious?" Ben Wayne's face broke into a wide smile. He slapped the back of his hand against his companion's chest. Jake rose from his seat.

"Holy shit!" Lance Harvey crossed the restaurant and embraced Jake. His teammates. Ben, Jake, and Lance had rounded out the varsity line-up as the only seniors on that state championship winning team.

"Good to see you, Lance!" Jake said. "But what the hell are you guys doing here?"

"Don't judge me," Lance said. "I like their taco salad."

"We're just picking up part of our lunch order to take back to the office," Ben explained. "What's your excuse?"

"I'm actually working," Jake said, spreading his arms wide, emphasizing the fact he was in a suit.

"Mind if we join you?" Ben said. "Damn, it's good you're back in town. I was telling Lance about Ryan's match. Lance's been doing some assistant coaching when he can get away."

"Ryan's a beast," Lance said. "Wild though. He doesn't listen worth a damn. I've been trying to work with him. We got a new baby at home now. Chris needs me around the house more."

"Wow," Jake said. "Lance, that's great. Congratulations."

Lance pulled out his phone and showed Jake a picture of a smiling, toothless baby with a perfectly round bald head.

"He's a cutie," Jake said.

"We named him Mitchell, after my old man."

"Good choice," Jake said. "I'm sure he's proud."

From the corner of his eye, Jake saw the swinging purple doors of the kitchen open. He heard her before he saw her. Her unique, raspy voice with the hint of a lisp she'd worked all through middle school to correct.

"You guys are early," she said. Lance and Ben stared straight at Jake, watching for his reaction.

"Jake?" she said, recognizing him, trying to process it.

Jake turned. A million memories flooded through him as he laid eyes on Anya Strong. Her laughter as she raced in front of him down the rickety dock his grandfather used to have over the pond. She would execute a perfect cannonball, squealing as her body hit the cold water. The black, strapless dress she wore that hugged her curves with the thigh-high slit up her thigh. Her father had threatened to ground her if she left the house wearing it. She'd actually changed into it in the back seat of Jake's old Ford Ranger on the way to Junior Prom.

She looked the same. God. How could she look the same? Wheat-blonde hair she wore piled up in front but long down her back. A pair of wide-set brown eyes and flawless skin.

"I heard you were back in town," she said, breathless. "Oh my God. Jake!"

Jake got to his feet. Anya ran up and hugged him. She smelled good. She smelled the same. Anya let him go, smiled up at him. Then slugged him in the shoulder.

"You should have called."

"Sorry," he said, rubbing his arm. "I've been a little busy." Anya's face fell.

"Judge Rand," she said. "I saw Sheriff Landry's press conference yesterday. Is he really dead?"

"I'm afraid so," Jake said. "Actually ... are you the only one working here?"

"Most weekdays, yes," she said. "I do the books for Melissa, the owner, too. We've got another waitress, but Mel only has her working weekends. We could use more help. God. I'm sorry. You've been sitting out here forever. Where's my head? What can I get you, Jake?"

Jake looked up at the mystifying menu. "Uh, I hear the taco salad is good. I'll try that. Just a Coke to drink."

"Oh," Anya said. "Sorry. We don't serve anything processed. We've got organic tea, juice of the day, strawberry or cucumber-infused water ..."

Jake put a hand up. "How about just regular water infused with nothing but ice?"

Anya smiled. It used to melt him. It still did. "Be right back. Don't let these two cause any problems for you. I'll spit in their food."

Anya turned on her tennis-shoed heel and headed back to the kitchen. Jake slowly sank back into his chair.

"I had no idea she worked here," Jake said. "It tracks though."

Anya Strong was a breed unto herself. Like a displaced flower child from the wrong generation.

"Yeah," Ben said. "We never could figure out how she put up with you all those years. You two couldn't be more opposite. You barely ate anything you didn't kill and she wouldn't eat anything that had a face."

Everyone always said that. No one understood. They weren't opposite at all. Anya and Jake had both been forged by their families' great tragedies. Once upon a time, she'd been the only person on earth who understood his soul.

"I could never figure it out either," Jake said. "Lucky for her, she came to her senses. I'm glad she's doing okay though."

"She's great! Got herself a husband with money," Lance said. Ben hit him under the table.

"Not so much money she can quit working here," Ben said, but Jake knew he was trying to cover.

"Easy," Jake said. "I'd already heard through the grapevine that she got married a few years ago. I'm sure he's a great guy. Come on, we broke up when we were nineteen. Almost half our lives ago. Relax. We're not in high school anymore."

"I don't know if he's great or not," Ben said. "Seems to make her happy though. He's just a geezer. I'm surprised you don't already know him. Tim Brouchard."

Jake had only been half paying attention to what Ben was saying. But the name stopped him cold. "Tim Brouchard?" Jake said. "Is his dad the prosecutor?"

"Not his dad," Lance said, smiling. "Tim *is* the prosecutor."

Jake tried to process it. His limited encounter with Brouchard hadn't been positive. He nearly helped Ed Zender muck up his crime scene for one. For another, he was old enough to be Anya's father.

Anya came back holding two paper bags in one hand, and Jake's salad in the other. She set it down in front of him and handed Ben the bags.

"We'll let you two catch up," Ben said. He pulled on Lance's sleeve.

"Yeah," Lance said. "We've gotta get back. Give me a call though, Jake. We'll go out for a beer."

"Sounds good," Jake said. As soon as they left the cafe, Jake looked up at Anya.

Tim Brouchard? He pushed it out of his mind. Anya had her own life. That part of it was none of his business. "Can you take a break for a few minutes? I didn't just come here for the salad."

She laughed. "Oh shut up. You didn't come here for the salad at all."

"No," he admitted. "I didn't. I'm working Judge Rand's homicide. I've heard from a couple of people that he was a regular here. Do you have time for a few questions?"

"Of course," she said, taking the seat Ben had just vacated.

"How well did you know the judge?"

Anya tucked a stray curl behind her ear. Jake couldn't help but notice the diamond ring on her finger. It was a big one. Tim Brouchard?

"He came in two or three times a week," she said. "Sat at this table, actually. He liked that it was usually pretty quiet for lunch. He didn't like eating at Tessa's or the deli close to the courthouse. He used to tell me too many people would bother him there. Also, I think it just made him sad going there."

"Sad?" Jake asked.

"Because of what happened to Nina, the Papatonis' daughter. You remember. And all those pictures they have of her up in the restaurant."

Jake shook his head. "I know she died. But it was after I left town. I can't say I knew Nina very well."

"She was raped and murdered after some college party, I think it was. Just awful. I'm ashamed to admit it, but it's what keeps me from going in there very often, too. Too many memories. I see Spiros and Tessa other places though. It's just hard. Nina was a fixture in that restaurant."

Anya's face got that faraway look he knew so well. She was thinking about her own older sister. Nicole Strong hadn't come home from a high school dance when Anya was just six years old. It made her an only child and the glue that held her parents' marriage together, until it finally, irretrievably broke. It was a hell of a lot to put on a young girl, but Anya shouldered it all.

"I can imagine," Jake said. He let Anya sit with her memory for a moment. It's one of the reasons they connected all those years ago. Neither of them felt the need to say empty words of comfort. It was enough to just sit in the silence sometimes.

Anya smiled. "Maybe we should form a club," she said. "Like the lonely hearts. Except it's for survivors of family tragedies and lost souls. You, me, Spiros, and Tessa."

"Sure," Jake said. "Or just a very depressing weekly Euchre game."

Anya laughed. She reached for him, sliding her hands into Jake's across the table. They stayed like that for a moment. Then, Anya let go, wiping away a quick tear before it had a chance to fall.

"The judge," she said, smiling. "I'll tell you what I can."

"Did he always eat alone?"

Anya nodded. "There was maybe one or two times when he brought Tony with him, his clerk."

"When was the last time you saw him?" Jake asked.

"I guess it was two weeks ago this last Tuesday. He told me he had a big trial the following week so he didn't know when he'd be in again. I gotta be honest, that's why I knew something was definitely wrong. He wouldn't have just disappeared when he had that trial. It's so awful, Jake. Do you have any idea who might have done this?"

"I've got a few leads," Jake said. "I'm just trying to get a feel for what he was up to those last days. Can you think of anything that might have been out of the ordinary with him?"

Anya shook her head. "He was just his normal, friendly self. He was a pretty happy guy overall. Never complained. Always had a big smile and a kind word. He had an ego too, don't get me wrong. The man loved being a judge. I really looked forward to seeing him. He'd order that taco salad and a strawberry water. He'd usually call ahead if he wasn't going to come in. Otherwise, I'd have it ready for him. I'd put a reserved sign on this booth. Oh, he loved that."

"I'll bet," Jake said.

"I'm sorry. I don't have anything helpful to tell you. But he was normal. Just ... normal Judge Rand. He'd eat every bite of that salad."

Jake took a bite of his. Dammit if the thing wasn't delicious. It had avocado and a southwestern tang to the dressing. He didn't dare ask what was actually in the vegan cheese shredded over the top of it. Even that was good.

"See? There's hope for you yet." Anya giggled. "Oh, it's good to see you, Jake. I think about you a lot. Wonder how you're doing. I see Gemma every now and again but I think she still holds a grudge."

"She never held a grudge," Jake said. "She's just ... well ... Gemma. She's salty with everyone."

"She loves her baby brother." Anya smiled. "It's why I like her."

"It's good seeing you too, Anya," he said. "It's been too long."

"So you're staying? In Worthington County? For good?"

That was Anya. Always direct. She'd learned at far too young an age, life could change in an instant.

Jake met her eyes. He could never lie to her. He had never wanted to. He found a smile. "I'm trying." It was the most honest answer he could give.

He reached for his wallet. Anya reached across the table and put a hand on his wrist. Her touch sizzled.

"Lunch is on me. Well, technically, it's on the judge. He paid in advance for his last lunch. He was supposed to stop in the Monday after he went missing."

"Fair enough," Jake said. He pulled his card out of his wallet. It was still generic county sheriff's contact information. Jake wrote his cell number down and slid it across the table.

"If you think of anything, on the judge, I mean."

"Of course," Anya said. She pocketed his card and stood.

"I'll see you around," he said, but doubted he'd ever have occasion to cross the threshold of the Vedge Wedge again.

"Sure, Jake," she said. "Be careful out there. Oh! That reminds me. I've got something for you."

She practically sprinted over to the counter. She pulled her purse out from behind it. Jake smiled. It was a monstrous, gaudy thing made of some sort of patchwork, quilted material. Anya pulled out a medallion and walked back to him.

"Keep this," she said. She pressed the thing into his palm. He looked at it.

"Saint Michael?" he said.

"It's for protection," she said. "I know it's hokey, but ..."

"No," Jake said. "It's perfect. Thanks."

He squeezed the medallion, put it in his pocket, and left.

He felt the weight of it as he walked the three blocks back to the Sheriff's Department. As Jake walked down the hallway to his office, he heard laughter coming from inside. Ed was there.

Jake stood in the doorway. Ed sat in his chair with his feet on the desk. A middle-aged man with graying dark hair sat in front of him. He was crying.

"Oh, hey!" Ed said, sitting upright. "I was hoping you'd show up."

Jake bristled at the snide comment. "Ed?"

Ed rose and put a hand on the man's shoulder, in a vice grip. He urged him to his feet.

"Jake?" Ed said. "This is Doug Lovett. We've been having a little chat."

Jake's blood turned to ice. Doug Lovett. Husband of Mandy Lovett. Sampson Rand's mistress. What in the hell was Ed doing talking to him without letting Jake know?

"Have you?" Jake said. "Ed? You mind stepping outside with me for a moment?"

Ed's eyes narrowed. Doug looked like he was about to throw up.

"Sit tight, Doug," Ed said softly to Doug. "I'll handle this."

Jake clenched his fists. He had a good mind to drive one into Ed Zender's throat.

Eighteen

"What the hell are you doing, Ed?" Jake asked. He took him further down the hall, far away from where anyone else could overhear them. Ed stood with his arms folded. He glowered at Jake, but his neck started to turn purple and the man was sweating.

"What do you mean what am I doing? I'm trying to help you out."

"How exactly is you hauling Doug Lovett in here helping me?"

"Look," Ed said. He put a hand on Jake's arm. Jake felt his whole body turn to granite. He concentrated on breathing, rather than his growing urge to put Ed into another wall. Ed felt it too. His Adam's apple bobbed and he let go, taking a step back.

"Doug Lovett is a material witness, Ed. It's for me to question him."

"Yeah?" Ed said. "Well, I didn't see you hotfooting it over here to get it done. It's after ten, Jake. Sorry to inform you, but we get an early start around here. We work for a living. Things are a little different here than at the eff BEE eye."

"Cut the crap, Ed," Jake said. "You know damn well it was for me to question Lovett."

"Relax, kid," Ed said. "Doug and me go way back. He feels comfortable with me. Maybe when you cool off, you'll see I was doing you a favor. And for the record, I didn't haul him in. He came in voluntarily. He called me. I'm telling you. Doug Lovett isn't your guy. He'd never hurt anyone. You'll see. He's a marshmallow. And you can read my notes. I'll tell you every damn thing he said. Like I said, he's comfortable with me. He'll tell me more than he'll tell you. That's why he called."

"He's comfortable with you?" Jake said. "I don't need him to be comfortable. And you telling me what he said doesn't cut it. I need to see the man's reactions with my own eyes. At the very least, you owed me a phone call or a text when he reached out to you. If I felt it would have been helpful to have you along, I would have asked. That's how it needs to be on this case. Are we clear?"

Ed shook his head. "Sure thing, hotshot. Whatever you say."

Ed turned and waved a dismissive hand back at Jake.

Fuming, Jake started to follow him back to the office. Their secluded conversation wasn't secluded anymore. A few heads poked out of the neighboring offices. Jake knew within the hour, the whole department would know he and Ed had words again. That would have to be a can of worms he dealt with later. Jake straightened his jacket and found a pleasant smile as he walked back into the office.

Lovett was on his feet. He wasn't a big guy. Five seven, five eight maybe. He had a head of thinning dark-brown hair and a doughy face. He looked nervously from Ed to Jake.

"This is my partner, Jake Cashen," Ed said. "The one I was telling you about."

Lovett extended a hand. Jake kept a poker face, but his brain spun with guesses as to what exactly Ed might have told Lovett about him. For now, it couldn't matter.

"Thanks for coming in, Mr. Lovett," Jake said. "You mind if we have a talk?"

"S-sure," Lovett said. "Ed said you'd want to. I want you to know right off the bat, whatever you need. Whatever you want to know."

It sounded rehearsed, like maybe Ed coached Lovett to say exactly that. Between this and the prints he left at the crime scene, Ed was doing a damn good job torpedoing this case if Jake ever did get to the bottom of it.

"I appreciate that," Jake said. "Why don't we step into the room across the hall? It's more private."

Lovett looked back at Ed. Ed smiled and held an arm out, gesturing for Lovett to follow Jake. Jake grabbed a pad of paper and pen and led Lovett across the hall to the interview room.

"So we're clear," Jake said as Lovett sat down. "This is an informal interview. The door's going to stay open. If you want to leave, you go ahead and leave. I'm just trying to get some things clarified."

"I understand," Lovett said, breathless. "Ed explained all of that to me too. He's been real nice."

"Good for Ed," Jake said. "I understand the two of you have a relationship?"

"Well, I've known him forever. Ed and I used to play on a bowling league together. My cousin dated him in high school."

"Got it," Jake said. "So I'm sure you're aware of the conversation I had with your wife yesterday."

Lovett gave him an almost manic nod. "I am. Mandy's beside herself. Inconsolable. She barely got her words out."

"I can understand," Jake said. "It's a difficult time. Do you mind sharing with me what she told you?"

Lovett was sweating through his dress shirt. Large pit stains formed. He kept wiping his brow.

"Can I offer you something to drink? We have bottled water. Maybe some coffee?"

"No. No, thank you," Lovett answered.

"Are you hungry? Did you miss lunch?"

"No," Lovett said. "I think if I tried to eat something, I'd puke. Thank you though. I'd rather just get this over with."

"Sure," Jake said. "So Mandy."

"Right," Lovett said. "She ... she uh ... she told me she and Sampson Rand were having a fling."

Lovett hiccupped on the last word and started to cry.

"That's gotta be a pretty tough thing for a man to hear," Jake said. "You didn't have any idea?"

"No!" Lovett shouted. "God, no. I feel like such an idiot. Mandy and me, we've been together a long time. Fifteen years."

"No kids?" Jake asked.

"No, sir," he said. "We tried. I've got bum swimmers, the doc said. Mandy always said that didn't matter to her. I believed her."

"Mr. Lovett ..."

"Doug," he interjected. "Call me Doug."

"Fine. Doug. Are you angry with your wife?"

He squeezed his eyes shut. "I don't know. I mean, yes. Of course. You should have seen her though. I was afraid she was going to give herself a stroke or a heart attack when she told me. I've never seen her like that. Not even when her mother died. I know I'm supposed to be enraged. It's there. Under the surface maybe. But at the same time, it does something to me seeing her like that. I don't know. I guess I'm still in shock. I don't know how to feel exactly."

"That's understandable. It's a lot to take in. I gotta be honest, I don't know how I'd feel either."

"Are you married, Detective?"

"No," Jake said.

"It's hard work. I thought I was doing it though. I know my job puts me on the road a lot. But I was already working for Mans Flooring when I met Mandy. She knew the deal. She liked it even. I've been able to take her on all these trips. Even the weekends away, she'd go on these girls' getaways. It was working. I thought she was happy, you know?"

"I'm sure you did the best you could," Jake said. "Women are a mystery to me. You're definitely one up on me getting one to actually marry you."

Lovett's face brightened. "Oh, give me a break. They always go for guys like you. You're young. Athletic. I remember you. From when you won states. I'm older by a few years and everything. But I remember. How many times did you cash that in to get laid?"

Jake smiled. "Oh, not as many as you might think."

"And you've got that badge now. I'm sure that doesn't hurt you in that department."

Jake sat back. He let Doug Lovett take him in.

"They say they don't, but that's what women are into. They say they want a nice guy. Somebody to talk to. But the minute some alpha male struts by, forget about it."

"So you suppose it was the robe Mandy went for?" Jake asked. "Judge Rand?"

Doug's face changed. He sneered. "Of course. She was always talking about whatever advice he was giving her. Judge Rand this. Judge Rand that. I'm such an idiot. She said he was like a father figure to her."

"So she was meeting up with him while you were in Fort Wayne?"

He clenched his fists. Doug Lovett's anger came out in the fire in his eyes. "Every month," she said. "I'm out there working my ass off. Sitting in godawful meetings and corporate team building events. Rope climbing. All kinds of crap."

"And she's out there screwing Judge Rand behind your back," Jake said. "Yeah. I don't know how you deal with that, Doug. She makes what? Thirty, forty grand working for the county? Gets six weeks a year off? I'm sure you don't get that. You've gotta have one of those jobs that's with you twenty-four seven."

"Exactly," Doug said. "It's a constant flow of crap every time my phone rings. And she gets to go on her girls' weekends with her piddly county money. Glamping. Where they sit there and sip champagne in a heated dome in the woods and call it camping."

Jake shook his head. "Unbelievable. Did she tell you the last time she saw Judge Rand?"

"Two weekends ago," he said through clenched teeth.

"While you were in Fort Wayne?" Jake asked.

Doug didn't answer at first. He just stared at the wall, his eyes flicking back and forth.

"At your last corporate retreat?"

"What? Yes. I was in Fort Wayne."

"Got it," Jake said. He scribbled on his notepad. "You stayed over. That's what Mandy said you said."

"Yes. There were a bunch of guys getting together at a bar downtown the next night. I decided to join them this time. I usually don't. I usually don't like being away from Mandy the whole weekend. I'm such an idiot."

Doug smacked his own forehead.

"Doug, I'm sorry about this. But I've got to ask you. Do you own a gun?"

Doug sat straighter in his seat. "I already told Ed all about that."

"Would you mind telling me? Technically, I'm the lead detective on this case. There's a form I have to fill out."

"Oh right," Doug said. "Yes. I bought one maybe six months ago. It was actually Mandy's idea. There was a group of guys taking a CCL course at the Elks Lodge. She thought it would at least be something social for me to do. She was always on me about getting out of the house more. Now I know why. Anyway, yes. I bought the pistol. I've never actually fired it though. It's still in the box."

"Gotcha," Jake said. Doug was already telling a different story than Mandy had.

"Wait a minute," Doug said. "Is that how he died? The judge? Someone shot him? I never asked. Mandy didn't say."

"It appears that way, yes," Jake said.

"Oh my God. You don't think I had anything to do with this. I didn't have anything to do with this. I told you. I was in Fort Wayne the weekend you asked me about. I wouldn't hurt a fly. Ask anyone. Ask Ed."

"Why did you call Ed, if you don't mind me asking?" Jake said.

"Because Mandy said you might be coming to ask me questions. Look, I'm sure you're a great guy. You seem like it. But I've known Ed for a long time, like I said. I figured he'd be the one to talk to. I wanted to make it clear I've got nothing to hide."

"And I really do appreciate that," Jake said.

"I'm angry," Doug said. "I just found out my wife was screwing someone else. But I still love her. Maybe in a few weeks or months, once I've had a chance to process it all. But right now, I don't want to lose her."

He broke down sobbing.

"It's okay, Doug," Jake said. He pushed a box of tissues across the table.

"She's my whole world. I knew she was out of my league though. You've seen her. And look at me. I'm not like you. I'm not like ... him." He spit the last word out.

"Is there somebody I can call for you?" Jake asked.

Doug shook his head. "No. But I need to get out of here. You said I could leave anytime I wanted. Can I?"

"Of course," Jake said. "But I'd appreciate it if you stuck around. I might have more questions, Doug."

"Sure," he said. He grabbed a handful of tissues. He blew his nose into them, sounding like a strangled goose. Then Doug Lovett practically sprinted out the door.

A moment later, Meg Landry walked in. "Well," she said. "What did you think?"

Jake rose. "I think it's time to get a warrant for Doug Lovett's phone."

NINETEEN

At sixteen, Ryan Stark had the kind of hard-cut muscles that turned his shoulders into perfect right angles. He was lean still and walked with that lowered center of gravity that would identify him as a wrestler for the rest of his life. He also bore more than a passing resemblance to his locally famous Uncle Jake. A fact pointed out to him on maddeningly frequent occasions by anyone in Worthington County born before 1990.

"Hop in the back," Jake said to his nephew. "Let Coach sit in the front."

Ryan climbed in, pulling his AirPods out long enough to say thank you. "I really appreciate you taking the time to do this," he said. "And Coach Borowski too. I know you're pretty busy with work and everything."

Jake's mouth curled into a half-smile. Ryan's words didn't seem quite natural for him, even if they were genuine. "Your mother make sure you said that?"

Ryan dropped his head and smiled. The kid's hair was too long. He and the rest of the team were doing some sort of ridiculous, unified growth of mullets. In Ryan's case, his was curling fast, making him look more Bob Ross than Joe Dirt. Jake knew he had no room to judge. His senior year, everyone on the team dyed their hair either blue or gray. It made half of them look like old men. Jake ended up shaving himself pretty much bald after states.

As they pulled up to Frank's two-story Craftsman-style house, Jake's heart clenched. Twenty years ago, he would come here for refuge. For a sense of normalcy. Coach would let him hang out and watch videos away from the chaos of Grandpa Max's house and the ever-present undercurrent of tragedy that seemed steeped in the walls.

Borowski saw Jake's truck pull up. He came through the front door waving a hand above his head. Coach had a big smile and color in his cheeks. He moved with nimble footing, practically sprinting to the truck.

"You ready?" Jake asked as Frank opened the cab door.

"Question is, are you?" Frank directed his question to Ryan.

"Everybody's really stoked you're coming into the room today," Ryan said. "Coach Purcell said he's been trying to get you to come out for years. He always appreciates having old-timers to help out."

Jake suppressed a laugh as Coach's eyes narrowed. He was pretty sure Ryan hadn't been going for sarcasm. Which made it even funnier.

"That's twice around the Gulag for you," Coach said.

Ryan put his head down and his face back in his phone screen. Wise move, Jake thought.

"So the team looks good this year," Frank said.

"Not bad," Jake answered. "Strong through the middle weights especially. Ben Wayne's kid Travis is doing a heck of a job at 106. He'll move up next year and that's going to hurt."

"How many seniors?" Frank asked.

"Just four on varsity," Ryan answered.

"Well, they'll need to set the tone," Frank said. "St. Iz is a powerhouse. How do you match up there?"

"They're deep in Ryan's weight class. Whoever wins it is going to contend for state champion."

"You think you're ready, son?" Coach asked.

"Hell, yeah," Ryan sneered. "I'm ready to beat some rich boy ass."

Frank laughed. "Yeah. We'll see how you work out today."

Jake let Ryan and Borowski off at the door while he parked. He needed a second to collect himself before he went into the practice room. He knew the smell would take him right back to eighteen years ago. For good or bad.

He was right.

All of it. The shouts from the practice wrestlers, the ear-splitting screech of rubber soles on the mat. Sweat.

Frank was already standing by Coach Purcell. The younger coach beamed up at him, star-struck almost. Every banner on that wall but one was earned under Frank Borowski's watch.

Jake joined them. He and Frank watched as Coach Purcell took the team through its warm-up. Stretches, rolls, dips, chin-ups, pull-ups. Enough to get a sweat going. It was the same warm-up done for decades at Stanley High School.

After that, the team broke off into groups. Jake found Ryan. He put a hand on his nephew's shoulder. "Listen," he said. "You're great on your feet but you need to work on your pinning combinations and on bottom."

Jake expected Ryan to say he knew or get defensive. Instead, the kid impressed him by saying simply, "Can you help me, Uncle Jake?"

Jake got right to work, showing Ryan the Gene Mills half-Nelson technique. It only took Ryan about a half hour to catch on. He was a natural. His poor Freshman partner took the brunt of the lesson. After being twisted into a pretzel enough times, the kid broke, stretched his neck and shoulders, and said to Ryan, "Pick a different partner tomorrow, man."

Winded, Jake grabbed his knees to catch his breath. Adrenaline still coursed through him. It was all right there. Eighteen years. Twenty. As if it had never happened. As if he'd never left. How many times had he relied on the same skills he learned in this room from Frank Borowski? They had saved his life on the street more than once. Maybe they had saved his soul.

He looked over at Frank. He stood bent over with his hand on Ben Wayne's son's arm. Frank jerked his hand upward, using his body as punctuation for the point he wanted to make. A wrestling coach's pantomime. A language only few could understand. Jake would until the day he died.

"He looks good." Coach Purcell came up to Jake. "Ryan could go all the way if he stays focused. It's hard to get him to listen. He's pretty headstrong."

Borowski was close enough to overhear. He burst into a hearty laugh and came to join the other two men. "He's like his uncle. You gotta break them down and build them back up. Forget about his ears."

"He just needs the proper motivation," Jake said. He put an arm around Frank. It was as close as he could come to a hug right now. He felt his emotions just below the surface. They weren't for anyone else. Not even Frank.

"I hope you can make this a regular thing," Purcell said. "Ryan's got a tough match with Blake McManus from St. Iz. He's not there mentally yet. Worst of all, he doesn't realize it. They'll meet up in their first dual right before Christmas."

"Plenty of time," Frank said.

"I'll work with him," Jake said. Even now, he watched Ryan squaring off against a teammate. Ryan worked top position with one of the varsity wrestlers two weight classes up and was putting him on his back at will.

"I don't know what you said to him," Purcell said. "But keep saying it."

Clapping his hands, Purcell headed over to Ryan and his partner.

"It's not what you said," Frank said to Jake. "It's that you're here, Jake. You're good for him."

Frank's words caught Jake off guard. He felt a pang he hadn't expected. Not for the first time since he'd come back to Stanley, he wondered how things would have turned out if Frank hadn't been there for him at Ryan's age.

"Well I don't know about you, but I'm ready for a beer and a damn shower."

"We can take off," Jake said. "Ryan's got a ride home."

"Sounds good," Frank said. They waved to Coach Purcell on the way out.

Jake was quiet on the way back. Frank was too. He intended just to drop Borowski off, but Frank wasn't having any of that.

"Come on," he said. "You look like you could use a drink too."

He knew, Jake thought. Frank knew being at this gym with him stirred up something Jake had tried to bury for a very long time. So Frank did the same thing he'd done hundreds of times when Jake was growing up.

He brought him home.

Twenty

Frank's house. Nothing had changed. Frank lived sparsely, not so much as a painting on the wall. His kitchen still looked straight out of the 1970s with dark paneling and olive-colored appliances. There had been a couple of ex-Mrs. Coach Borowskis but Frank had never let them redecorate. Jake knew it was one of many reasons they became exes.

"Forget the beer," Frank said. He walked over to the liquor cabinet. Jake followed. He whistled low, impressed with what he saw. Blanton's, Elmer T. Lee, Buffalo Trace, Four Roses, and Jim Beam Black.

Jake picked up an unopened bottle of twenty-three-year-old Pappy Van Winkle Family Reserve.

"Where the hell did you find this?" he asked.

"More than half of that stuff came from my retirement party. Haven't had the nerve to crack open a lot of it. That one though. The white whale. I found that at a barn sale. The woman running it had it marked for five bucks. I gave her a crisp fifty-dollar bill and made her day. I'm saving it for a very special occasion."

"Pretty special," Jake said. It was a six-thousand-dollar bottle of bourbon.

Frank pulled out a bottle of Four Roses Small Batch and poured a shot into each of two crystal bourbon glasses. Each glass had an image of the Worthington County Sheriff's patch laser-etched into it.

"Got those at my retirement party too," Frank said. He slid a glass over to Jake.

"Thanks." Jake brought the glass nose first, then took a sip. It was so smooth going down with a hint of vanilla and caramel.

"So," Frank said. "I've been hearing some rumors Ed's causing you problems."

"Rumors, huh?" Jake said. "You mean Ed called you?"

Frank smiled.

"He's having a tough time letting go," Jake said. "And it's becoming a problem."

"How so?"

"He was sloppy at the scene. That's going to come back to bite us in the ass. He's off conducting his own interviews of the main person of interest."

"You got to get that locked down, Jake," Frank said.

"I'm trying. Believe me. The thing is, I can deal with all of that. I've worked with a hundred guys like Ed Zender, and worse. I don't even take it personally. I just think this is more than his ego in the mix. It's like he's actively trying to sabotage this to get back at Meg Landry."

"How do you like her as a boss?" Frank asked.

"So far, so good. She does what she says she's going to do. It'd just be nice if people like Ed would simmer down and give her a fair chance. The way things stand, she's going to have a tough time holding on to O'Neal's seat in the next election."

"Any idea who's running against her?"

"Haven't paid attention," Jake said. "I've got my hands full with Rand's case."

"I heard on the news Reese Sheldon got popped over in Marvell County. You think that's related to Rand? I can't say I was ever a big fan of Sheldon's. He was up to his elbows with the Hilltop Boys."

"You think they hit him?" Jake asked.

Frank shrugged. "Wouldn't put it past them. Maybe they had a falling out. Maybe they were worried Sheldon was going to sell somebody out. Who knows?"

"Then why take out Rand too?" Jake said. "All that's doing is making more people ask the same questions."

"Dave Yun catch that one?" Frank asked.

"He's turning it over to the Feds."

"Smart," Frank said. "How's that going to mess with you?"

"Shouldn't," Jake said.

"Hmm. Listen. I gotta level with you. I got a phone call the other day from Yun. He said he met you. He said you hotfooted it away from his crime scene right before a certain Special Agent Lilly showed up. Then Special Agent Lilly had some choice words to share with Yun about you. Anything you want to get off your chest?"

"Nope," Jake said. "I don't even know Lilly. Any beef he's got with me he's borrowing second-hand. Not my circus anymore."

"Yun asked me if he can trust you," Frank said. "Sounds like Agent Busybody told him he shouldn't."

"Why are you telling me this, Frank?" Jake asked. "Something happen to make you think Yun can't trust me?"

"No. God, no. I just think you should be aware, is all."

"Believe me," Jake said. "I'm aware." He finished the last of his bourbon and set the glass on the table. "Thanks for the drink, Coach. And thanks for today."

"Jake," Frank said. "This is me. This is you and me. I know you. Something happened and you're holding it inside so tight it's practically choking you."

"It's nothing," Jake said, but of course Frank knew he was lying.

"Right," Frank said. "Sure. You came back here to Worthington County for a reason. But it's not the one you've been trying to shovel to everybody else. Greg O'Neal wouldn't have put you in field ops to start with unless you asked him to. You're running from something. Or you're hiding from something. Maybe both. What is it? What happened with the Bureau to make you leave the way you did?"

"It was just time," Jake said.

"Bullshit," Frank said. "You're not a quitter. You were at the top of your game. I know about Operation Black Box. That's a career maker, not an ender. What'd they do to you, Jake?"

Jake felt good being there, in Frank's house. He knew it was partly the bourbon talking, but it felt like home. He stared at his empty glass, then looked up at Frank. Before he knew it, the words just came.

"The RICO case on the Blood Money Kings was pretty much over. Either everyone pleaded out or made deals to testify against the bosses. Anyone left over saw the writing on the wall. Not one trial in the whole case."

Frank leaned over and poured another shot into Jake's glass.

"I had an ace informant, Catalina Renya. She was the girlfriend of the second-in-command. The guy in charge of logistics with the cartel. I never had to name her so I thought she was protected. She had a sister, Lupe. Lupe was basically a pin cushion for the soldiers on the crew and was always jealous of Catalina's standing in the gang.

"Catalina called me one night after hours on a Saturday. She was frantic. She said she heard there was a hit out on her and saw some cartel-looking guys hanging around her apartment complex. They definitely were not from her neighborhood. She said she needed some quick cash to get out of town."

Jake saw the knowing look on Frank's face. There was no judgment in it, but Frank seemed to know where this was headed.

"She got to you," he said.

"Listen, Frank, I know how to handle informants. They are not your friends. You never totally trust them and you definitely don't screw them. I do treat informants like human beings though. I know a ton of guys would have just said "oh well, got what I needed out of you, you're on your own." That's not me, and this is where I screwed up big time. That is the *only* thing I screwed up. I swear to God."

Jake wanted to stop. He never intended to tell anyone this story again. Ever. He took another sip of bourbon.

"I told Catalina I'd meet her in our usual spot, an hour later after she called. I was alone, no partner, no backup. I was just going to give her five hundred dollars to get her through the weekend until I could get her under protection."

Frank made a hissing sound. "Let me guess, all against Bureau policy."

Jake nodded. "Absolutely, but it was the right thing to do. I never would have made that case without her. She risked everything. If she was made ..." He paused. He let his gaze drop.

"So I meet with her," he continued. "Give her the cash and tell her to take a bus to Milwaukee and get a hotel room and fly under the radar. Gave her a burner and told her to only call me. She gave me a hug and we went our separate ways. That was that."

"Except it wasn't, was it?" Frank said. "What happened?"

Jake shook his head. "I got a message early that Sunday morning. A text from another burner phone. It was a picture of Catalina and me hugging. Somebody either followed me out there or was waiting the whole time. Texter said if I didn't pay ten grand, they'd report me. I was going to go straight to the office with it. I knew I'd be screwed for violating Bureau policy by meeting with this girl alone. But by the time I walked into the office Monday morning, the shit had already hit the fan. My pinhead boss pokes his head out of his office and calls me in. Peter Nathan. You probably know a thousand guys like him. Career paper-pusher out of D.C. Never investigated a real case in his life, but was a favorite of some of the elitists at HQ. So they put him in charge of the task force after my old boss got promoted. The HQ brass thought this would be a feather in his cap on the next promotion at HQ. The task force guys barely acknowledged him and their command went through me for anything they needed. He made a fool out of himself in briefings and operations, always giving his *sage* advice. The task force guys would laugh out loud at him. This really pissed him off and he resented me for it."

Frank put a hand on Jake's forearm. Jake looked up. The bourbon warmed him. He'd been quiet for so long that now, once he started talking, he couldn't seem to hold back.

"Nathan was looking for a reason to jam you up," Frank said. Jake nodded.

"I went into his office. He had a guy from OPR waiting for me."

"OPR?" Frank asked.

"Office of Professional Responsibility. Like Internal Affairs."

Frank's expression turned sour.

"I swear to God I went into the office that morning ready to come clean about all of it. But they already knew everything. They started accusing me of having sex with my informant. They had the pictures and a statement from Catalina's sister, Lupe, laying out this whole, false story."

Frank went very still. "Jesus."

"It was a lie!" Jake shouted. "A set-up. I did one thing wrong. Just one. I met with Catalina alone. But the OPR guy had the pictures of us together from the Saturday before. The one where I was hugging her. Frank, Catalina was scared to death. I told them everything I told you. But it didn't matter. Nathan was just looking for a reason to get me out and he thought he found it."

"You think your CI set you up?" Frank asked.

"I went over that and over that," Jake said. "I think Lupe was acting alone. She swore out this statement that Catalina and I were having a sexual relationship. She was out there, waiting with a camera when I showed up. I never saw her. I couldn't disprove her version other than with my word. My word wasn't enough. Nathan told me my choice was to hand in my badge, gun, creds, and phone or get suspended."

"So why'd you leave?" Frank asked. "It was her word against yours. Forget about the pictures."

"What I did was bad enough," Jake said. "I met with an informant alone. That's a fireable offense in and of itself. Nathan wanted more though. He was going to bring me up on charges. He might have been able to get them to stick. But at the last minute, Catalina came forward. She somehow caught wind of what was going on. To this day, I don't know how. But she filed a statement denying everything Lupe said. The prosecutor's office told Nathan to pound sand."

"But Nathan had enough to fire you anyway," Frank guessed. "Because you violated one bullshit policy."

"OPR made a deal with me: resign and I'd get to leave in good standing as far as the FBI was concerned. I thought about telling them to go to hell but even if I kept my job in the Bureau, I'd be blackballed forever with a target on my back. It was the right decision to take the deal ..."

"What's to stop this stroke, Nathan, from spinning stories about you anyway?" Frank asked.

Jake smiled as he took one last sip. "This place. This job. I was just going to do my own thing and fly under the radar here for a while."

Frank smiled. The two men sat in silence for a moment. Finally, the conversation drifted back to the familiar old ground of the wrestling season.

"Ryan. That boy reminds me of you," Frank said. "Not just how he looks. He's hungry. Starving, actually. Not just for the win. He hasn't had much in the way of good male role models. He looks up to you."

"You sound just like my sister," Jake said.

"Yeah," Frank said. "I'll shut up. I'm just here for you, Jake. Anything you need. I've got your back. You know I always will. But what happened back in Chicago? Maybe you should tell someone else. Before someone writes the story for you."

"No," Jake said. "I'm taking that one to the grave."

"Well," Frank said. "Anyway. I've said my piece. My offer to handle Ed for you still stands."

"Screw Ed," Jake said. "Screw the Bureau too." God. He thought Worthington County would be far enough to run. But sooner or later, he knew Frank Borowski was right. If he didn't write his own story, someone else would do it for him.

TWENTY-ONE

The Monday after Thanksgiving, when Jake saw Darcy the dispatcher's ID pop up on his cell phone, he knew it wouldn't be good news. He braced himself, considering just letting the call go to voicemail, but knew she'd figure out another way to find him.

"Hey, Darcy," he said.

"Hey, yourself," she said. "Why so down in the dumps?"

"I don't know," he said. "But why do I get the feeling you're going to tell me?"

"Yeah. I'm sorry, Jake. But I think you're going to want to head out to the County Road 9 exit off US-33."

"You know I'm in the Detective Bureau now, right? I mean, I know you know."

Silence. She took a breath. "Right. It's just, I think you're gonna want to see this one for yourself before anybody else breaks it to you."

"See what?" he asked. Jake was already halfway to his car. He planned to head over to the office to check the status of the phone dump on Doug Lovett.

"Um," Darcy said. "I gotta go, Jake. Just get out there. Trust me. You'll know when it smacks you in the face. And you might want to hurry. Before anyone else finds you first."

She clicked off with that cryptic message. Jake held his phone away from his face, scowling at it as if Darcy could see him.

Unbelievable. Luckily, or maybe not, Jake was only about a ten-minute drive from that exit. There was nothing there but a truck stop and a little country store that housed one of the county's hidden gems. Polly's Little Eats. A deli counter that served up some of the best food you could get.

Jake expected to see patrol cars or maybe a group of people gathering somewhere. There was nothing that would otherwise arouse suspicion or necessitate a homicide detective's attention.

Then Jake looked up.

"Holy ..."

And up.

The County Road 9 exit was the main way to get in and out of Worthington County from anywhere else. Literally everyone in town would use it at some point during the week, often multiple times. It made the billboard one of the most coveted pieces of advertising space money could buy. They had a waiting list years long to rent it. And this year, Gemma had scored the winning ticket. She had professional headshots done. Her smiling, six-feet-tall pearly white teeth shined down on him with her name and branded catch phrase:

Gemma Stark-Gerald, I'll Help You Make it Home ...

Today though, there was also a ten-foot-long, red spray-painted dick jutting straight from her mouth. Above it, on his sister's forehead, the word "H-O-R-E" was spelled.

His phone rang again. Darcy.

"You there?" she asked.

"Yeah," he said.

"Sorry, Jake," she said. "I just figured ..."

"Yeah," he said. "I get it, Darcy. You sending somebody out here to take a report? Maybe somebody at the truck stop saw something."

"There's a crew coming out. This'd be Gary Majewski's case. He's already aware and knows you were going to take a look. I'm sure he'll start ..."

"I've already got a pretty good idea who might have done this, Darcy."

"I figured that too," she said. "Do you want to wait for Gary?"

"No," Jake said, still staring up at the sign. "I mean, send him out. I'm on my way over to Jordy Gerald's. My ex-brother-in-law's been staying there."

"Okay, Jake," she said. "I'll tell Gary."

Jake slipped his phone back in his pocket, got behind the wheel, and peeled out of the truck stop parking lot, spinning gravel behind him.

J ordy Gerald lived in a rickety, rundown trailer in Maudeville. His was easy to spot. He still had political signs draped across the side of the trailer from two elections ago. Dickie's beat-up green Silverado was parked in front. Jake walked by it and his blood boiled. There were three red spray paint cans rolling around the bed.

Jake stormed to the front door and pounded on it. The whole trailer shook.

"Get your ass out here, Dickie. We need to talk."

Nothing. Jake heard a thump from inside. Then whispers. He pounded harder, half certain his fist might bust straight through the siding.

"You got about five seconds to drag your sorry ass out here or I'm coming in!"

More thumping from inside. Finally, the door opened and Dickie squinted against the sun.

"Well, hey, brother," he said.

Dickie wore a tank top and a pair of jeans he looked like he'd just pulled on. The fly and buttons were undone. His muscled arms were covered in tats, but also the faint but unmistakable trace of red spray paint.

"Why don't you step outside, Dickie," Jake said.

Dickie looked behind him into the trailer. "You got a warrant?"

"Outside," Jake said. "Unless you want me to lose my temper again."

"Well that sounds threatening," Dickie said.

"Yeah? Then let me be less vague. Get your ass out here before I smash your face into the concrete."

Jake took a step back, keeping his hand resting casually, but noticeably on his weapon. Dickie noticed. He was all bravado, but he checked behind him again.

"Your brother in there?" Jake asked. "You in there, Jordy?"

"He's sleeping," Dickie answered. "He worked a double shift. Some of us still have to work around here, Jake. That is, if you still want your nephew to be on the baseball team."

"It's wrestling season, idiot," Jake said. "And you haven't spent so much as a dollar on that kid since Gemma threw you to the curb."

"Is that what this is all about? You trying to shake me down?"

"No," Jake said. He put an arm up, caging Dickie against the side of the trailer. "This is about those paint cans rolling around in the back of your truck. And the stains all over your arms and shirt."

Jake jabbed a finger into Dickie's chest. Dickie smiled and held his arms up.

"What business is that of yours? And you've got no business searching my truck. That's a violation of my civil rights."

"Maybe don't try thinking so hard, Dickie," Jake said. "You'll hurt your brain."

"You're trying my patience, Jake. I came out here as a courtesy. But I'm done talking."

"You're done when I say you're done. Now, you want to tell me what Jackson Myers is going to find when I ask him to pull his security cameras out at the County Road 9 truck stop?"

Dickie said nothing.

"You felt like expressing your artistic side on private property, is that it?" Jake asked.

Still nothing.

The door of the trailer opened. Jordy Gerald stepped out. He looked exactly like Dickie, only scrawnier. He wore his head cropped close in a buzz cut. He ran a hand over it and blinked against the bright sunlight. He wore a black tee shirt and Jake spotted track marks on the inside of his left arm. It was hard to tell under his tattoos, but Dickie's arms were clean except for the paint.

"He said you'd probably come tearing out here, accusing him of all kinds of shit," Jordy said. "Whatever your crazy sister's been saying is a lie."

"Oh yeah?" Jake said. He pushed off of the trailer, letting Dickie go. "When I need your opinion, I'll ask for it."

"Dickie had nothing to do with what happened to that judge. I can prove it."

"I wasn't asking," Jake said. "But since you're in the mood to talk, let's hear it."

"Don't have to hear anything," Jordy said. "I was planning to come on down to the sheriff's and do you a favor. Do your job for you anyway."

Jordy reached for his back pocket.

"Do *yourself* a favor, Jordy," Jake said. "Keep your hands where I can see them."

"Calm yourself," Jordy said. "I got a piece of paper. You want to know where Dickie was the night that judge showed up dead? I can prove he was here. All night. All weekend. Just like he told you."

"On a piece of paper?" Jake asked.

Jordy turned, wiggling his rear end at Jake. Then slowly, he slid his hand into his back pocket and pulled out a crumpled piece of folded notebook paper.

"You can log in and see for yourself," Jordy said, handing Jake the paper. "Better do it quick though. I'll change the password tomorrow."

"What is this?" Jake asked. Jordy had written down an email address and a password.

When Jake looked back at him, Jordy pointed to a small solar panel hanging loosely off the side of the trailer.

"You've got a Ring camera?" Jake asked, incredulous. "On this piece-of-shit trailer?"

"It's in my interest to see who's coming and going," Jordy said. "That's my login. Dickie and me got nothing to hide."

Jake tucked the paper into his jacket breast pocket.

"Dickie," he said. "I'm going to need you to step away from the trailer and put your hands behind your back. You're under arrest."

"What for? Jordy just told you he can prove I had nothing to do with Judge Rand's murder," Dickie said.

Jake delivered his Miranda rights in a monotone. He slapped cuffs on Dickie.

"What are the charges?" Jordy asked.

"Vandalism," Jake said. "For starters. As for you, Jordy? You better hope that footage doesn't show you tearing off with this idiot last night with those paint cans in the truck."

Jordy's face went white. It was as much as an admission.

"Dickie, you said ..."

"Not another word," Jake told him. "Walk yourself back inside that trailer. You can bail his sorry ass out tomorrow morning."

With that, he left Jordy swearing up a storm behind him. Dickie more or less came quietly, but Jake found himself praying he'd resist.

Twenty-Two

J ake handed Dickie off to Gary Majewski. The security cameras at the truck stop clinched the crime. He captured clear shots of both Jordy and Dickie climbing the ladder up to the billboard, paint cans in hand. They were clearly high or drunk or both. Now if Jake could just get someone out to clean off the sign before Gemma saw it and went ballistic.

With Majewski busy processing the Gerald brothers and Ed Zender off doing who knew what, Jake had the office all to himself. He logged into Jordy's Ring account and pulled up the weekend of November 1st.

Friday at 3:10 in the afternoon, Dickie was clearly visible parking his pickup, exiting, spitting on the ground, then entering the trailer. Jordy's camera was pointed so that Jake could see the entire parking area and halfway down the street. Dickie's car didn't move.

The motion sensor on the camera captured two more videos that evening as Jordy came home followed by two women Jake recognized as local prostitutes. Then nothing. No movement until noon the next day. Saturday. Well after Tony Byers had started texting the judge with no response. The women were seen leaving. At four in the afternoon, Saturday, Jordy left again, probably to score.

He returned an hour later carrying a paper bag. Dickie wasn't seen on the camera again until ten o'clock Sunday morning looking like hell, staggering out to his truck.

Unless something earth-shattering happened, Jake knew he could cross Dickie off his list of suspects in the Rand murder once and for all.

His phone rang for about the seventh time. Most of them had been Gemma. He'd deal with her after work when he had more to tell her. He promised Ryan he'd work out with him after practice. The kid was coming along. He had his first match-up with the McManus kid from St. Iz in three weeks.

When his phone rang yet again, he almost didn't pick it up. This time though, the text came in from Meg Landry.

GET UP TO MY OFFICE.

Puzzled, Jake pocketed his phone and switched off his computer monitor. When he got to the second-floor corner office, he found Landry pacing in front of her desk.

"Close the door," she said.

Jake looked behind him. There was no one else in the hall. He did as she asked.

"Sit," she said, gesturing to one of her desk chairs.

"Why do I get the feeling I'm better off standing and leaving myself a clear escape plan?"

"Don't," she said. He didn't know all of Meg Landry's tells yet. He hadn't known her long enough to understand how she processed things. But right now, something had her good and pissed.

"I got a call from a Peter Nathan with the FBI," she said. "It wasn't a good one, Jake."

Jake felt his shoulders tighten.

"Do you want to guess what he had to say?" Landry said.

"Not really, boss."

"He got Dave Yun over in Marvell County asking a lot of questions, I can tell you that. I heard from him too. What happened with you and the Bureau, Jake? It says in your file you resigned. Is that the truth? Or did they force you out?"

Jake didn't answer. It was everything Frank had warned him about. Someone else was trying to write his story. Peter Nathan.

"Fine," Landry said; she wore a path in her carpet. "I really wish you'd have told me this before. And that's not the only phone call I got. You want to guess who else?"

"You know, I'm not really a fan of the guessing game, Sheriff. If there's something you gotta say to me, I'd rather you just got to it."

"Fine," she said. "I'll say it. A particular county commissioner gave me an earful. Rob Arden. You sure did something to piss him off, too."

"I haven't seen Rob Arden in probably twenty years," Jake said.

"He's your uncle," she said. "Your mother's brother."

"I'm aware. Though I suppose that's not something he likes to admit to. And I suppose that's the general nature of what he had to say."

"What's his beef with you? The truth, Jake."

"You'd have to ask him that."

"I did. It's the first thing I said when he called me demanding that I fire you. He's the one who suggested I call your ASAC at the Bureau."

Jake finally did take a seat. He rested one leg on the opposite knee and stared straight ahead as Landry came around and sat on the edge of her desk.

"You're telling me Rob Arden, my dipshit uncle, told *you* to call Peter Nathan?" he asked.

"Not a lot of people like me in this town," she said. "Turns out some of them like you even less. So now, I'm asking you for your side of it."

"My side of it? I don't have a side. My mother was Sonya Arden before she was Sonya Cashen. That's all I can really speak to. What my uncle Rob Arden and Peter Nathan are doing talking to each other, I couldn't tell you."

"He hates you, Jake. Rob Arden essentially told me if I want to keep my job, I gotta take yours. You should have told me there was bad blood between you and the Ardens."

"As far as I'm concerned, it's just blood. I've never done anything to Rob Arden except exist."

"Come off it, Jake. The truth. I can't defend you if I don't know your side of it," she said.

Blood roared in Jake's ears. "I didn't ask you to defend me. My family history is a matter of public record. When I was seven years old, my dad shot my mom then he shot himself. I'm sure there's a file somewhere in the archives. Look it up. Or spend five minutes over at Papa's Diner and wait for somebody to start gossiping. I'm sure you won't be disappointed."

"I'm not interested in rumors. And I'm not interested in dusting cobwebs off some twenty-nine-year-old case file. I want to hear it straight from you. I owe you that courtesy. Why in God's name does Rob Arden blame you for whatever your father did when you were seven years old?"

Jake gripped the side of the chair.

"Jake," she snapped. He gritted his teeth and looked up at her.

"Again, you'd have to ask Uncle Rob."

"Come off it, Jake. I don't have to tell you how precarious my position is here. Turns out your position is directly tied to it."

"You want me to quit?"

"Would you?" she asked, getting directly in his face. Jake met her eyes. Landry searched him. Was she bluffing? Was he?

"No," he said quietly.

"Good," she said.

"You gonna fire me?"

"That depends," she said. "Tell me what happened with you and the Ardens?"

He took a breath. "Nothing. That's the God's honest truth. Nothing. You've been through Ardenville. You've seen that gaudy-ass shrine they've got put up in that cemetery."

"The new one? The marble one with the waterfall and the bench?" she said. "I pass by it every day."

"Me too," he said. "That's where my mom is buried."

"Oh God," Landry said, finally starting to understand. "But the Ardens don't even live near there anymore. They've got that compound up on Hart Lake in Carlow Township."

"You got it," Jake said. "That's the way it's always been. The Ardens owned their little company town but wouldn't deign to live in it. Now they just want the peons to still worship their princess at that mausoleum. Or maybe they just figured it was a way for them to stick it to my old man and the rest of us every time we drove through to Stanley."

"But what happened, Jake? Honestly."

"I don't know," Jake said, dropping his tone an octave. "I really don't. We don't talk about it. My dad just snapped. I don't remember anything unusual."

"Were you there the night it happened?" she asked.

Jake stiffened. He spent almost thirty years training himself not to think about it.

"No," he said. "I was at a friend's house. At Ben Wayne's. It was a Friday. I was spending the night. My sister ... she came home from school and ..."

Landry put a hand to her mouth. Jake hated it. It's what everyone always did.

"What was she?" Landry asked. "Twelve? Thirteen?"

"Twelve," Jake said. "Gemma was twelve. Look, it's all probably in that report. Read it."

"Have you?" she asked.

Jake turned to stone. "No. And I never will."

"I'm sorry, Jake. That must have been awful for you. Both your parents."

"They tried to put us in foster care," he said. "I can't prove it, but I think the Ardens might have had something to do with that. There was a court fight. Grandpa Max finally got a guardianship."

"The Ardens were your family too," she said. "You're telling me they were going to let you and your sister get split up in the system? Because you know that's what would have happened."

Jake shrugged. "Grandma Rose always said Paul Arden, my other grandfather, warned my mom that my dad would drag her down. Destroy her. That we were nothing but a bunch of hillbilly troublemakers. She was too good for our blood. Something like that. After it happened, they all just figured Paul was right. He never wanted anything to do with us."

"You're his grandchildren," she said. "The only thing left of his daughter. I just don't understand."

"Don't try," Jake said. "And don't feel sorry for me. It is what it is. I've never needed anything from the Ardens. My sister? She's another story. She's been trying to seek their approval her whole life. That's what that damn billboard was for. So they'd see."

Landry bit her lip. "Yeah. I saw that on my way in. I told Detective Majewski to make it a priority."

"Oh it wasn't tough to crack that case. Dickie and Jordy Gerald are downstairs being processed. I just gotta find somebody to clean it up before the end of the day."

"Jake," she said. "Rob Arden isn't kidding around. I told you. Rob Arden and Peter Nathan have been in contact. I think he can make real trouble for you if he wants to. Like I said, if I know what I'm up against, I can handle it. But as it stands, Rob Arden seems to think there's grounds for firing you. He believes you lied about your severance with the FBI and therefore your application here. You swear to me he's wrong?"

Jake's jaw popped, he was clenching it so hard. "Yes," Jake said. "He's wrong."

"Because he said his contact told him you resigned right before they were going to fire you. Is that true?"

Jake met Landry's eyes. "I resigned. O'Neal checked my references. Don't tell me you didn't too before you asked me to help you with Judge Rand's case."

"You're right," she said. "I did. But that's not what I just asked you. Were they going to can you?"

Jake stared at the wall. "Yes."

She folded her hands in her lap. "Would they have been making a mistake?"

"Yes."

"Okay," she said. Jake had gone so rigid, he almost didn't hear her say it.

"What?"

"Okay," she repeated. "I trust you. But someone's still got it out for you over there. And they've figured out your Uncle Rob could be their ally in screwing you over, Jake. But I'm rarely wrong about people. And I think you're worth sticking by. So I will. Just don't make me regret it."

He met her gaze again. Sheriff Landry rose. "So tell me something good," she said. "What's going on with your investigation?"

"Well," he said. "I've pretty much cleared Dickie Gerald. The only thing he seems to be guilty of is poor spelling and a fuzzy grasp of male anatomy."

Landry laughed. "Yeah, that giant billboard dick sure did seem to take an odd left turn."

"But," Jake said. "He appears to have a solid alibi the weekend the judge got himself killed. I'm waiting for the phone dump on Doug Lovett. If I can confirm his alibi from that, I'm back to square one on local suspects. It's looking like Dave Yun's case in Marvell might yet be connected."

"Good," she said. "Keep me in the loop. I need something to tell the county commissioners. I won't lie to you, Jake. I said I'll go to bat for you. But if you don't clear this case and soon, we're both going to be out of a job."

Twenty-Three

Sunday morning, Jake woke up to a sharp, solid knock on the door. Instinct kicked in and he grabbed his gun off the nightstand.

Another thump. "Let's go, Sleeping Beauty." His grandfather's raspy voice cut through Jake's brain fog. For a second, he felt ten years old. It was how the old man woke him up every weekend morning. It was usually followed by a few hours' worth of log splitting, or moving heavy piles of something from one end of the property to the other for no good reason. Jake's back ached already.

"What time is it?" Jake muttered. He put the gun down and reached for his phone. Grandpa kept right on pounding on the door.

Jake grabbed his jeans off the floor, wriggled into them, and came out to the front room.

"Quit banging," he said as he swung the door open. "You'll wake the dead."

"That's the idea," Grandpa said. He stood on the porch wearing a suit and tie. Jake checked his smart watch. It was nine o'clock. Sunday morning mass started at 8:30.

"You're late," Jake said. He had no intention of going to church himself, but his grandfather rarely missed it.

"Don't like the new priest," Grandpa said. "He's a windbag who likes telling me how to vote."

"Yeah," Jake said. "I don't think they're supposed to do that."

"Come on," Grandpa said. "Get the lead out. We're going up the hill."

"I'm not dressed," Jake said. "I need a shower. What's your hurry?"

"It's time," Grandpa said, as if that explained everything. "You wanna keep freeloadin', you'll walk with me up the hill. Rosie's waiting."

"Yeah, I don't think Grandma is going anywhere. She's not going to mind if I at least brush my teeth and find a shirt."

"Watch your mouth," Grandpa said. "You got five minutes."

Jake knew once his grandfather got a hair up his ass about something, there was no talking him out of it. So Jake found a clean tee shirt, ran a quick toothbrush over his teeth, and grabbed his Carhartt jacket off the hook. He slipped his boots on outside the door.

"Take the four-wheeler," Grandpa said. He walked down the three porch steps sideways, as old men do, and toddled over to the ATV. The keys were sitting on the seat.

Jake climbed in and prayed the thing wouldn't start. He hated going up this particular hill and hadn't since he came back to town.

The thing started on the first try. Grandpa held the dashboard, bracing himself as Jake put it in gear and drove them up the hill.

The Cashen family cemetery took up the flat land at the base of the largest oak tree on the property. A dozen limestone crosses formed an ever-widening semi-circle facing the tree. Years ago, Grandma Rose had put a bench there. For reasons Jake never understood, she had liked to sit there in the rain. Grandpa had placed her headstone right beside the bench.

Jake climbed out and went to the passenger side, offering a hand to help Grandpa out. He waved him off with a grumble and climbed up the rest of the way, depositing himself on the bench. The old man pulled a comb out of his pocket and smoothed back the few white strands he had left across the top.

"You look fine," Jake said. "Grandma always liked that suit on you."

Grandpa murmured something, eyes closed. A prayer, perhaps. Jake gave him a moment, then came to sit beside him on the bench.

"Look who's come back," Grandpa said, staring at his wife's headstone. Breast cancer had taken her when Jake was a junior in college. Her funeral had been one of the few times he'd come back. She'd put up a valiant fight for four years, getting her diagnosis when Jake was only seventeen. Those had been hard years. Both he and Gemma thought Grandpa would join her soon after he put her in the ground. He hadn't though. Now, fifteen years later, he was just as ornery and alive as ever.

"Don't be rude," Grandpa said. "Tell her hello."

"Hi, Grandma," Jake said. He knew his grandfather didn't think spirits could talk to you. But manners still mattered to him as long as they weren't his own.

There was another headstone right beside Rose Cashen's that Jake didn't like to look at. Not ever. And yet his eyes were always drawn to it.

It's a hell of a thing seeing your own name etched on a grave. But there it was. Jacob McGreavy Cashen. The man he was named for. The man he remembered teaching him how to bait a hook with patient care. Who would sit on the edge of his bed when thunder shook the house. Who danced a Texas two-step in the kitchen with his laughing bride as she looked up at him with the brightest smile Jake had ever seen. The man with a deep laugh and clear green eyes just like his own.

The man who took his mother away.

"Your sister never comes up here," Grandpa said, his voice cold.

"She's got a lot on her plate, Gramps," Jake said.

"She's got plans," he said, wiggling his fingers in the air on the word "plans."

Jake knew a rant was coming.

"She tell you them?" Grandpa asked. "She wants to sell off the land right out from under me and put me in a damn nursing home. I'll die here. You got that? You set her straight."

"She doesn't want to sell the land from under you," Jake said. "She just wants to rent some of the acreage by the road. She says people will pay over three hundred a night. Blackhand Hills is turning into a real tourist spot."

"Yuppies." He spat the word. Jake smiled.

"Yeah," Jake said. "I don't think that's what they're called anymore."

"They want to run all over the place. Tear up the trails. Not a chance."

"She's worried about you," Jake said. "She's trying to make sure you're taken care of."

"I told you," he said. "She's greedy. Wants to put me in a home."

"I won't let that happen," Jake said. "But maybe you could let her get you some help. You know. Just to check on you. Do some housework so you don't have to. So Gemma doesn't have to. I told you. She's got a lot on her plate. She's not getting a lot of help from either Ryan or Aidan's fathers."

"She sure can pick 'em," Grandpa said.

Jake couldn't argue that particular point. He wondered if his grandfather had seen or knew about the billboard graffiti. He hoped not. As far as he knew, Grandpa hadn't been in town for a couple of weeks. Jake got a cleaning crew up there the night before. Dickie was out on bail, but he'd probably end up doing another ninety-day stint out of the whole thing.

"Anyway," Jake said. "Just think about it. Having a girl come just once a week would be good for you."

"So she can steal from me? No thank you."

"Nobody's going to steal from you," Jake said. Grandpa huffed, unconvinced. But he grew quiet again at least.

Jake's eyes went to his father's headstone, though he'd tried to resist. Maybe it was the conversation he'd had with Sheriff Landry, but today that ghost just wouldn't rest.

"We never talk about it," Jake said. He leaned over and brushed a pile of dried leaves away from the base of his father's cross.

"Nothing to talk about," Grandpa said.

"It's just ... did you know? Did you and Grandma know? Try to get him help? Did Mom?"

Jake watched his grandfather. He wouldn't answer, but his eyes misted as he stared at his son's grave.

"How do you help a thing like that?" he said. "He talked to the priest."

Jake balled his fists. "I mean a professional. A psychiatrist. Hell, even a regular doctor. There are medications."

"Pills," Grandpa spat. "He had enough of pills."

"What about when he was growing up," Jake asked. "You didn't see any signs?"

Grandpa dropped his chin to his chest. "She asked herself that a lot," he said. "Your grandma. Blamed herself for years. Tore her up. Then it turned to cancer."

"You think her guilt turned into breast cancer?" Jake said.

Grandpa snapped his head up and glared at Jake. "As sure as I'm sittin' here. Yes. Where else would a mother's sorrow settle and fester? And what good does it do? It eats away at you. Well I won't let it."

"It wasn't her fault," I said. "I'm just trying to understand."

Grandpa shook his head. "Can't be understood. Don't waste your time trying."

Jake knew it was as much as he'd likely get out of his grandfather about the illness that ravaged his son's brain, twisting it into the thing it became that awful Friday night, twenty-nine years ago.

So Jake stopped asking. He let his grandfather sit and pray. After a few more minutes, Grandpa put a gnarled hand over Jake's. "Do you think he went to heaven?"

The question tore through Jake like a gunshot wound. He had no good answer. He just held Grandpa Max's hand and brought it to his heart.

In the space where his mother *should* have been laid to rest, there was another, smaller headstone. Jake brushed some dirt off of that one as well.

Fiona Rose Jarvis. Jake's breath caught as he read the date. He'd forgotten. And now he knew why Grandpa insisted on coming up here today of all days. Twenty years ago today, Gemma had given birth, and then lost her firstborn child. Beside him, Grandpa Max said the Hail Mary.

"Come on," Jake said, when he finished. "I'll make you some breakfast." He wrapped his arm around the old man and the two of them walked back to the ATV.

There were no more questions from either of them as Jake made eggs over easy and toast up at the big house. There were plates in the sink already. When they finished eating, Jake washed and dried them all then put everything back the way his grandmother used to prefer it. He collected the garbage and ran a vacuum while Grandpa napped in his recliner in front of the TV.

He was still sleeping when Jake was ready to leave. He didn't want to wake him. So Jake simply loosened Grandpa's tie and carefully slipped off his shoes and set them on the mat by the door.

His phone rang. Jake quickly grabbed it, clicking the ringer off before Grandpa could wake. Carrying the garbage over his shoulder, he went out the back door, heading for the dumpster. His caller ID showed Mark Ramirez from BCI.

"Hey, Jake," Mark Ramirez said as soon as Jake answered. "Sorry to bug you on a Sunday. But I figured you'd want me to."

"What's up, Mark?" Jake asked.

"We got the phone forensics back on your suspect Doug Lovett. I'm looking at it right now. I'll have a disk couriered over to you later this afternoon if you want."

Jake heaved the sack of garbage into the dumpster and closed the lid. He kept on going down the hill, finding the trail that led straight to his cabin. The cell reception was better there.

"Can you email me the report now?" Jake asked. "I'd like to take a look at it."

"Already done," Mark said.

"Any highlights you care to share?" Jake asked.

"Nothing that jumped out at me," Mark said. "But I don't know your timeline or your geography so that might not mean much. He texts his wife a lot. There was nothing that'd make you think they were having trouble. Pretty mundane. If I didn't know they were married, I'd think they were just roommates or something. Never once talks to her about sex. Who doesn't text their wife about sex?"

"Good question. Thanks. I'll take a look at what you sent."

"No problem. Let me know what else you need."

Jake clicked off just as he got to his own back door. He left his laptop on the bistro table in the kitchen. He fired it up and checked his email. He would wade through the minutiae of Ramirez's report later, but the first page told him most of what he feared.

Jake pulled up a county cell phone tower map he kept bookmarked and cross-checked it with the places Doug Lovett's phone pinged the weekend Judge Rand got killed.

He was lying. Doug Lovett was lying. Friday night at eight p.m., Lovett's phone pinged the tower in Arch Hill Township closest to Sam Rand's house.

The son of a bitch never went to Fort Wayne. He was parked right outside the judge's house the night he was killed.

Jake called Meg Landry's private cell. She answered right away and Jake explained what he was looking at.

"What do you want to do?" Landry asked.

"I need to write a warrant for Doug Lovett's house and car," he said. "If it turns up what I think it will, I might be able to make an arrest by tomorrow evening."

TWENTY-FOUR

Judge Finneas Cardwell concealed a secret under his robes and behind his bench. He had bunions so bad he only wore flip-flops or slippers as he presided. Now, as Jake sat in his chambers at eight o'clock Monday morning, he had a clear view of the man's bare feet as he burst through the adjoining courtroom door and peeled his robes off with a flourish. He twirled the thing like a matador before hooking it on the coat rack beside his desk and taking a seat.

"Whatcha got, Detective?" he said. "I've got a busy docket."

"I appreciate you making space for me," Jake said, sliding his freshly minted warrant across the desk. "I know you're doing double duty while they figure out your replacement in Muni Court. Congratulations, by the way, we're glad to have you in Common Pleas."

"Trying to butter me up?" Cardwell said, peering at Jake over his readers. He held his pen poised over the warrant. He read it line by line, humming to himself.

"Doug Lovett, huh?" he said.

"Yes, sir," Jake said.

"Welp, I'd say you better get to it then. This one's going to cause a stink."

He signed the search warrant, stamped the copies, and handed those back to Jake. "You think he's it, Lovett?"

"I think I've got probable cause to search his home," Jake said, folding the warrant copies and placing them in his pocket.

"Good answer." Cardwell smiled. "Are you going to cost me a court reporter?"

"Did you know?" Jake asked, ignoring the question. "You were close with Rand. You know your number came up on his phone. That group text."

"I hate that thing," Cardwell said. "Tried to get my daughter to figure out how to delete me from it. Like I give a damn if Tim Brouchard's eating eggplant parm on a Tuesday."

"Reese Sheldon's also in that group text," Jake said. "You heard what happened to him?"

"You really think that's connected to Sam's murder?"

"I can't be sure yet," Jake answered.

"You think any of the rest of us have anything to worry about?" Cardwell asked.

"Unlikely," Jake said. "But you make sure you let me know if anyone threatens you. In court. Out of court. Anything. Just in case."

"I sure will," Cardwell said. "Good luck with that." He gestured toward Jake's breast pocket where he'd stuffed the warrant.

"Thanks, Judge," Jake said. "And like I said, we're glad to have you stepped up to Common Pleas. I hope they find a good replacement for you in the lower court."

"Yeah." Cardwell sighed. "So far, nobody wants the damn job. I swear, this place is about to implode. It'll get better once you get cuffs on somebody for killing Sam. And not for nothing, but I think Commissioner Arden is a douche nozzle. You tell your boss not to back down. He's a bully."

Jake smiled. "Will do."

Cardwell was already up and grabbing for his robe. Jake bid him goodbye and headed down the hall, pulling his phone out of his pocket.

"Hey, Sarge," he said as Sergeant Hammer picked up. "How quickly can you get me a couple of field ops out at Doug Lovett's place on Canterbury Road? Cardwell just signed off on my warrant. I'd like to get out there before the whole county catches wind of this."

"I can have a crew meet you out there in a half hour," Hammer answered.

"Is Ed in yet?" Jake asked.

"He's down in the lobby. Darcy brought in a whole box of breakfast pastries. I seriously hope nobody else gets murdered or burgled in the next hour. I got the whole department down there. You better hurry if you want something."

"I'm good," Jake said. "You think you could peel Ed away and have him meet me out at Lovett's, too?"

Hammer went silent for a moment. "You sure?"

"Yes," Jake said.

"That's a good idea, Jake. I know Ed's been difficult, but he really does mean well."

"I know," Jake said, though he didn't. But he figured he'd try throwing Zender a bone. Better to keep him close and out of trouble.

"Good deal then," Hammer said. "I'll get you set up."

"Thanks, Sarge," Jake said, clicking off.

The elevator doors opened and Jake found himself face to face with a flustered Mandy Lovett. Her eyes went big when she saw him. She'd been crying.

"Detective Cashen," she said. "Can we talk?"

Jake bristled. He didn't have to be psychic to know what was on her mind. It was a small courthouse. With the tears in her eyes, no doubt some busybody had already tipped her off as to why he came to court today.

"It's not a good time, Mrs. Lovett," he said.

"It has to be now," she said. "Please. I know you've got a warrant for our house."

Jake ground his teeth. "I can't talk to you about that right now."

"Please!" she shouted. It drew the attention of people standing in line at the County Recorder's Office just across from them.

"Please," she whispered, pulling on Jake's arm. "You have to listen to me. Doug didn't do this."

"Mrs. Lovett, I can't discuss this with you."

"You have to," she pleaded, trying to drag Jake to the first-floor jury room.

"Mrs. Lovett ..."

She whipped around to face him. The woman looked half-crazed, her eyes bugging out, her lips a bloodless line.

"This is my fault," she said. "I should have told you when we first talked. I was afraid. I thought ..."

Jake looked behind him to make sure no one else was listening to their conversation. Then he placed a light hand on Mandy Lovett's back and ushered her into the jury room, closing the door behind them.

"Sit," he said. "And so there's no ambiguity. This is a formal interview, Mrs. Lovett. Anything you say to me ..."

"I know, I know," she said. "I waive my rights. I'm talking to you voluntarily. I'll sign anything you want."

Jake took his cell phone out and pulled up his dictation app. He placed the phone on the table between them and instructed her to say it all again. She did. Pulling up a chair, she took a seat. Jake joined her.

"Now, what didn't you tell me the first time we spoke, Mrs. Lovett?"

"I was afraid," she said. "I know what those people are like. I didn't want to cause any trouble."

"From the beginning," Jake said.

"There was something going on with Sam," she said. "He was in some kind of trouble."

"How do you know that?" Jake asked.

"He would take meetings," she said. "Once a month, when we met out at the Dreamfield Inn, sometimes I'd wake up. You know. To pee. And he wouldn't be in the bed beside me. He wouldn't even be in the room. The first time or two, I looked for him. I saw him outside in the parking lot talking to somebody. When I asked him about it, he blew me off and told me he just needed air. Or one time he told me he was having trouble sleeping so he went out to smoke his pipe and he knew I'd be angry. Only he was lying. He didn't come back smelling like pipe smoke ever."

"Did you confront him about that?" Jake asked.

"No," she said. "I didn't want to nag. When we were together, we both just wanted it to be simple. I wasn't his wife. He didn't want a wife. And I already have a husband. So what do I care if he goes out there and smokes a pipe? He could go smoke crack if he wanted to. It just wasn't my circus, you know?"

"Sure," Jake said.

"But he was meeting with somebody. I couldn't ever see who. It was this truck. This blue pickup truck. Sam would go over and kind of lean into the driver's window so I couldn't see who it was. They'd talk for a while. Then that was it. Sam would come back. I'd pretend I was sleeping and we'd carry on."

"A blue truck," Jake said. "Make? Model?"

"It was a big one. F-350. Beat up. Lots of rust. The back window was cracked."

"Did you ever get a license plate?" Jake asked. She'd just described half the trucks in Worthington County.

"No," she said.

"And you never saw the driver?"

"Not never. Mostly never. Only, the last time we met out there, something happened. They got into an argument."

"Judge Rand and the driver?"

"Yes," she said, crying again. "I woke up, um ... you know. To pee again. Sam wasn't there. I heard shouting. Real loud. At first I thought it was just somebody else in another room. But like I said, Sam wasn't in bed. So, I went to the window. He was out there with this real big guy. Like, he towered over Sam. And he started jabbing his finger into Sam's chest. Hard enough Sam stumbled backward."

"Could you hear what they were saying?" Jake asked, dubious.

"Not what he was saying," Mandy answered. "But I heard Sam say over and over, you can't, you can't."

"What'd the guy look like, Mrs. Lovett? Besides, big. Was he black? White?"

"He was a white guy," she said. "Wearing one of those wife beater tank tops. Lots of muscles. Motorcycle boots. Real shitkickers. And he had a tattoo all over his left bicep. Wrapped all the way around his arm."

"Can you describe this tattoo? Would you recognize this guy if you saw him again?"

"I think so," she said. "His ink was ... look, you have to understand. This isn't easy for me."

"Mrs. Lovett?" Jake said. "Your husband is a liar. Did you know that? He wasn't in Fort Wayne the weekend Sampson Rand was murdered. He was here. In Worthington County. He went to the judge's house."

Her fingers trembling, she covered her mouth. "No. You can't really think Doug did this. He wouldn't ..."

"Hurt a fly," Jake spoke along with her. "That's what you keep saying. But your husband went to pretty great lengths to cover his tracks. So you're going to have to forgive me if your story seems a little too convenient on the brink of me serving a warrant on your house."

"It was a grim reaper. His tattoo. With a smoking gun, okay? You know what that means as well as I do. This guy Sam was seeing, he was a made guy. The Hilltop Boys have those."

"So why didn't you share this with me before? You're not stupid, Mandy. You knew I was going to have serious questions about Doug."

"I was afraid," she cried. "I'm still afraid. Somebody shot Sam. Killed him. And you're right. I'm not stupid. Last week, somebody killed Reese Sheldon. Everybody knows who Sheldon represented. Bobby Long. He's got one of those tattoos, too, Detective. What if they know I'm the one who was with Sam all those times out at the Dreamfield? Can you guarantee they won't want to come after me next? I know what happens to snitches. But I'm telling you. If Sam was murdered, it was one of the Hilltop Boys. I don't know what he was talking to that guy about. I never asked. I minded my own business. But if you actually think my husband is a murderer, well, I'm telling you, you don't know everything. Doug is innocent of this. I don't know what he was doing over at Sam's. It was a coincidence. Or maybe you're wrong. You have to be wrong."

Jake reached over and clicked off his recorder.

"Come with me," he said, pocketing his phone. He got up and went for the door.

"You'll leave Doug out of this now?" she pleaded, rising to join him.

He gripped the doorknob. "You know it's far too late for that, Mandy. Right now, I need you to come to my office with me. I need you to sit tight and not talk to anybody. Do you understand?"

Sobbing, she followed him out the door.

TWENTY-FIVE

"Sit," he said to Mandy Lovett. Glad he found an empty interview room, he meant for her to stay put until he could figure out what to do with her.

She was still crying. He handed her a box of tissues. "I'm supposed to handle a hearing in probate court after lunch," she said.

"Get someone to cover for you. I need you right where you are for now."

She nodded. "And then what?"

"Where's Doug now?" Jake asked.

"He's on the road today. Sales calls. I don't expect him back until dinner."

"Is anyone at your house right now?" he asked.

"No," she said. "My neighbor comes over every day at eleven to let the dog out."

"Mrs. Lovett," Jake said. "You know I have a warrant to search your premises."

"Fine," she said. "That's fine. Whatever you need. You can even take my key. The alarm code is 1482. Same as the garage door code. If you go through the garage, the alarm won't trip. Take anything you want. We don't have anything to hide."

Jake stopped himself from reminding her she'd been hiding things since the very beginning.

She pulled a set of keys out of her purse and gave them to Jake. "The one with the yellow tag goes to the front door. The silver one opens the shed in the backyard."

"I appreciate it," Jake said. "What kind of dog?"

"Lacey? She's a teddy bear. She won't give you any trouble. She's a Maltipoo. She sleeps in her crate most of the time. The crate's locked. She might bark your crew to death, but she's no bother."

"All right," Jake said. "Stay here. I'll be right back. And hand me your phone. You don't talk to anyone until you hear from me again. Got it?" The last thing he needed was her calling her husband before he had a chance to either talk to him again or serve the warrant.

He pocketed Mandy Lovett's keys and phone, then headed upstairs to his office. He ran into Ed Zender on the way.

"What took you so long?" Ed asked. "Hammer has a crew out at Lovett's waiting with their thumbs up their asses. I was about to head over there without you."

"Thanks for waiting," Jake said. "Something's come up. I ran into Doug's wife on the way back from Cardwell's office. She's now claiming she saw Rand meeting with a guy she thinks might be affiliated with the Hilltop Boys."

Ed's face fell. "She's telling you this now? I thought you interviewed her already."

"I did," Jake said. "She says she was scared of snitching. I don't know if I believe her. She's given me keys to the house. Doug's out on the road. She claims he doesn't know about what she just told me."

"Great," Ed said. "Just great. These two just keep on digging a deeper hole for themselves, don't they?"

"Look," Jake said. "Do you think you could sit with her? I don't want her talking to Doug until either I get to him first or we get this warrant executed. She says this mystery thug Judge Rand met with had ink like the Hilltop Boys wear."

"Do you believe her? This all seems pretty convenient coming right after she catches wind of your warrant."

"I don't know," Jake said. "A lot is going to depend on what we find over at Lovett's house. I know you were planning on heading over there with me. It would really help me out if you could sit with Mandy."

Ed nodded. "I'll talk to her. She trusts me. Maybe I can help her remember more about this guy."

"Yeah," Jake said, though he hoped Ed knew better than to try coaching her.

"Sure," Ed said. Jake couldn't tell from his expression whether he was pissed or not. Mandy Lovett wasn't the only one he wanted to keep out of trouble for the next two hours.

"I really appreciate it, Ed," Jake said. "You know the players with the Hilltop Boys a little better than I do in terms of what they look like. We might get lucky."

"I got it," Ed said. "I'll handle Mandy. You better head on over to Lovett's though. Better to get that done before Doug gets back."

"Thanks," Jake said. For once, Ed was acting like a real partner. He hoped it was a fresh start for them. It would be nice to both be pulling in the same direction.

Two hours later, Jake had searched every corner of Doug and Mandy Lovett's house, even the dog crate. The lab guys would go through Doug's home computer. He'd have to run ballistics on the handgun he found in Doug's safe, but Jake wasn't expecting anything to come from it. It was, as Doug Lovett described, still in the box he'd bought it in.

Jake sat outside the Lovett house as the last of the crew packed up and left. It was a quiet little street on a pear-tree-lined cul-de-sac. A fair number of the Lovett's neighbors had pressed their noses to their windows watching the proceedings. One old lady kept walking by with her little white dog, glowering at Jake. There would be plenty for them all to talk about at the next HOA meeting, for sure.

It was all there. He had a lying, cuckolded husband with a reason to put a bullet in Sampson Rand's head. Doug's alibi had fallen apart and his cell phone put him where he shouldn't have been right when he shouldn't have been there. And yet, something didn't feel right about Doug Lovett. Mandy had every reason to lie about what she saw, but did she?

Jake checked the time. He'd left Mandy with Ed almost three hours ago. He punched in Ed's number. It rang a few times, then Ed finally answered.

"Hey, Ed," Jake said. "We're just finishing up. Nothing too exciting yet. How'd it go with Mandy?"

"Uh, fine. Nothing new from her though. She gave me the same story as you about the guy with the tats. Grim reaper with a smoking gun. That's the Hilltop Boys insignia all right. But I believe her. She doesn't know who it was. She might be able to pick him up out of a line-up or a photo array though. We can start putting one together."

"It's a good thought," Jake said. "Thanks, Ed."

"Jake," Ed said. "I don't think Mandy's your problem at the moment. I know you don't want her talking to Doug before you can. She hasn't. But she got a call from Doug's secretary. She was pretty worried. Doug's AWOL."

"What do you mean?" Jake asked.

"I mean he was supposed to check in a few hours ago. He missed a sales call. Nobody knows where he is."

Jake gripped his steering wheel even harder. "Copy that," Jake said. "I'm on my way back in."

TWENTY-SIX

Twenty-four hours later, Doug Lovett still hadn't come home. He wouldn't answer Mandy's calls and he'd never made it to his last two sales calls of the day. He'd sent Mandy home with strict instructions to call him if Doug got in touch.

"I just can't believe it," Ed said as they regrouped at the end of the next full day. "Doug's acting beyond stupid."

"What he's acting," Jake said, "is guilty. You know him better than I do. Do you think you could start running down family members or friends he might try reaching out to? I'll work up a warrant for his bank and credit card. He's not going to make it far."

"Mandy's worried he might try to hurt himself," Ed said. "I gotta be honest. So am I. He knows you caught him in a lie. He's gotta know maybe there's something on that computer he doesn't want you to find. Any word on how long that's going to take to get back?"

"A day or two," Jake said. He had a small gym bag by the break table in the corner of the office. It was Wednesday. He'd been working out with Ryan and the team once a week. Tonight, Coach Borowski agreed to go again. He was already fifteen minutes late picking him up.

"Go on," Ed said, seeing Jake eyeing the gym bag. "There's not much more you can do here today. We don't have enough for probable cause to arrest Doug. He'll either show up tonight or he won't. You want me to try texting him?"

Jake wasn't sure he wanted Ed talking to Lovett without him there. At the same time, he and Ed were going to have to start trusting each other.

"I'd appreciate it," Jake said, slinging his bag over his shoulder. "You'll let me know if you hear from him? I don't care what time of night it is."

"You got it," Ed said. "Good luck with Ryan tonight. He's got that big match coming up with St. Iz. We're all rooting for him."

Jake pursed his lips and nodded. He shot a quick text to Frank to let him know he was on his way.

"Thanks, Ed," Jake said. "I know Doug's your friend."

"We're not friends," Ed said, his tone gruff. "I've just known him a long time."

"Well, either way. I appreciate having you pull in the same direction with me."

Ed grumbled. Jake figured it was as much as he'd get from the guy. He'd take it. He gave Ed a last wave then made his way out of the building, heading for the high school.

A half an hour later, Jake had changed into his gym clothes and warmed up.

Practice went well. Jake started a new cradle series and Frank worked with Ryan on hand control for escapes.

It was good work. Hard work. By the end of practice, Jake was covered in sweat and every muscle in his body ached. But it cleared his mind.

"Good job, son," Frank said, patting Ryan on the back. "You keep using your speed off the bottom like that with good hand control and nobody will keep you down."

Jake could see real improvement with him, too. Whether it would translate to victory against the McManus kid from St. Iz, would remain to be seen. But there was no denying McManus should be just as worried about the match as Ryan was.

Frank practically danced on the balls of his feet as Jake found him again. Adrenaline still fueled him. Jake hadn't noticed it until just now, but Frank looked like he'd lost a good ten or fifteen pounds since he'd started working out with the team again.

"You ready?" Jake asked. "You want to grab a burger or something on the way back?"

"Nah," Frank said. "I gotta pot roast in the crock pot. You can help me eat it. I owe you a beer, anyway."

Jake's stomach growled. He didn't envy the rest of the team. Ryan had about seven more pounds to cut before his next match. It'd be salad and ice cubes over at Gemma's house tonight.

"Sounds good," Jake said, following Frank out.

Frank Borowski's venison pot roast might just have been the best damn thing Jake ever tasted. He devoured a heaping plate of it as Frank slid a cold Bud Light across the table to him.

"Secret recipe." Frank winked. "I'll take it to my grave. I'll box some up for you though. Give it to your grandpa."

"He'll love it," Jake said. "Thanks." He sipped his beer. Later, he cleared his plate and joined Frank out in his rec room. There was a hockey game on. Frank was a diehard Red Wings fan.

Something nagged at Jake. He worried he might stir drama by bringing it up, but here, far away from the Sheriff's Department, Jake knew Frank was probably the only person he could talk to about it.

"Out with it," Frank said, pointing the neck of his beer bottle toward Jake. "You've been pussyfooting around whatever question you want to ask me since we left the gym."

Jake smiled. "That obvious?"

"I've known you since you were five years old and your mom first started bringing you to wrestling club. She was going out of her mind with what to do with you. Said you were bouncing off the walls determined to kill yourself with whatever daredevil scheme you cooked up. She told me you tried to turn the basement stairs into an indoor toboggan run with a piece of cardboard. Split your head open on a radiator when you crashed into it coming down. She pretty much handed you off and told me to wear you out."

"I forgot about that," Jake said. Truth was, he didn't really remember not knowing Frank.

"You weren't easy," Frank said. "Wouldn't listen to save your life. Constant case of the wiggles. I finally started giving you jobs before practice even started, just to give you something to focus on. Taking out the trash, rolling up the mats. Then I had you running with the bigger kids when I saw you doing circles around your age group. Once I got you good and tired out, then you could start real practice."

Jake laughed. "Well, I'm sure my mom appreciated it."

Frank's smile faded a bit. Everyone's always did when they remembered Sonya Cashen. They couldn't think of her without thinking of how she died. Of everything his father took from him, that was the thing Jake blamed him for the most.

"So the rumor is Doug Lovett looks good for killing Judge Rand?" Frank asked, deftly changing the subject.

Jake finished the last of his beer and waved off another. He still had to drive home. "Can't keep a secret in this town, can we?"

"I don't think it's through the whole town," Frank said. "But I hear things."

"You wise asses," Jake said. "You going to tell me Adamski, Thompson, and Nutter weren't wagging their tongues yesterday? The ink wasn't dry on my search warrant before Doug's wife threw herself at me in the courthouse. I was literally coming out of Judge Cardwell's chambers."

"Poor Mandy," Frank said. "She's gotta be losing her mind."

"You had no idea she was screwing Rand?"

Frank shrugged. "I mean, there were rumors he had some girl on the side. He was always a cagey son of a bitch, though. Steered clear of Papa's. But no, I didn't know it was Mandy. I gotta be honest. I would have thought she was out of his league. She have Daddy issues or something?"

"Or something," Jake said. He stared at the framed pictures on Frank's wall. There was one of him when he graduated from the academy a million years ago. Young. Fresh-faced, standing in between his beaming parents who were long since dead. There was another of Frank at his retirement party. He was the newest member of the Wise Asses. The rest surrounded him, toasting him with a bottle of Wild Turkey. Another picture of Frank holding up his prize-winning barracuda on Captain Russ's charter with the Florida sun beating down on them. Jake looked closer. It was from the trip Frank took him on when he was fifteen years old. He'd been a skinny, but muscle-bound kid on the cusp of manhood. Jake's throat got thick as he realized Frank had no other family photos on the wall. It was just the two of them.

"What's the matter?" Frank said. "I told you. I know that look. Something's bothering you about Doug Lovett."

"It's just a gut feeling," Jake said. "He had every reason to kill Sampson Rand. He lied about being in town that night. He probably lied to his wife about when he found out. And to me. He bought a gun a few weeks ago. It's just … I don't know. This just feels bigger."

"Bigger how?"

Jake turned to him. "It's actually something Ed said. I just find it a little hard to believe that Doug's this dumb."

"How's that working out?" Frank asked. "You and Ed?"

"We're getting there," Jake said. "He's at least doing a good job pretending he wants to work with me, not against me."

"It's a start," Frank agreed. "But if you don't think Doug Lovett capped the judge, who do you think did?"

"I told you Mandy practically tackled me in the courthouse. She said the judge was meeting with somebody on these weekend getaways of theirs. Like he was using it as a cover."

"Meeting with who?" Frank asked.

"I'm still trying to figure that out. She didn't recognize the guy. But she recognized his tattoo. Grim reaper with a smoking gun pointed right at you. That's Hilltop Boys ink. Even Mandy knew that. It's why she was reluctant to give me that detail the first time I interviewed her."

"Jesus," Frank said. "She's just now bringing you that little tidbit?"

"I know. The timing is suspicious. Convenient. As soon as the net starts tightening around her husband."

"Ya think?" Frank said, his voice rich with sarcasm.

"I know. It's probably garbage. It's just ..."

Frank set his beer on the end table beside him. "Your gut," he answered for Jake.

"Right."

"But she wasn't able to ID who this mystery thug was?"

Jake shook his head. "Not yet. She gave a description. Bald. Muscles. Drove a beat-up blue pickup with naked girls on the mudflaps."

Frank laughed. "Well that describes about a hundred different county shitkickers."

"I know. But she was scared. Terrified. It wasn't just about the heat I'm bringing to her husband. I believe she's truly scared about what happens if the wrong people find out she snitched. She said the last meeting Rand and this guy had, they got in some kind of argument. Judge came back fuming mad. Wouldn't tell her what was going on and gaslighted her when she told him she saw him talking to the dude. She let it go."

"Until now," Frank said. "Like you said, pretty damn convenient."

"Look," Jake said. "You know the lay of the county land a little better than I do. I've been gone a long time. You think Rand was on the take?"

Frank blew out a breath. "Shew. I don't know. Never got that vibe since he took the bench."

"What about before that? When he was a prosecutor?"

Frank flapped his hands in defeat. "Nothing I can red line. He's been a good judge for cops. That drug court he set up has made a real difference. He never put up with crap from any of the lawyers who appeared before him. Respected our time when we got called in to testify. And this? You know how I feel about this being a Hilltop hit. It's just not their M.O."

"I'm just trying to figure out why Rand would be meeting with one of them less than two weeks before someone blows his brains out," Jake said.

"This just isn't their M.O.," Frank repeated. "They're bad dudes. They've been running guns and drugs through here for a couple of decades now. But there's a code, if you know what I mean. They don't hit judges. Politicians. Cops. None of that. Hell, I don't have to tell you that, Jake. You spent enough time in organized crime for the Bureau."

"Yeah," Jake said. "But Rex Bardo's been in federal prison for a long time."

"Six years," Frank said. "But trust me. King Rex is still running the show. I told you before. If anything, things have been smoother since he went inside. He's protected."

"But then there's Reese Sheldon," Jake said. "Sheldon was in Rand's courtroom defending Bobby Long, one of King Rex's lieutenants, three months ago. He lost. Rand sentenced him to five years."

"I'm telling you," Frank said. "This just doesn't sound like something Rex Bardo would sanction."

Jake considered Frank's words. He made sense, but Jake still couldn't shake the feeling that something bigger might be coming.

"Jake?" Frank pressed.

"I'm just worried," he said. "Worried maybe Rex is losing control of the organization. Like maybe somebody's decided to clean house now that King Rex lost his latest appeal. Maybe they saw Sheriff O'Neal's death as an opportunity. I know that's what Meg Landry's worried about. It's why she roped me into investigating the judge's murder in the first place."

"Whoo, boy," Frank said. "I sure hope you're wrong. You're talking about a civil war, Jake."

Jake didn't answer. He's said far more than he should. But as he said goodbye and thanked Coach Frank for the pot roast, he'd already made a decision.

He needed to ask for an audience in the court of King Rex Bardo.

TWENTY-SEVEN

Nobody told Rex Bardo who was coming to see him. Jake wanted it that way. It was a risk. Bardo could have refused to come. But Jake banked on Bardo's curiosity getting the better of him. A gambit that would put Jake in control from the downstroke.

He flipped through the thin file he had on Rex Davis Bardo IV. King Rex. If he lost all of his appeals, King Rex would spend at least the next twenty years in here. At fifty-two, that might as well be a life sentence. It had been six years for him already. Maybe he'd lost hope of ever getting out. He'd figured out how to run the family business behind razor wire. By all accounts, he'd barely missed a beat. Virtually every gun runner, drug dealer, or pimp in Worthington County could be traced back to the Hilltop Boys. Business was booming.

Jake sat under the harsh fluorescent light of the smallest interview room they had at the Glenmoor Federal Penitentiary. He'd called in a favor to get in this soon. That, too, was a gamble. Jake's currency with the federal justice system dwindled by the day. Peter Nathan, his ex-ASAC, made sure of that.

The steel door opened. Jake rose to his feet as the guard led King Rex Bardo in. He was big. Huge, actually. The man had gone from a two hundred and seventy pound doughy frame the day of his indictment to a muscle-bound behemoth. Bardo had a thick head of wavy, jet-black hair he wore loose to his shoulders. A few silver strands blended in. He had a square face with a flat nose, crooked from old breaks. He stared at Jake through a pair of piercing gray eyes.

"You want me in here?" the guard asked. He was just as big as Bardo. The buttons on his gray uniform shirt strained as he reached for Bardo's wrists, ready to remove the cuffs.

"I think we're all right here," Jake said. Bardo sized him up. He saw the badge on Jake's belt, of course. The suit. If he was surprised, he didn't show it. Bardo only allowed a slight curving of his mouth as a reaction.

"Thanks for meeting with me, Mr. Bardo," Jake said as the guard removed the cuffs. Bardo absently rubbed his wrists and grabbed the nearest chair. He sat down with force, flicking his head to keep the hair out of his face.

"Be right outside," the guard said. "Just let me know when you're done."

Jake took his seat. "My name is Cashen," Jake said as soon as the door shut behind the guard. "Jake Cashen. I'm working a homicide case for the Worthington County Sheriff's Department."

He let Bardo process it. The last name, at least, would mean something to him. He'd know at least that Cashens were mill workers. Jake folded his hands in front of him on the table, letting Rex see the ring he wore just for today. His state championship ring with the large, fake sapphire. A tiny detail for Rex to file away. It might matter to him. It might not. But Jake wanted Rex to at least think it mattered to Jake. Let him draw conclusions about it. Sure enough, Jake watched as Rex clocked the ring.

"Who died?" Rex asked. It was a bullshit question. Of course, Rex would already know.

"Sampson Rand," Jake answered anyway. "Worthington County's Common Pleas Court judge."

No change in Rex's expression. He waited for a beat. Jake let him.

"We believe Rand was shot in the head," Jake said.

"You believe?"

"No body," Jake said. "But whoever killed him was sloppy enough we don't need one."

"Tough break for the judge then," Rex said. "But why are you here talking to me about it? My alibi is what you'd call airtight." Rex smirked at his own joke.

"I thought it was long past time you and I met, Mr. Bardo. I know we have mutual interests in Worthington County. I know you know Sheriff O'Neal brought me on."

"Well, that's nice for you. But I don't really have my finger on the pulse of county politics anymore. I've got my own problems here."

Jake took a more casual posture, leaning back in his chair. "That's a nice story. Only I know it's bullshit. The reign of King Rex is still alive and well, according to the people I've talked to."

Rex scratched his chin. "Well, that doesn't say much for your sources."

Jake let it go. He wasn't interested in that particular dance. And he wasn't here to get Rex Bardo to admit anything. He was here to get his attention.

"It can't be easy," Jake said. "I'm sure there are plenty of people who are still trying to push you out. They're who made sure you wound up here in the first place, aren't they? That's a hard lesson to learn, I suppose. The first time you trusted people outside the family, they turned on you, didn't they? Served you up to the Feds and now you're sitting here facing life."

Rex smiled. "You sure about that? That's not what my lawyers are telling me."

"Your appeal? Those are pretty hard to win, I'm told. Judicial deference, is that what they call it? Really tough to get one judge to second guess another one."

"You here to offer me some deal?" Rex said. "You think you're the first?"

Jake shook his head. "No deal. I told you, I'm with the Worthington County Sheriff's Department. That's a federal mess you're in."

"So what, you just thought you needed a meet-and-greet with me? You want my autograph? You trying to score some big dick points with your county boys? Tell 'em you came here to jerk my chain? You wouldn't be the first for that either."

"Maybe," Jake said. He resisted the urge to ask Rex what he meant about him not being the first. The minute he did, Rex would think he had something Jake really wanted. "But maybe I'm here to do you a favor instead."

Rex leaned forward, resting his forearms on the table. Jake got a good look at the tattoo snaking up his right arm. Though the grim reaper's head was hidden by the orange sleeve of his jumpsuit, the smoking gun was pointed right at Jake.

"You and the family probably aren't part of Sampson Rand's fan club. He caused some trouble for one of your boys recently. Bobby Long. Sent him up on assault charges a little while ago," Jake said.

Rex's eyes narrowed, but he said nothing.

"So if somebody from your crew was trying to settle a score off it, I'd say that means you've got a bigger problem than staring down a life sentence in here. I'd say that means somebody's not following the rules."

Still, Rex Bardo said nothing. But he was listening. It's what Jake came for.

"You don't go after judges. You don't go after cops. You don't go after families. I know the code, Mr. Bardo."

"You don't know shit, Detective Cashen," he said.

"I told you, whoever offed the judge was sloppy about it. Left some evidence behind that's going to make my job easier."

"Good for you ... Jake," Bardo said.

"You need to know," Jake said. "One of your boys was meeting with the judge at least once a month over the last year. Out in the open. In front of a few witnesses. Witnesses who can identify him. Saw his ink. Big guy. Bald. Bad attitude. Drives a blue pickup truck with a busted-out back window."

Bardo laughed. "Other than the ink, you just described about a hundred Blackhand Hills dipshits."

"Maybe," Jake said. "But I know that's the family crest." He pointed to Bardo's tattoo.

"You done?" Rex asked.

"Just about. I told you. I'm doing you a favor. Consider this a friendly heads-up. Get a hold of your boys. Whatever control you thought you had, it's slipping. Somebody's not afraid of you out there. That's going to cause you problems. And it's going to cause me problems."

"You got some balls on you, I'll give you that," Rex said. "You've been gone a while though. They kicked you out of the FBI is what I heard."

It was Jake's turn to smile. Of course, somebody tipped him off to Jake's arrival. He'd done his homework, too.

"I resigned," Jake said.

"Whatever you say, Detective. How's your granddad? Heard your sister's trying to force him off that hill."

Was it a veiled threat?

"You've got some experience with that," Jake said. "Way I heard it, *your* granddad sold all your family land right out from under them fifty years ago. Aren't too many Hilltop Boys actually living on the family hill anymore, are there? But I gotta imagine there are still some people who remember. Hold a grudge. Maybe biding their time once they know you're really never getting out of here. You've never sanctioned hits on judges before. Sam Rand made plenty of enemies. So one of them's decided now's the time to do something about it. You're in here. What are you going to do?"

He stayed mute, but Jake watched Rex's eyes flick back and forth. He was getting under his skin.

"You know Greg O'Neal is dead," Jake said, pressing his advantage.

"You think I know something about that too?" Rex asked, laughing.

"I think you know Meg Landry isn't Greg O'Neal. That might be a problem for you, it might not. I'm still deciding whether it's a problem for me. But I'm going to figure out who put a bullet in Sampson Rand's head. If you already do, it might pay you a dividend down the road if you tell me now, Mr. Bardo."

"Yeah," Rex said. "Like you said. A county deputy can't do shit for me. So I'd say this conversation is over."

He rose, went to the door, and tapped on the window. The guard peeked in, making contact with Jake. Jake gave him a nod. He opened the door.

"Time to go," Rex said.

"Think about what I said, Mr. Bardo," Jake said, rising.

Rex cocked his head to the side. "It's Rex," he said.

Jake stayed stock still. Showed no reaction. But he recognized Rex's words as a sign of respect he didn't casually throw around. This meant something.

It was a start.

Twenty-Eight

Ryan Stark had a good day. A very good day. His senior opponent, the 138-pounder from Claymore High School, finished third in the state last year. He was taller than Ryan. More experienced.

Jake yelled from the side of the mat, "Inside tie-up! Work to double, under hooks!"

Ryan caught the kid in a headlock and pinned him in seventeen seconds.

Seventeen seconds.

Jake pumped his fist. Coach Purcell clasped his arm and pulled him into a quick hug.

"Damn," he said. "He looks good, Jake. Really good."

Ryan tore off his green ankle band. The ref raised his arm in victory. Ryan bounded over to the corner and went right into Jake's arms.

"Good job," Jake said. "Way to hustle."

Ryan shook his coach's hand then went to rejoin the rest of his teammates. The 144 match was next.

"You sticking around?" Purcell asked. "Something I want to run by you when we're done here."

Jake nodded. "I'll come find you. I gotta go deal with Gemma."

Purcell laughed. Gemma's nerves got the better of her today. Jake could see her huddled under the bleachers, biting her nails to the quick. One of the other wrestling moms found her and whispered the results of Jake's match to her. The tension went out of her and her booming yell echoed through the gym.

"That's my boy! That's what I'm talking about!"

Ryan turned beet red, pretending he couldn't hear her.

"I've got her," Jake said to the other mom as he pulled his sister out from her hiding spot.

"Seventeen seconds?" Gemma asked. "My boy!"

"Come on," Jake said. "Take it easy. The other kid's mom is sitting right over there."

"He's a beast!" Gemma crowed. Jake had a mind to put a hand over her mouth. She wasn't wrong though. Ryan was looking better and better. The trick would be to make sure the kid didn't peak too soon.

He and Gemma climbed back to the seats she'd saved for them with her coat and two coolers. She got high fives and congratulations from the rest of the Stanley High parents. Jake no sooner sat down before a woman walked into the gym and caught his eye.

It was Anya. From this distance, it was like twenty years had just melted away again. She wore her hair in a messy ponytail. No makeup. She'd never needed it. He watched her scan the stands, looking for someone she knew. Was she looking for him?

"Well, look who the damn cat dragged in," Gemma said.

"Zip it," Jake said.

"Haven't seen her at one of these before," she said. "She doesn't have any kids wrestling. She doesn't have any kids at all."

Anya spotted Jake. Her whole face lit up as she waved.

"I'll be right back," Jake said. He apologized as he scooted past the same four people on his way back down the row. Anya waited against the wall, making sure she wasn't blocking anyone's view of the next match.

"Hey!" she said. "I was hoping I'd see a familiar face here."

She hugged Jake and put a quick peck on his cheek.

"Ryan just finished," Jake said.

"I saw," she said. "Jake, he looks so much like you. It's almost eerie. How does he feel about that?"

"He's bearing it," Jake said.

"You think he can make it to states?"

"If he keeps his head straight, yes."

"I'm so happy for you. I watched you out there too. You're in your element, Jake. It was good to see."

The next match ended with another pin for Stanley. The crowd erupted in fresh cheering.

"Come on," Jake said. "We can talk out in the hall."

"Oh, I don't want to interrupt you."

"It's okay," Jake said. "Was there something you wanted to talk to me about?"

Anya bit her lip. "There was something, yes. I suppose I could have just called you at work. But since we were coming tonight anyway."

From the look on Anya's face, he knew whatever she had to say had been bothering her quite a bit. She still got this little crease right between her eyes. Jake took her by the elbow and led her to the alcove under the stairs off the gym entrance. It was quiet enough there.

"You said if I could remember anything unusual about Judge Rand. To be honest, I'm a little embarrassed I didn't think of this sooner. It's probably nothing. I probably should just mind my own business."

"Anya," Jake said. "It's okay. Just tell me what you saw."

"The last week or so, before he disappeared. Um ... died. He left a lot of food on his plate. Like, he barely touched his salad. I really didn't think anything of it. It slipped my mind."

"His salad?" Jake said. It was an odd thing for her to mention, and not like Anya at all.

"I know," she said. "It's stupid probably. And that alone wouldn't maybe be a big deal. But there was something else. Again, I completely forgot about it. We get really busy at lunchtime and I didn't always have the time to sit and chat with the judge the way he liked. But he took a call. I mean, he always took calls. There was this one though. He left the table and went out the back into the alley behind the restaurant. Even that he'd done before. The cell reception is better out there. Anyway, I didn't hear what he was saying. Not the whole conversation. Just the tail end of it. Anyway, I remember him saying to whoever it was not to call him on that number again. He hung up on him. The judge seemed really angry. I asked him if everything was okay and he said it was fine. He said it was a reporter. And that was that. I told you, it's probably nothing. Only I know you look at cell phone records, right?"

"Yes," Jake said. "But you said this call was a few months ago? It'd be tough to narrow down when ..."

"That's the thing though," she said. "I think I've got that figured out. See, I was having back trouble. I had to get those cortisone shots. I took two days off work. And I remember, because I forgot the judge was out in the alley and I went out to take out the trash. He asked me if he could help me. You know. So I didn't lift the bag into the dumpster and strain anything. It was my first day back at work. So I know. I looked at the scheduling calendar app we use. It was September 14th. The judge always came in during his lunch hour between eleven thirty and twelve thirty. So maybe if you see who would have called him during that time on that day ..."

The gym door opened. Gemma poked her head out. Anya's back was to her.

"Anya, that's great. That could be helpful. I really appreciate it," Jake said.

She put a hand on his arm. "Oh good. I was hoping you wouldn't think I was insane. I was just turning it all over in my head and ..."

"You forget something?" Gemma said. She let the gym door slam shut behind her. She stared lasers at Anya, her hands on her hips.

"Oh, hey, Gemma!" Anya said. "Jake ... I mean, Ryan, looked so great! You've got to be so proud!"

"Uh huh," Gemma said. "And you've got to be missing your husband." She put emphasis on the word husband.

"Gemma," Jake warned.

"Oh look," Gemma said. "There he is now. Tim! You better be careful. It looks like your wife got lost!"

Jake looked up. Tim Brouchard was heading toward them.

Anya's cheeks flushed as she came out from under the alcove and went to Tim's side. He put a possessive arm around her.

"Hey, Jake," Gemma said. "Have you met Tim Brouchard? Anya's husband?"

Jake had to force his jaw not to clench and put on a smile.

"Good to see you," Tim said. "I was actually hoping to run into you. Any luck with Doug Lovett?"

"Is that who you think killed the judge?" Anya asked.

"Ah, that's not ... I haven't ..."

"Oh, pipe down, woman," Tim said. "You know he can't comment on that. Why don't you head back into the gym? I'll come find you."

"Maybe you should too, Gemma," Jake said. He had visions of strangling her.

"Come on, Anya," Gemma said. "I'll help you find a seat."

She snaked an arm around Anya and shot a glare over her shoulder at Jake. He shot one right back. Tim waited for the gym door to close on the women before turning his attention back to Jake.

"I didn't realize you and Anya were married," Jake said.

Tim smiled. "I get that a lot. I still can't believe my luck either. That's a rare woman I've got. Believe me. I know it."

"What did you want to talk to me about?" Jake asked.

"Doug Lovett," he said. "How close are we to making an arrest? I got a call from a friend of mine in Broward County. Down in Florida. He's a family law lawyer. Apparently one of Doug Lovett's fraternity brothers. Anyway, Doug's down there advising him. So, I'm wondering how close you are to writing a warrant."

"Dead in the water for now," Jake said. "Not enough for probable cause."

"Well, Doug's being advised to stay put until you do. You think he's our guy?"

"I don't know, Tim. I really don't. I need more time. I've got a few more leads to chase down."

"Anything you care to share?" Tim said, his voice dripping with sarcasm. Meanwhile, the gym door kept opening and closing. About a dozen people lined up a few feet away at the concession stand.

"We'll talk later," Jake said. "Not here."

"We'll talk when I say," Brouchard said, his face turning purple. "We're talking about a well-liked judge, Jake. Folks aren't going to sit still for this. This can't happen on my watch. I won't let it. I'm counting on you to make sure it doesn't." Brouchard actually shoved a finger in Jake's chest. It took everything in Jake not to crack the thing off and shove it up Brouchard's ass.

He realized then, this was all bluster. Brouchard wanted people to hear him asking. He was doing it to get attention. Rumor was, Brouchard had some real competition in the next election.

"I said we'll talk later," Jake said. He swatted Tim Brouchard's hand away and started to walk down the hall. The match was breaking up. The team started to file down to the locker room. Couch Purcell caught Jake's eye.

"There you are," he said. "Walk with me?"

Jake looked back. Tim Brouchard had recovered, straightened his tie, and started to glad-hand as the spectators poured out of the gym.

"Sure," Jake said.

"Listen," Purcell said. "It's been great having you in the room these last few weeks. I was hoping you'd consider something more official."

Jake was still watching Brouchard. Anya hadn't come out of the gym yet. He wasn't sure he could stomach seeing her with that asshole again.

"What?" he said to Purcell.

"I got approval from the A.D. to hire an assistant. I'd like it to be you. It's not much money. Three grand a year. But if you're coming into the room anyway. Ryan's got two more years after this until he graduates. I just figured ..."

Jake's cell phone rang. He pulled it out. The caller ID was from the Marvell County Sheriff's Department.

"Brian," Jake said. "I'm sorry. I have to take this. But I'll think about it."

Purcell nodded. "Think hard. We could really use you. I mean, if you're planning on sticking around."

Gemma emerged from the gym. Her eyes flicked to Brian Purcell, then Jake. He begged off as his phone kept ringing.

"Cashen," he answered, plugging an ear against the noise of the gym.

"Hey, Jake," the caller said. "Dave Yun. Sorry to call you after hours. But we've got a break in Reese Sheldon's case. I thought you'd want to know."

"What'd you get?" Jake asked.

"How soon can you get here?" Yun asked.

Gemma wasn't close enough to hear, but she was close enough to read Jake's body language. And he read hers. She knew he was going to leave. Her shoulders sagged and she turned her attention to another group of moms coming down the hallway.

"Give me thirty minutes," Jake said to Yun, then he clicked off the phone.

TWENTY-NINE

"Tawny Rafko and Jed Kendall," Yun said. He tossed down two freshly minted mugshots. Jed Kendall's bloodshot eyes stared back at Jake. The kid was a beanpole. A buck ten at five feet six. He had dirty brown hair slicked back with sweat. Tawny Rafko stared at the camera with vacant eyes and a painful grimace on her tear-stained face.

"You're sure?" Jake asked. He sat in Dave Yun's tiny office, a pot of stale coffee warming in the corner.

"They left DNA soup all over Sheldon's bedroom," Yun said. "Kendall cut his hand on the broken window glass. Bled a trail all the way down the hall. Some of Sheldon's blood sprayed Rafko's shirt. She was standing right next to Kendall when he pulled the trigger. We found the shirt wadded up in a trash bin right outside their trailer. We got a call from a pawn shop out on Decatur Road. Kendall came in two days ago trying to pawn Sheldon's wristwatch. His cleaning lady said he always kept that on the dresser. We've got the security tape from the pawn shop owner. It's Kendall. No doubt."

"What's their connection to Sheldon?" Jake asked.

"Tawny's brother was one of his clients. We brought him in for questioning. He flipped on these two geniuses pretty quick. They're a couple of strung-out meth heads. The brother said they broke into his house two weeks ago looking for cash. Sheldon got him a settlement from the trucking company where he worked. Wasn't much. Ten grand. Anyway, the guy said Rafko and Kendall smashed his desk apart. He didn't have any cash, but the settlement papers were in there with Sheldon's name all over them. His home address was pretty easy to find online."

Jake scratched his chin. "Well ... shit."

"It was almost too easy," Yun said.

"Yeah. I'm glad for Sheldon's family. Don't get me wrong. My gut was just in a completely different place."

"Well, it's good news though," Yun said. "As much as this kind of thing can be. I was worried we had something bigger on our hands. But whatever happened with your judge over in Worthington County, it's not connected to Reese Sheldon's bad luck."

"Yeah," Jake said. "Well, I appreciate you sharing all of this with me. I'm curious though. You could have told me all of this over the phone."

Dave Yun squirmed a little. He got up, shut his office door, and sat back down. His odd behavior confirmed Jake's suspicions. Yun hadn't just wanted to talk about the Sheldon murder.

"Look," Yun said. "I don't know you. But I've asked around a little. You seem like a decent enough guy. And if you're gonna keep your current job with Worthington, chances are this won't be the last case we have in common. So, I figured I had nothing to lose by giving you a heads-up."

"I'm listening," Jake said, though he knew exactly what Yun was going to say. Landry had already filled him in.

"I told you I brought in the Feds on this one. You were pretty quick to get lost when Special Agent Lilly showed up. And he was pretty quick to make sure I knew how he felt about you. He's trouble, Jake. You need to know."

"I appreciate that," Jake said. "He ran his mouth to Sheriff Landry too."

"Figures. Guy's got a big fat mouth, if you want my honest opinion. Also these guys, some of them anyway, they waltz in here acting like we're all a bunch of country bumpkins, Barney Fifes. Meanwhile, most of them suck at real detective work."

"Dave," Jake said. "I'd surely appreciate it if you'd make your point."

"Oh, right. Sure. Well, Lilly had plenty to say about you. He said I shouldn't trust you as far as I could throw you and that the Bureau should have fired you outright but they were too afraid. He said you're dirty. Now I didn't get that vibe from you at all. And I knew Greg O'Neal pretty well. He would have done his homework and not brought you on if he had even a whiff of that kind of stink on you. So, I figure Lilly doesn't have the whole story. And I don't like gossip. So I'm asking you to your face."

"You're asking me if I'm dirty?" Jake said.

"Well, yeah."

Jake smiled. "And you think I'd just admit it if I were?"

"No. No."

"I told you," Jake said. "I don't really know this guy Lilly. So whatever he's telling you isn't coming from a firsthand source. I've never worked with him. I couldn't care less what he thinks of me."

"Right. Right. I was figuring to hell with that guy. But like I said. Maybe you need to know what guys like him are spreading about you."

"I appreciate it," Jake said, though he wasn't sure he did.

"Anyway," Yun said. "You don't have to worry about any of that crap with me. I judge people based on what I see with my own eyes. But maybe you need to watch out. I've seen guys like that really screw with people's careers."

"Well," Jake said. "I'm not looking to go back to the FBI."

"Sure. Sure. Yeah. Well, anyway. I just thought you should know."

"Thanks, Dave," Jake said. He'd heard enough. He'd had enough. He shook Dave Yun's hand and showed himself out.

Jake would have to deal with the Agent Lillys of the world later. He had a murder to solve. And with Doug Lovett still his prime suspect, he knew he was really back to square one.

THIRTY

Mandy Lovett's instinct to protect her husband quickly evaporated when Doug refused to come back home. He left her hung out to dry, alone, and facing all the tough questions the town had for her. So today, she sat in an interview across from Jake and Ed Zender, ready to play ball for real.

"Do I need a lawyer, Ed?" she asked.

"You're not under arrest, Mandy," he answered. Ed sat at the table in front of her. Jake hung back, leaning against the wall. She cast a nervous glance at him, but Jake tried to keep his face neutral.

"When's the last time you spoke with Doug?" Ed asked. He and Jake developed a loose game plan for how this interview would go. Ed would focus her on all things related to Doug. They were old friends. He would play up his legitimate concern for Doug and Mandy's well-being. Hopefully, he'd be able to put her at ease when Jake started in on the real reason they brought her here.

"Last night," she said. "It's getting bad, Ed. Doug blames me for all of this."

"He lied to you too," Ed said. "He knew about you and the judge. He went out to the judge's place behind your back. Even after you knew Rand was missing, he kept that from you."

"He doesn't see it that way," she said.

"Mandy," Jake said. "Has he said anything at all that would make you think he's still lying?"

"I've asked him point blank," she said. "I said Doug, did you kill Sam? He swears he didn't. He was so angry with me that I even asked the question."

"Do you believe him?" Ed asked.

"I don't know anymore," she said. "Yes. I guess. I mean, it's still Doug."

"Mandy," Jake said. "Did you ever hear the judge take a phone call that upset him?"

"Did I ever hear him get mad on the phone? Like ever?"

"In the weeks leading up to his disappearance," Jake said. "There's a waitress at the Vedge Wedge who says she overheard him talking to someone. He was pretty upset. She said it was unusual for him."

"Oh," Mandy said. "You mean Anya Brouchard. Sam really loved her. I think she's half the reason he'd go into that place. He said she treated him like a king."

"This would have been in the middle of September," Jake said.

"Well, Anya's probably got pretty good instincts where Sam was concerned. I used to worry she would pick up on something between us. Don't let that sweet demeanor of hers fool you.

Anya's as shrewd as they come. She pretty much runs that place. They're going to be screwed if she ever decides to quit. Nobody would have thought a vegan place would last in Stanley, that's for sure."

"Is that a no?" Jake said.

"Oh, the phone calls. Yeah. No. I told you, I saw Sam meet with and get really upset with that guy with the tattoos. He didn't answer his phone when we were together."

Jake had placed a tablet on the table in front of Mandy. He reached over and tapped it on.

"Do you think you'd recognize the guy if you saw him again?" Ed asked her.

"From a picture?" Mandy asked.

"Yes," Jake answered. "I'd like you to take a look at a photo array. See if there's anyone you recognize."

"Sure," Mandy said.

Ed took the tablet and scrolled over to the first set of photos. He placed it in front of Mandy.

"Just keep scrolling," he said. "Stop if there's anyone familiar."

Mandy took the tablet. Her brow furrowed as she concentrated. She scrolled through page after page.

Jake subtly cleared his throat. It was a signal. They'd been questioning Mandy for about an hour.

"Why don't you take a little breather," Ed said. "Can I get you some coffee? How about a sandwich? It's getting close to lunchtime."

"That'd be great," Mandy said. "A sandwich. I'm not picky. And a bottle of water, maybe?"

"You got it," Ed said. "Sit tight."

Ed and Jake left her and walked back into the office across the hall.

"She's telling the truth, Jake," Ed said. "About Doug."

"Yeah," he answered. "I think so too. You think you could sit with her for a few minutes? I've got Darcy doing a Lexis/Nexis search. The date of that phone call Anya Strong … er … Brouchard said she witnessed, there's only one incoming call during what would have been the judge's lunch hour. I'll see if she's come up with anything."

"Oh I got this," Ed said. "You go do you."

Ed went back in with Mandy. Jake followed him back out of the office and watched from the one-way mirror for a moment. Mandy just kept on scrolling. Jake finally stepped out and called Darcy.

"You got anything for me?" he asked.

"Hello to you too," Darcy said.

"Sorry. It's been a day."

"It's been a month," Darcy agreed. "And the answer is yes. I looked up your number. It's a landline registered to a Mary Alice Doyle. 231 Glanville Road. It's a farm off County Road 13."

"Mary Alice Doyle?" Jake repeated.

"Yep," Darcy said. "And cuz I know you'll ask, I looked into her already. She doesn't live there anymore. She died two months ago at the ripe old age of ninety-eight. No kids. No husband.

And I checked. Nobody's been paying the phone bill for that particular line since she died. It's disconnected now."

"Huh," Jake said, puzzled. "I appreciate you dropping everything to look this one up for me. I owe you."

"Oh, you owe me plenty," she said. "I'm keeping a tally."

"I'm good for it." Jake laughed. He hung up. Darcy's answer wasn't what he expected. He figured the number would come back to a burner phone. He might never prove it, but his gut told him whoever called to harass the judge was either the same guy, or calling about the same thing Mandy witnessed.

It had been three days since his jailhouse meeting with King Rex. Though the guy played it as cool as they come, Jake knew he'd rattled him. It all depended on how much.

"Hey, Jake," Ed said, poking his head back in the office. "Mandy's got something. I think you better come take a look."

Jake walked back across the hall and into the interview room. Mandy's face was white. She practically curled into herself on the other end of the table.

"Mandy," Ed said. "It's okay. Tell Detective Cashen what you just told me."

Mandy kept her eyes locked on Ed.

"Go ahead," Ed said, more forcefully.

Nodding, Mandy broke Ed's gaze and pointed a shaky finger at the tablet screen. "Him," she said. "That's who I saw."

"Where did you see him, Mandy?" Jake asked.

"That's the guy I saw Judge Rand meeting with outside the Dreamfield Inn. He's the one Sam got into an argument with the last weekend we spent together."

"You're sure," Ed asked.

She nodded. "But you can't tell anybody. Nobody can know I was in here."

"It's okay," Ed said. "You did the right thing, Mandy." Ed picked up the tablet and handed it to Jake.

Jake stared down at the photo Mandy picked. He was tanned and bald. He had dark-brown eyes that almost looked black. The guy wore a black sleeveless shirt, his Hilltop Boy ink clearly visible. Jake tapped the screen, pulling the guy's copious rap sheet . But it was the name that struck him more than anything.

Zeke Bardo.

"You know him?" he asked Ed.

"Yep," Ed said. "King Rex's nephew."

There was no mistake. Sampson Rand had somehow run afoul of a blood member of the Hilltop Boys.

THIRTY-ONE

"Good luck finding him," Ed said just before he bit into his gyro. Papa's Diner for lunch was Ed's idea. They'd just let Mandy Lovett go. She'd offered to wear a wire next time she spoke to her husband.

"Tell me about your run-ins with Zeke," Jake asked. He'd opted for a Greek salad with a side of stuffed pepper soup. Tessa called it Nina's Special. According to her mother, the girl had lived on it for most of her teen years.

"Not much to tell," Ed said. "I think Zeke's King Rex's sister's boy. No dad to speak of. The kid's a blowhard. A poser, if you ask me. Always thrusting his chest out, making sure everybody knows he's a Bardo. Except he isn't really. He's a bastard whose uncle took pity on him, or maybe just got worn down by Rex's sister long enough to let him keep the name."

"He never appeared before Rand," Jake said. "I checked his docket. I checked with Tony Byers. There's no good reason for Zeke Bardo to have anything to do with Rand."

Ed took another big bite. "Who knows? The kid's nothing more than a dumb thug trying to show what a big man he is. I don't think King Rex ever trusted him with much more than moving low level product. And he couldn't even do that without making too much noise. There's no way King Rex is going to let that idiot anywhere near Rand."

"Well, I still want to talk to him," Jake said.

"And like I said," Ed said. "Good luck finding him. Haven't seen him around in a good while."

"You mean, since before Sampson Rand died?" Jake asked, trying to keep the sarcasm out of his voice.

The bell rang over Tessa's door. Frank Borowski walked in.

"You're late!" Tessa shouted. "Your food's already cold."

Jake hadn't noticed, but Tessa had put a burger and fries on the counter.

"There's a sight for sore eyes!" Ed bellowed. "Drag your fat ass over here, Borowski. Jake here's got some big ideas."

Jake knew Frank's expressions better than Ed did. Borowski smiled with a tight jaw. Jake knew if he could have, Frank would have knocked the smirk right off Ed's face. He grabbed his burger and sat in the empty space next to Jake.

"We were just talking," Ed said. "You remember Zeke Bardo? King Rex's moron of a nephew?"

Jake balled his fists under the table. They weren't alone. Never mind Frank, there were two full tables just across the way. Plus Tessa and Spiros and two busboys.

"Keep your voice down," Jake said.

Frank took a bite of his burger.

"I was telling Jake what a screw-up Zeke's always been. Remember that time you busted him for possession, Frank? When Zeke was a juvi and he tried to swallow that bag of dope on you? Moron choked on it. You had to give him the Heimlich and broke a couple of his ribs. Cried like a little baby. You saved his miserable life and all he could do was whine about police brutality. We still talk about that. I always wondered what his old Uncle Rex did to him after that. I'm surprised that the kid has managed to stay out of jail for as long as he has. You seen him around lately?"

Frank shook his head. "Not in a few years. I'm retired, Ed. This crap is your job now. And I see you've still got a big mouth. Lower your voice."

Ed looked wounded by Frank's words. All the bluster went out of him. Ed wiped his hands on his napkin and threw it on his plate. He still had mustard on the corner of his mouth, but Jake decided not to bother telling him.

"Well, I'm clocking out," he said. "I got a dentist appointment at three. Jake, can you tell Lieutenant Beverly to OT me?"

"Sure, Ed," Jake said. "See you tomorrow."

Ed said a quick goodbye to Tessa, then walked out of the diner.

"Guess I'm paying for lunch," Jake said. Frank moved to the other side of the booth as one of the busboys came and cleared Ed's plate.

"Typical Zender," Frank said. "I probably should have warned you. But it seems like you two are getting along okay. That's good, right?"

"It's good," Jake said.

"The key to Ed is giving him stuff to do where he can't cause too much trouble."

"I'm finding that out," Jake said.

Frank stabbed his French fries into his ketchup. "So what's this about Zeke Bardo?"

Jake debated saying any more. But Ed had pretty much spilled whatever beans there were to spill.

"There's a chance he had some involvement with Sam Rand over the last few months," Jake said.

Frank's eyes went up. "He's a suspect?"

"He's just somebody I'd like to talk to."

Frank shoved his fries in his mouth and took two twenties out of his wallet.

"Lunch is my treat," he said. "Let's go take a walk."

Frank hadn't even finished his burger. But whatever he had to say, he was in a hurry to say it and knew there shouldn't be witnesses. Not for the first time, Jake wished Frank was still on the job instead of Ed.

"Thanks, Tessa," Jake said as he followed Frank outside.

"Come on," Frank said. "We'll drive around the block." Frank's car was parked right out front. Jake climbed in the passenger seat and waited for Frank to pull out. When they'd made it three blocks away from downtown, Frank pulled into an empty space at the curb and put the car in park.

"Frank?" Jake said.

"What's Zeke done?"

"I don't know yet," Jake said. "Ed's saying Zeke's always been trouble for Rex."

"That's true," Frank said. "That's the problem with Rex's business model. You can't pick your family. But most of the time, you can't trust anybody else. He learned that one the hard way. It's how he ended up in federal prison. He brought in outside help and they turned on him. I don't think he'll ever make that mistake again."

"I talked to him," Jake said.

Frank's eyes got wide again. "You talked to Rex? No kidding? How did that go?"

"Not sure yet," Jake said. "I was just throwing chum in the water."

Frank nodded. "Risky move."

"I'm hitting a wall, Frank," Jake admitted. "I got a witness who positively ID'd Zeke as someone the judge met with on a regular basis. I don't know why. But the man ended up with a bullet in his brain not long after. I've got a jilted husband who everyone assumes is guilty, including his wife now. Only I can't make probable cause. He's hiding out in Florida and I haven't got a shred of physical evidence connecting him to the crime."

"Plus," Frank said. "You don't think Doug Lovett did this."

Jake didn't answer.

"But you're sure? Zeke was meeting with Sam Rand? You can prove that?"

Jake hesitated, then let go. "Yeah. I'm sure. And whatever was going on, Rand was getting pretty pissed about it. But I can't find a damn thing. No unusual payments coming into his accounts. No cash in his house that shouldn't have been there.

No big purchases. If he was on the take, he was hiding it well. Which doesn't make any sense if he was careless enough to be seen talking to Zeke Bardo. So, I need to find this guy. I need to talk to him. But as Ed said, he's gone to ground."

"And that alone is enough to make you want to talk to him. Listen, there's something you should know."

"What?"

"Ed doesn't know this. No one does. But Zeke was one of my CIs."

Jake held his breath. "No shit?"

"Ed's right that relations between his Uncle Rex and Zeke were strained. And to be clear, Zeke never ratted on Rex. It was mostly to do with some of their competition in the drug trade. Zeke was an idiot, but he was more loyal to the Hilltop Boys than people give him credit for."

"And Ed didn't know?" Jake said.

"Nope," Frank said. "No one did. Not even Sheriff O'Neal. When I retired, I offered to put Zeke in contact with Ed. Zeke didn't want anything to do with that. He only trusted me. And I gotta be honest. The last couple of years, Zeke gave me garbage. I think he and Uncle Rex were in a better place by then. Now? I don't know."

"Do you feel comfortable reaching out to him now?"

Frank considered the question. "I don't know. But it's a moot point. I wouldn't know where to find him."

Jake fingered the slip of paper where he'd written Mary Alice Doyle's address.

"I think I might," Jake said. "I think I might know where he was calling the judge from, at least part of the time."

Frank looked behind him, toward the restaurant. "You let Ed think you didn't know where to find him. Is there something going on I should know about?"

"No," Jake said simply.

"He won't talk to you," Frank said. "I told you. Zeke's twitchy that way."

"So come with me," Jake said. "Introduce me. Tell Zeke Bardo he can trust me."

Frank gripped the steering wheel. Jake knew it was a big ask. When Frank Borowski walked away from the Sheriff's Department, he'd walked away.

"An hour," Jake said as he saw the corner of Frank's mouth lift in a smirk. "Give me one hour. Then dinner's on me."

"Oh, I plan on being hungry, Jake. Starving." Frank reached over and opened his glove box. He pulled out his 40 cal Sig Sauer. "And it's surf and turf night over at the Red Horse Grille. Lobster's fifty-eight bucks a pound."

"Drive," Jake said. Frank put the car in gear then peeled away from the curb.

Thirty-Two

"I know this place," Frank said. He had just turned down Glanville Road, a dirt road off County Road 13. The absolute middle of nowhere. The nearest operating farm was a good three miles away.

"He can't be living here," Jake said as Frank slowed to almost a crawl. There was one house nestled in the hills with the woods beyond that. Frank stayed far back and came to a stop.

The house itself looked ready to fall in on itself, covered with silver Tyvek that had weathered at least a few winters. The roof had a clear dip to it such that the chimney tilted almost parallel to the ground. It looked like someone had tried to put in new windows but even from here, Jake could see large gaps where any manner of critter could find its way in.

Oddly though, on the back of the property sat what looked like a brand-new pole barn.

"I think this belonged to Zeke's Aunt," Frank said. "I'll be damned."

"How was she connected to the Bardos?" Jake asked.

"His deadbeat dad's sister. Her name was Molly or Mary something. She's gotta be dead by now."

"The township rolls have a Mary Alice Doyle listed as the owner," Jake said. "A caller from the landline registered to this property showed up on Rand's cell phone records. Anya heard one of the calls. She said the judge seemed pretty upset by it."

"Yep," Frank said. "Mary Alice. That's the aunt's name. Welp, I'd say let's get this over with. Just, maybe don't touch anything when we get inside."

"Or don't knock too hard on the front door. The whole thing's liable to topple over."

Frank pulled into the driveway. As soon as he did, Jake saw the rusted blue pickup truck with the knocked-out back window Mandy Lovett had described.

"That's Zeke's truck," Jake said.

"We'll take that as a good sign," Frank said as the two of them stepped out of the car. They made it about five feet toward the house before a snarling, enraged, distinctly hoarse bark of a pit-bull stopped them cold.

The dog came tearing around the side of the house. Jake got his hand on his weapon and moved in front of Frank.

The dog stopped short, two feet from them as he ran out of chain. He was wrapped around a huge oak tree sitting midway between the house and the barn.

"Christ!" Frank said. The dog foamed at the mouth and bared its great, lethal set of teeth in a jaw that looked wide enough to bite off a human skull. "I'm way too old for this shit, Jake."

Jake smiled. "Good for me then. I figure all I gotta do if he breaks loose is outrun you."

"Smart ass," Frank said. "I'll go see if he's home. You check the barn. See those tire tracks leading up to it?"

"I do," Jake said. It had snowed and thawed the day before so the ground was still soft and wet. The tracks through the mud were narrower than the truck would have made and looked fresh. Jake gauged the length of the pit bull's chain. And prayed.

"Zeke!" Frank called out as he approached the front door. The dog had a bark that cut through Jake's brain. Jake hung back, waiting, not wanting to let Frank out of his sight. Frank knocked on the door, staying off to the side of it. He peered through the window, cupping his hand over his brow.

"See anything?" Jake asked.

Frank shook his head. "He's gotta be here though. Zeke's not one to leave that dog out there all day. Zeke! Open up. It's Frank Borowski!"

Still nothing. Jake thought he saw a shadow move across the window in the pole barn door. He jerked his chin at Frank and pointed toward the barn. Frank nodded. Jake began his approach.

The dog was having none of it. He tracked Jake, lunging straight at him. Jake's heart pumped. That bark set his every nerve ending on fire.

"Good dog," Jake muttered. The dog strained against his chain. He got to the door on the pole barn, turned his body sideways, and knocked.

"Zeke?" he called out. "I'm Jake Cashen. With the Sheriff's Department. I've got Frank Borowski with me. You got time to talk to us?"

Jake peered through the window. It was dingy and dark inside, but he could make out a red Ford Focus parked in the middle. It still had melting snow on the hood. He saw garden and lawn tools hanging on the wall and a workbench in the corner. As he knocked on the door again, something crashed to the ground inside.

"Zeke?" Jake called out. He used his sleeve to wipe the dirt off the window and looked again.

Something big and black popped up then banged on the window. Jake dropped to the ground. He heard the telltale screech of a barn cat. Then the thing darted out a side window, brushing across Jake's legs.

The dog pretty much went berserk after that. Jake half wondered if the pit might rip the tree he was tied to straight out of the ground and drag it behind him.

Jake tried the barn door and found it unlocked. He found the light switch and turned it on. The building was completely empty, now that the cat was gone. He put his hand on the hood of the car and found it cold. No one was here.

Jake pulled the door closed behind him. The pit was straining against the chain on the opposite side of Jake now, far more interested in whatever the barn cat was up to. Still, Jake made sure to stay far outside the chain's perimeter as he headed back up to the house.

He heard it before he saw anything. A cracking shotgun blast. Instinct took over and Jake dropped to the ground.

"Frank!" he yelled. Another round racked. Jake saw the barrel poking out behind the house.

"Frank!" he yelled again. On his belly, Jake aimed his gun, trying to lay eyes on Frank before he fired. Fire exploded out of the shotgun barrel.

"Zeke!" Frank yelled. "Hold your fire!"

Then he heard six quick, rapid-fire rounds from Frank's gun.

Jake ran toward it, keeping his gun aimed high.

"Goddammit!" he heard Frank cry out.

"Police, drop your weapon!" Jake yelled. But he had no eyes on anyone. Not Zeke. Not Frank.

Jake dropped low as he came around the back of the house.

A man, Zeke Bardo, lay flat on his back, his arms and legs splayed wide. His eyes were open, frozen in shock as a pool of blood widened beneath him.

"You okay?" Jake asked. Frank had his weapon still drawn, his back against the side of the house. Panting, he slowly sank to his knees, nodding.

"We gotta check the house," Frank said. His own weapon still drawn, Jake walked over to Zeke's lifeless body. He kicked the shotgun out of his reach.

Frank was up. He pushed the back door open. They entered side by side, Frank heading left, Jake heading right.

One by one, they cleared each room. There was only the kitchen off the back, a living room, and two bedrooms down the hall.

"Clear!" Frank called out as Jake lost sight of him down the hall.

Jake nodded. He rejoined Frank.

"What the hell happened?" Jake asked.

Frank shook his head, still panting. The two of them walked back out of the house.

"Came out of nowhere," Frank said. "Tried to blast a hole in me."

"I see that," Jake said as the two of them stood over Zeke Bardo's body. Zeke let out a moan.

"Shit," Frank said. "He's still alive."

Jake pulled out his cell phone and dialed Darcy's direct line.

"Hey, Jake," she said. "I knew you couldn't live without me."

"Darcy," he said, his tone flat and serious. "We've got shots fired out on Glanville Road off County Road 13. I'm gonna need an ambulance."

"You okay?" she asked.

"Yeah," he said. "But get 'em out here quick. I've got a single victim, gunshot wound to the chest. He'll probably bleed out before they get here."

"On it," Darcy said.

Jake slipped his phone in his back pocket. Frank stood over Zeke. Zeke let out an ominous, rattle breath. He was dying. Jake took off his jacket and pressed it into the wound.

"Why'd you go and do that, huh?" Jake asked. "I just wanted to ask you a couple of questions."

Zeke coughed up blood. His eyes began to turn red. He kept them locked on Frank.

"Help's coming," Jake said. "Zeke, can you hear me? Can you talk?"

Zeke blinked, but wouldn't look at Jake. Frank leaned down next to him.

"It's gonna be okay," he said. "We got an ambulance coming."

Frank met Jake's eyes. They both knew, no matter how fast the EMTs got here, it would be too late.

"Zeke," Jake said. "Did you kill Judge Rand? Is that what happened?"

Finally, Zeke's eyes flicked briefly to Jake's. They were vacant though. Jake doubted Zeke could even process what his words meant. Then he turned his head and stared at Frank again.

"Zeke?" Frank said. Zeke tried to draw in a breath. His body contorted from the effort. Then he let out one last, slow, wheezing breath and his eyes went blank.

Jake drew a hand across his neck. It was over. Zeke was gone.

"Son of a bitch," Jake whispered.

Frank sat back on his heels, shaking his head. "Stupid bastard. I had no choice."

"I know, Frank," Jake said. "I know."

It was then that Jake noticed a spot of blood on Frank's shirt. It was growing.

"Frank?" he said. He released the pressure on Zeke Bardo's chest and went to Frank. He grabbed him, feeling along his chest, looking for the wound he now knew was there.

"Jake?" Frank asked. He had the oddest expression in his eyes. When Jake pulled his hand away, it was covered in blood.

Jake pulled his phone back out and hit redial. "Darcy?" he said, breathless. "Tell them to get here. Tell them to get here now! I've got an officer down."

As soon as he got the words out, Frank Borowski collapsed to the ground.

THIRTY-THREE

The minute Jake heard Frank swearing in Polish, he knew Coach would be okay. That was, if the nursing staff didn't smother him with a pillow to shut him up.

Jake paced by the nurse's station. Frank let out a particularly spicy word. A young doctor came out from behind the curtain, red-faced. His badge read Zalinski, so Jake knew the kid could translate.

He caught Jake's eye and walked over. "Does he have a wife? Any other family, Detective?" Zalinski was reading the badge hanging around Jake's neck as well.

"Uh. No. A couple of ex-wives. Otherwise, it's just me."

Zalinski nodded. "Well, he looks and sounds worse than he is."

It was then Meg Landry rushed down the hall flanked by three deputies. "Jake?" she said, her voice hoarse.

Jake put a hand up. "It's okay. Doctor Zalinski is just about to give me the rundown."

"He's okay?" Meg asked.

"He will be," Zalinski said . "A chunk of buck shot basically carved a nice channel through the meat of his shoulder, but didn't hit bone or anything else we can't stitch up. He'll be sore as hell and have an ugly scar. I'd like to call in plastics on that but he won't let me. Told me to use glue."

Jake put a hand over his mouth and faked a cough so he wouldn't laugh. Meg rolled her eyes.

"Thank you," she said. "And I apologize for whatever he said that you're not repeating."

"Ah," Jake said. "So you *do* know Frank pretty well."

"We've crossed paths," Meg said. "And Greg loved him, of course."

"You can go in and see him," Zalinski said. "Try to convince him to calm down and rest. He's pushing to get out of here. Like I said, his wound is mostly superficial, but I don't like his heart rate or his blood pressure at the moment. I want to observe him for a little while here. He's got a valium on board so that should help."

"I'll talk to him," Jake said. "Thanks again."

Zalinski nodded, then scurried to his next patient down the hall. Jake started toward Frank's curtain.

"Wait," Landry said. "What the hell happened out there?"

"It was fast," Jake said. "Mandy Lovett ID'd Zeke Bardo as the guy Judge Rand met with the week before he died. We went out to talk to him and the guy came barreling around the back door with a shotgun. Frank had no choice. It was a clean shoot."

The lines in Landry's forehead didn't ease. "You two shouldn't have gone out there by yourselves. And you shouldn't have gone out there without telling anyone else. Frank's not one of us anymore, Jake."

"He'll always be one of us," Jake said. He walked further down the hall to a small, empty waiting area. He'd rather no one else heard what he had to say.

"You shouldn't have gone out there yourself, Jake," she repeated.

"All I wanted to do was ask Zeke a few questions. I don't need a whole crew for that. As far as Frank, he's got an established rapport with the guy."

Landry reared her head back like he'd slapped her. "Some rapport. I'd hate to see what happens when Frank runs into someone who hates him."

"Look," Jake said. "I told you. It was a clean shoot. Completely justified. I'll have my report to you and Tim Brouchard by the end of my shift."

"You think Zeke killed Rand?" she asked.

Jake let out a breath. "I don't know. We'll search the house."

"Do I have a war on my hands?" she asked. "If the Bardos killed the judge, and you guys turn around and kill Zeke, certain people might think that's quid pro quo."

"Zeke shot at us," Jake said. "This wasn't an execution. Now I need to see Frank before he flat out assaults Doc Zalinski when he tries to put a stitch in him."

Landry nodded. Jake left her and passed the elevators to get back to Frank. They opened. Tim Brouchard stepped off, looking pissed. He took a breath to speak and Jake cut him off.

"Talk to Landry," he said. "You'll have a formal statement from the both of us in a few hours."

"Look here," Brouchard started. Meg Landry got to him before he could say anything else. She pulled him away as Jake went to Frank.

Jake peeled back the pink curtain. A nurse was busy adjusting a blood pressure cuff around Frank's beefy good arm. Jake could already tell the valium was starting to work. Frank looked at him with hooded eyes and smiled.

"Fight's gone out of him," the nurse commented. "Blood pressure's coming down. Looks like I might not have to muzzle you after all, Mr. Borowski."

Frank's smiled deepened. He gave the red-headed nurse a salute. She was right. Frank Borowski had been temporarily defanged. Jake pulled up a stool and waited for the nurse to leave.

"You okay?" Jake asked.

Frank wagged his index finger at Jake. It had a pulse oximeter taped to it. Frank marveled at the little red light.

"Man," Jake said. "You are stoned."

"Only way to fly," Frank said.

"You kinda scared me there, Coach. Glad you're okay."

Frank found a big, cheesy smile. "That was something."

"You're a regular gunslinger," Jake joked.

"Old man's still got it," Frank answered. "He was aiming at you, Jake."

Jake didn't know if he was joking or not. But Frank said it just as the curtain pulled back again. Jake turned. Anya stood there, pale-faced, holding a giant brown grocery bag under her arm.

"Jake," she said, her voice small, scared.

"Hey, Anya," he said.

"I was ... I drop off a lunch order for the E.R. staff on Wednesdays. I ran into Tim, he said ..."

"Hey, pretty lady," Frank said, all charm.

"Hi, Coach," she said. Anya put the bag down on the table inside the room and went to Frank. She smoothed his hair back and put a kiss on his forehead.

"She was always one of my favorites," Frank said. "Way too good for your sorry ass." Frank winked at Jake.

"Oh, hush," Anya said. "Do you need anything? I can bring you back some food?"

"That vegan crap?" Frank said. "Nah. But I wouldn't say no to Tessa's chicken orzo."

Anya smiled. "I'll come back with some. As long as you promise to do whatever the nurses tell you to and don't act up."

"Ohh," Jake said. "That'll be a hard promise for him to keep."

Frank mumbled something, but his lids were heavy. Within a few seconds, he was snoring. "Nice work," Jake said.

"Come on," Anya said. "Better let him get some rest. You know he won't the second they let him out of here."

She picked up the grocery bag and followed Jake out of Frank's cubicle. He pulled the curtain closed behind him.

Jake waited as Anya delivered her food order. Brouchard and Landry had moved off somewhere down the hall. When Anya came back, Jake could see she'd been holding back tears.

"I was scared to death, Jake," she said. "On my way over, it came over on the news that there was an officer involved shootout on Glanville Road. They wouldn't identify anybody but they said it was a detective."

"Oh geez," Jake said.

"I thought ..."

Anya's whole body trembled. "You're okay?"

"I'm okay," he said.

"They said on the scanner, it said the coroner had been called. My heart just dropped. Tim wouldn't tell me anything. I just ... I had to come over. I had to see if ..."

He hugged her. Anya sank against him. "It's okay," he said. "I'm fine. Coach will be fine. It's over."

She pulled away. "Okay. Okay. I'm sorry. I'm embarrassed. But it would be so like you to go and get yourself shot to death just when we're starting to be friends again."

She tried to laugh but it came out as a hiccup.

"Well, I appreciate the concern," he said. "And I know Coach does too. But we're good. Though I'd like to throttle whatever news idiot put that out there. If Gemma ..."

Anya and Jake locked eyes. They uttered the words together as the elevator doors opened once more. "Oh shit, Gemma."

Jake's sister came barreling toward them, blonde hair flying, her high-heeled red boots clacking on the tile floor.

"Jake!" she yelled, then broke into a run.

"Anya, I better ..."

Gemma launched herself at her brother. He barely got his arms up before she tackled him.

"Gemma," he said. "I'm okay. Fake news. I'm good."

"You!" she said. She took a light swat at him. "You scared me half to death!"

"Gemma ..." Jake started. His sister's eyes were wild with worry. She turned on Anya.

"And you," she said. "I think I saw your husband coming down the hall. Scoot!"

Anya's jaw dropped. Jake gave her a slight nod over Gemma's head, signaling her. Better she left now before Gemma really revved up. Anya gave him a quick smile, then disappeared back down the hall.

Gemma pounded on Jake's chest.

"Ow!" he said. "Calm down, woman!"

"Calm! I'm supposed to be calm! While you're out there getting your head half blown off?"

"Gemma," he said, keeping his voice soft. "I'm fine. I'm touched by your concern."

Gemma blinked rapidly, holding back her tears. "Don't you dare joke with me. Don't you dare ..."

She put a hand up to her mouth. A tremor went through her and Jake's tough big sister finally broke down and cried.

He put an arm around her. All the bluster had gone out of her as Jake pulled her along and got her seated in a waiting room chair.

Gemma clung to him. It took a good five minutes before she pulled herself back together.

"I'm sorry," he said. "I'm sorry, Gemma."

"You should have called me," she said. "You should have answered your texts!"

"I've been a little busy," he said. "Besides, how many times have I told you, if you haven't heard from me, there's nothing to worry about? If something bad happens, someone will come find you."

"You can't leave me, Jake," she said. Then Gemma erupted in a torrent of words. A dam had clearly broken inside of her.

"I need you," she said. "We need you. You saw Ryan the other night. He crushed that kid from Claymore High. That was you. That was you working with him, but it was more than that. It's just having you around. He needs a father figure. And Aiden too. I don't know what I'm doing with them half of the time."

"You're doing great," Jake said. "You're a great mom."

"It's not enough," she said. "Do you know how much I lie awake at night worrying about what they'll become? They're not afraid of me."

"Gemma," Jake smiled. "I don't know too many people who aren't terrified of you. Me included."

"Oh no you're not. You should be. But you're not."

"Well, I'm here now," he said.

"Are you? Are you really? Because if you aren't, you might as well leave now. It'll be harder when you leave later."

He froze. He knew he should have said he wasn't going anywhere. But something made him stop.

"And don't even get me started on the old man," she said.

"Grandpa's doing fine, Gemma. I promise."

Gemma looked at the ceiling and shook her head. "He's lying to you. And you refuse to see it."

"What are you talking about?"

"Jake, he's going blind."

Her words hit him in the chest. He shook his head. "He can't be. We just went up to the graveyard together."

"Did he drive himself there? Did he walk himself? Let me guess. He asked you to take him. He held on to your arm or something, saying something or other about his knees. Was that it?"

Jake swallowed hard. She was right.

"He doesn't come to Ryan's matches anymore because he can't see them, Jake. The doctors told him he'll probably be completely blind within a year. That's why he had so much trouble at the Dollar Kart. He couldn't count the change they gave him because he can't see the dollar bills clearly enough. He shouldn't be driving. His license is expired already and he knows he won't pass the vision test."

"Christ," Jake said. "Why didn't you tell me? Why didn't he?"

"He's in denial. He blames me for everything. It's easier for him to have a bad guy. I'm it. Why can't you just see it?"

Jake dropped his head. "I'm sorry."

"He's gotten very good at covering," she said. "But Jake? I'm so very tired of doing all of this alone. So if you're planning on going out in some blaze of glory ..."

"I'm not," Jake said. He pulled his sister against him and let her fall apart. She let loose into a big, sobbing, ugly cry.

"I love you, you asshole," she said.

He kissed the top of her head. "I know. I love you too, you crazy bitch."

She tried to laugh but it came out in a sort of strangled goose cry. They both laughed together.

"Come on," he said. "I'll take you to lunch or something. But do me a favor. Go easy on Anya."

"Oh, don't get me started on that one," Gemma said. And she was back. His bossy, tough sister was back. She nagged at Jake all the way to the elevators.

THIRTY-FOUR

"Hey, Sunshine," Ed Zender said first thing Monday morning. He had a huge smile on his face as he leaned so far back in his desk chair Jake worried he might overbalance the thing.

"What's up, Ed?" Jake asked. He knew the guy well enough by now to read his look. Ed couldn't wait to drop some pearl of wisdom on him.

"Oh, nothing," he said. "Only I just solved all your little problems."

Jake stood at his desk, holding a pile of mail Darcy handed him as he walked by her desk.

"I'm fine, Ed," Jake said. "Thanks for asking. Frank's fine too. Doc says he's lucky to have just walked off with a chunk taken out of his shoulder. How was your weekend?"

Ed waved him off. "Gonna take a lot more than that to stop Frank Borowski. No. Your problem. Doug Lovett. He's coming in. I've arranged for him to turn himself in."

Jake put his mail down. "There's no warrant for his arrest yet, Ed. I don't know that there ever will be. I've still got to execute the search warrant on Zeke Bardo's house."

"The words you're looking for are you're welcome. Doug will be here the day after next. Only he insists I be there when you interview him. You have a problem with that, hotshot?"

"I do not," Jake said. He had a whole host of other things to say to Ed, but his cell phone started ringing. It was a number he didn't recognize. One he'd normally just ignore. But it made the perfect excuse to step away from Ed's insufferable blustering.

"I gotta take this," Jake said. "We can work out the logistics of Doug Lovett later on. Thanks though. I definitely need to hear what he has to say."

Jake walked out in the hall and accepted the call.

"Cashen," he said.

"Hello, Detective. I hope I didn't catch you at a bad time."

Jake froze. He'd only met him once. But there was no mistaking that deep, gravelly voice. It was Rex Bardo.

"How did you get this number?" Jake asked, then instantly realized the futility of it. It was also futile to ask Rex how he got a hold of a burner phone in prison. This was King Rex, after all. Still at the top of his reign, no matter how much he wanted law enforcement to believe otherwise.

"Can you talk?" Rex asked. "Are you alone?"

Jake looked both ways down the hall. He was never truly alone in the building. He made a beeline for the stairs and walked outside to the alley between the Sheriff's Department and the courthouse.

"I am now," Jake said. "What do you want, Rex?"

"Just making sure you're all right. Hard to know what to believe on the news."

Jake leaned against the wall. "Well, I sure appreciate your concern, Rex."

He had to know by now his nephew, Zeke, was dead. His network was wide enough he clearly also knew Jake was involved. Meg Landry's fears were at the forefront of his mind. Jake shared them.

"Do I have you to thank for my nephew's fate? That part was unclear."

Jake let out a hard breath and closed his eyes. There it was.

"What do you want, Rex? Zeke drew on my partner. Did that part of the news make it your way? He shot at a police officer."

Silence on the other end. Jake spoke first.

"Do we have a problem?"

He could hear Rex breathing on the other end of the phone. In the distance, other voices. "I hope we don't," Rex finally said.

"Do you? Because it got me thinking. Maybe your nephew was carrying out an order. You knew he's the one who met with Judge Rand, didn't you? I gave you his description. The make and model of his truck. You knew I'd figure out who he was. Did you set me up, Rex? Tell him I'd be coming to talk to him? Did you tell him to try to kill me?"

Rex let out a haughty laugh. "I suppose I should be flattered. That's a hell of a lot of credit you're giving me. It's my kin lying in a body bag at the morgue right now. You seem to be fine. Your partner, if that's what he was, is fine."

"Only because Zeke's a lousy shot, Rex. Cut the shit. Why are you calling me?"

"I like you, Jake," Rex said. "Whether you believe it or not, I was glad to hear you're okay. That makes things easier."

"Yeah? For who? I think Zeke being dead is what makes your life easier. In fact, I think maybe things played out at that shithole of a house exactly the way you wanted them to. I think maybe we did you a favor. Is that what you hoped would happen when you tipped Zeke off we were coming?"

Rex didn't answer. It was enough of an affirmation for Jake.

"You didn't want him talking to us. You didn't want Zeke telling us whatever he knew about Judge Rand's murder. Is that it?"

"Jake," Rex said. "I'm gonna say this as plain as I can. I had nothing to do with Sampson Rand. Nothing. I'm actually sorry he's dead. It's not good for the county. What's bad for the county is bad for me. I know what you're worried about. But let me tell you, I've got no beef with you. There will be no retribution for what happened to Zeke. Whatever that boy did or didn't do? It's on him."

"Well I'm real glad to hear you say that, Rex," Jake said. "Only I still don't know what Zeke had to do with Judge Rand. Why were they meeting? You know I'm not going to stop until I find out."

"And I give you my word," Rex said. "I'll say it again. I got no beef with you. Zeke's been a thorn in my side since he was a boy. But what was I gonna do with him? His daddy took off before my sister squeezed him out. I've tried to do right by him. But the way he ended up? I'd say that's been coming to him for a long time."

"We're not square, Rex," Jake said. "He shot at us. If my partner weren't a better shot than Zeke, he'd be dead right now."

"Is that so?" Rex said. There was an oddness to his tone that made Jake think twice. Was Rex implying Zeke meant to die? Was this suicide by cop?

"You were going to kill him yourself," Jake said. No answer from Rex. "Goddammit, Rex." Jake had his answer. The only way Rex Bardo could let the death of his nephew slide is if he wanted him dead anyway. Why?

"I've got something you want," Rex said. "Call it a gesture of goodwill. So you know. As far as I'm concerned, Zeke's death is what he deserved."

Jake fumed. He was tired of the games. Finally, he said, "I'm listening."

"Good," Rex said. "I had nothing to do with most of what Zeke got himself into. But I asked around for you."

"I'm touched," Jake said.

"One of these days, Jake," Rex said, "you're going to have to show me some faith. I think what I'm about to do for you will be a good first step."

Jake gripped the phone tighter, but didn't answer.

"There's somebody you need to talk to," Rex said. "Somebody who I think can help you fix your Judge Rand problem."

"Still listening," Jake said.

"Good. You'll need to get moving though. He's only going to be there for an hour."

"Rex," Jake said. "You're going to have to forgive me if I'm disinclined to walk into another Bardo family ambush."

"No ambush," Rex said. "You've got one hour. A nice and public place. You know the truck stop on Exit 68? Just into Kingman County? The one with the cow statue on the roof?"

"Yeah, Rex," Jake said. "I know it."

"So get there. There's a guy you'll want to talk to. He'll be sitting in the last booth along the window. He'll wait until ten thirty for you. But he won't talk to anybody but you."

"You want me to come alone," Jake said. "Rex, I don't think ..."

"You listen," Rex said. "This meeting is the first favor I'm doing for you. But here's another. You need to be careful who you trust in that building of yours. There might be somebody who doesn't want you to solve this particular case."

"Who, Rex? No more games."

Rex clucked his tongue. "I've said what I'll say. You're a smart guy, Jake. You'll do the right thing. Get going. Now you've got forty-five minutes. Then I can't promise this guy will ever want to talk to you or anybody else again."

"Rex ..."

But Rex had already ended the call. Jake knew if he tried to call him back, it would go nowhere. Odds were, within the next few minutes, Rex would destroy the phone.

Jake checked the time on his. Forty-four minutes before this mystery man would allegedly disappear. He knew he should just ignore it all. Playing by Rex's rules couldn't end well.

And yet, Jake couldn't shake the nagging sense that Rex was telling the truth. He knew he might catch hell for it. He knew he'd likely regret it. He headed for his car. If he hurried, he'd make Exit 68 with about five minutes to spare.

Thirty-Five

J ake hadn't been to The Sixty-Eight since he was in high school. Ben Wayne's little sister used to work here as a waitress. She'd give them free breakfasts on weekends until her manager found out and docked her for it. Birdie, Jake had always called her. On account of the fact she had knock-kneed, skinny legs until she hit puberty. She took it well, considering. But rumor was Birdie had grown into a real knock-out and joined the army. Ben said she lived in Hawaii now.

The place looked exactly the same. Red faux leather booths patched up with duct tape in places. A long counter with case after case of fresh-baked pies. Jake scanned the room. He spotted a short-order cook in the back, slinging eggs. Two teenage girls acting as servers. Three old men sitting in the corner drinking coffee. Then, in the back booth along the wall, his mark.

A skinny white guy with stringy blond hair under a weathered John Deere ball cap. He was smoking, jabbing his butt into an ashtray. There was, of course, a no smoking sign in the window but places like this tended to shun state-mandated smoking bans. It was too bad for business.

Jake walked over. As soon as the guy saw him, he put both hands flat on the table, scared. He already seemed to know Jake was a cop. Jake stood over him.

"You Jake?" the guy asked, his voice cracking.

Jake put his hands on his hips, spreading his suit jacket enough so the guy could see his gun and badge, just so they were both clear.

"I'm Detective Cashen," he said. One of the teenage girls walked over with a coffeepot. Jake nodded, thanking her as she poured some into the overturned mug on the table in front of him. Jake sat down.

"Black is fine," he told her. She cast a nervous glance at Jake's booth-mate, then hurried back behind the counter.

"I guess you know Rex Bardo sent me," Jake said. "So maybe you should start by telling me who the hell you are."

The guy shook from head to toe. He was wearing a black tee shirt. Jake looked for track marks but couldn't find any.

"You can call me Coleman," he said. "Freddy Coleman."

"Okay, Coleman. I gotta say, I don't like walking into meetings when I don't know what they're about. So let's cut to it. Do you know who I am? What I'm working on?"

Coleman reached for another cigarette from his pack. "You mind?"

"Whatever gets you through," Jake said.

"You want?" Coleman asked as his cigarette now dangled from his lip.

"No, thanks," Jake said. "Coleman, I'm working a murder investigation. Judge Sampson Rand in Worthington County.

Our mutual acquaintance, Rex Bardo, seems to think you might have something to tell me about that."

Coleman shook his head. "I don't know nothing about who killed that judge. That's the God's honest truth. And I don't want to be here."

"So why are you?"

Coleman took a long puff. "Did you kill Zeke Bardo? Is he really dead?"

Jake folded his hands. "He's really dead."

Coleman nodded nervously. He was tapping his foot beneath the table.

"Coleman, I know Zeke was meeting with Judge Rand before he died. I got the feeling maybe you know why. I also think you're here because Rex wants you to tell me. How am I doing?"

Coleman shook his head. "I got nothing to do with Rex. I gotta make that clear. I never met him. Was never on his payroll. A guy like Rex Bardo wouldn't so much as spit in my direction. Not back in the day. Not now. You need to know that."

Jake didn't doubt it. But he was getting good and tired of guessing.

"Fine," Jake said. "You don't work for Rex. Never did. You work for Zeke?"

Coleman nodded. "Been a long time. Nearly eight years. I was in a bad state back then. Real bad. I did some shit I ain't proud of. But I got out of it. Started over."

"Coleman," Jake said. "What did Zeke have to do with the judge?"

"We're clear though, right? I don't work for Rex. But if Rex wants to get a message to me, he's got the means. That's why I'm here. I'll do what he said. But that's it. After that, it's on you."

"Get to it, Coleman," Jake said. "What did you do for Zeke?"

"Tucker Macon. He's who introduced me to Zeke. Eight, nine years ago ... Tucker was Zeke's boy. Zeke set him up. He walked around with rolls of cash. I knew Tucker from when we were little. His mom and my mom were best friends from the neighborhood. I asked Tucker how he was doing so good. Could I get in on it? So he told me. He brought me up. Introduced me to Zeke."

"You were running drugs?" Jake asked.

"Pill mills, yeah," Coleman said. "Zeke would round up buses full of junkies, send 'em around to the pain doctors. They'd load up on whatever. Oxy was big, but anything. Xanax. Other pain meds. Steroids too. You can sell anything. I'm ashamed now. I'm clean. But I was in on it. Man, for a while, we would clean up. Hundreds of dollars a day. I never seen that kind of money up close. We were rolling in it."

"Sure, Coleman," Jake said.

"Zeke was a big talker. Kept promising Tucker more and more. Told him he was gonna take over for his Uncle Rex. He was the heir apparent. Only it started feeling like bullshit. There were times I overheard Zeke trying to talk to Rex on the phone. Sounded like Rex wanted nothing to do with him. Zeke would get pissed. Then he'd come back and lie to us when I knew what I heard with my own ears."

"Rex wasn't a big fan of his nephew, Zeke," Jake said. "I get that."

"No, sir," Coleman agreed. "Tucker played it off. Kept telling me all these things Zeke was gonna do for him once he moved up in the organization. It was all bullshit. And Tucker? He was hitting the product hard. That boy was strung out. And the nasty stuff, too. Heroin toward the end. I knew it was gonna end bad. I wish I'd a done something. Only I don't know what. Should have just left, that's what."

"What happened with Tucker?" Jake asked.

Coleman's whole body changed. He stopped shaking. He hung his head and all the color drained from his face.

"One night, we were out at Digby's. That old hole-in-the-wall bar out in Maudeville. It's not even there anymore. Burned down a few years ago. Good riddance. That place was cursed. Anyway, Tucker was tweaked off his ass. High as hell. He was a maniac. They should have thrown him out only he was friends with the bartender or something. Anyway, there were these girls playing pool. College girls. Damn fine ones. They were nice, too. Clean. The one, the brunette. She even joked with Tucker for a bit. She was sweet."

The server came back with more coffee. Jake politely waved her off. Coleman waited until she was out of earshot. Even so, he leaned in and started whispering the rest of his story.

"Tucker started getting too fresh, you know? Came over bragging how he was gonna get with her later. How he was gonna make her beg for it. Well, we knew he was full of shit. A girl like that? With Tucker's junkie ass? No way. Maybe we shouldna busted his balls so much. Tucker had a nasty temper. But he was always doing crap like that. Big man. Thinking he was all that and making sure to rub your face in it. It was all bullshit. So I had enough. I called him on it. I dared him. God. I shouldna done that. Man, I swear. I wish I could take it back."

Coleman started to cry.

"Coleman," Jake said. "What did Tucker do?"

"He got real handsy with that girl. The brunette. She got pissed. She was with some friends, but whatever Tucker said to her, she was mad enough she wanted to go home. I guess she had her own car or something cuz the friends she was with didn't want to go. She stormed off. I saw Tucker head for the john. I didn't think much of it then. Figured he was off to go lick his wounds. Whatever. Anyway, I don't know how long it was after that, but I was getting tired and wanted to go home. Tucker was my ride. I realized he never came back to the table. I gotta tell you. You gotta know. I was pretty much on my way then, too. I smoked some meth earlier and it was really starting to hit. I wasn't thinking straight."

"What did Tucker do?" Jake asked again. He felt a cold chill creep up his spine.

"I couldn't find him," Coleman said. "I went out to the parking lot. He had this big, ugly Suburban he drove. All brown and rusted out. We used to give him shit that it looked like he was driving his mom's car. Anyway, he always parked it way out at the edge of whatever lot. Used to drive me nuts. Well, I saw it out there. I had to take a piss, so I went to the side of the building and did my business. That's when I heard him."

Jake clenched his fists.

"That noise," Coleman said. "I mean, you can't mistake it for much else. That sick, wet thumping. He was grunting. I heard him say stuff like, you like that? How's that feel? You know you wanted it."

"Where was he?" Jake asked.

"I thought, well, hell, looks like Tucker followed through for once. There was a little hill, like a knoll on the edge of the lot. I saw Tucker up there. He was on the ground. I could see that girl's legs under him. Spread out. She was wearing these purple cowboy boots. I wouldn't have bothered him. I would have gone back inside. Only I heard her like whimper. God. I'll hear that until I die. I froze. I just froze."

"He raped her," Jake said. "The brunette."

"Yeah." Coleman sobbed. "That sound. I swear to God it sobered me right up. But Tucker heard me or saw me or something. He called me over. I should have run the other way but I didn't."

"What did you see, Coleman?"

"You couldn't even hardly see her face anymore. Like she didn't have one. Tucker had beat her to a pulp. Her eye was half out. Her lips were all cut up. He had these brass knuckles."

"But she was still alive?"

"Yeah," Coleman said. "Barely. I said, Jesus, Tucker. What've you done? He asked me if I wanted some after he was done. I tried to pull him off her. I swear to God I did. I told him we needed to call an ambulance. That girl was dying. Hell, she was already dead. Tucker came off her. I tried to help her. I swear. I picked her up and checked for a pulse. She kind of looked at me for a second with her one good eye. Then it was just over. She was gone. That's when Tucker figured out maybe he went too far. He panicked."

"You didn't call the police? For help?" Jake asked.

"Nah, man. No. Tucker freaked out. He got me freaked out. At that point, I was covered in her blood, too. Tucker picked her up and stuffed her in the back of his car. He told me to get in. He told me if I didn't help him, he'd tell Zeke I was in on it."

Jake sat back. "Coleman, I get it. You felt like you were in a bind. Rex Bardo is who he is, but I don't suppose he'd be keen on Zeke's crew committing a murder in a public place."

"That's just it," Coleman said. "That's what we were afraid of. We knew we had to get a hold of Zeke. That girl? I knew she had to have people. She wasn't some strung-out whore. This was gonna land somewhere bad. I knew that. Tucker even knew that."

"So what did you do?" Jake asked.

"We drove like hell. I was in a trance or something. I don't know. Like I couldn't believe it was happening. Tucker drove home and grabbed some stuff out of the garage. Then he took us out to that apple tree farm on County Road 19. He took a shovel out of his car and had me start digging. He stuffed her in a garbage bag and threw her in it. He had some lighter fluid and emptied the thing all over her. Then he lit a match."

Coleman broke down for a moment. Then, he met Jake's eyes. "She started screaming, man."

"She was still alive," Jake said, his stomach turning.

"Yeah," Coleman cried. "I don't know how. But as soon as she started burning, she started screaming. I hear that sound in my nightmares, man. And I don't know what's worse, that she started screaming, or when she finally stopped. Then ... Tucker just started covering her up. He buried her."

Jake ran a hand over his face. "What about Zeke?" Jake asked.

"Tucker called him. Told him what happened. But it was all twisted up. He said she was just some junkie he hooked up with

and it went sideways. I was scared out of my mind. I knew if
Zeke knew the truth. If King Rex did. We'd be toast. This was
back when he was under investigation by the Feds. They ended
up making that RICO case against him the next year. We knew
no matter what Zeke said, Rex wasn't gonna risk anything for
our sorry asses. We were on our own."

Jake rubbed his forehead. He had the makings of a screaming
headache. "You called Zeke? You told him what happened?"

"No. I told you. Tucker did," Coleman said. "That idiot actually
thought Zeke wasn't gonna lose his shit over it. Well, he did.
Beat the living piss out of Tucker. I think he was gonna kill
him."

"What does this have to do with Zeke and Judge Rand,
Coleman?"

"After Zeke calmed down, he told us just to keep our mouths
shut and that he'd take care of everything. He told Tucker he
had a connection. Somebody he knew could make it all go away.
All we had to do was lay low and stay quiet."

"A connection," Jake said. "Who?"

"I didn't ask," Coleman said. "Not then. I should have. That's
the one really stupid thing I did."

Just the one? Jake thought. But he kept his mouth shut and let
Coleman unload.

"For a little while, I did what I was told. But what Tucker did?"
Coleman said. "That poor girl? I know what you'll think of me.
But that day saved my life. I quit cold turkey after that. Off
everything. Pills. Booze. All of it. Started going to meetings.
They tell you. You gotta make amends."

"The ninth step," Jake said.

"Yeah. I couldn't live with myself. I knew it might get me dead. But like I said, at the time, King Rex had enough of his own shit going on so I figured maybe it was safe. Maybe I'd have a chance. Anyway, that girl? I told you. I knew she was somebody with people. There were fliers up all over town with her picture on it. There were these candlelight vigils. So finally, I went to the cops. I told them everything. I told them where to find her. They cut me a deal."

"Who was she?" Jake asked.

"Her name was Nina," Coleman answered. "Nina Papatonis. Her folks own that restaurant over by the courthouse."

The air went out of Jake's lungs. Papa's Diner. God. Nina Papatonis. Her picture. Her brown pigtails and wide smile as she ran through the sprinkler in Spiros and Tessa's backyard. The stories the Wise Men told of her serving them eggs off a tray bigger than she was. The hollowness to Tessa's eyes even this morning as she smiled.

"What the hell happened?" Jake didn't know the ins and outs of the case. It happened well after he left town.

"I told you, they cut me a deal. Put me up in a motel outside of town. They were gonna arrest Tucker. I was all set to take the stand. Then he came."

"Who came?"

Coleman let out an exasperated sigh. "Rand!"

"Rand," Jake said. "Eight years ago he would have still been the prosecutor."

Jake's ears buzzed. His chest felt hollow. But the pieces began to fall into place.

"Rand was Zeke's connection," Jake said. "Rand was in Zeke Bardo's pocket back when he was prosecutor? You're telling me he was dirty?"

Coleman let out a frustrated sigh. "That's what I'm saying. I walked right into it. Tucker kept telling me Zeke knew somebody who would take care of it. I should have believed him. I just couldn't. I had to tell somebody. What Tucker did wasn't right. It just wasn't right. Only Rand knew where I was staying. They kept moving me. But he knew. Rand showed up one night, jerked me right out of bed. He told me he had a message for me. Said plans had changed. If I didn't want to end up burned alive and buried like that girl, I needed to vanish. He gave me ten grand, cash. Told me to go disappear, get a job on an oil rig in Alaska or something. Any place that was as far away from Ohio as I could. He said the Bardos were gonna kill me if I didn't. Told me they had him over a barrel too."

Jake's head spun. Rand. Sampson Rand.

"What'd you do?"

"I did like I was told. I took the money and split. Went to Canada. I did find a job on a fishing trawler. I heard after that the case against Tucker fell apart. There wasn't any physical evidence tying him to the crime. He burned that girl up pretty good. There was no DNA. Tucker got rid of the Suburban too. Well, not long after that, Tucker disappeared. I figured Rand probably made that happen too. Made him a deal like he made me."

"But Rex found you?"

"Zeke did," Coleman said, exasperated. "Maybe three months ago now. I was living near Seattle by then. Zeke showed up on my front door. Scared the hell out of me. I don't know how he did it, but he tracked me down. He said it was okay now. He said

it was okay for me to come forward and say what I knew about
Tucker and that girl and Judge Rand as long as I kept Zeke's part
out of it. Said he'd kill me if I mentioned his name. Man, as
freaked as I was to see Zeke, I was relieved too. I've been living
with this thing for so long. Every time I try to do the right thing,
somebody else ends up dead or disappeared."

"Right," Jake said. "And now Zeke's dead."

"Right," Coleman said. "And nobody can find Tucker. So what
good does it do? That's what I told Zeke. Well, he told me if I
just sat tight, he'd make it so I could come back home. My
mom's getting on in years. I'd like to be able to see her again. I'd
like to be able to help her."

"Sure," Jake said.

"And then Sam Rand ends up dead. So I figured it's not safe. But
I stayed put. I've been living in a little farmhouse about a mile
from here."

"Zeke put you up," Jake said. "But I'll ask again, why didn't you
go to the cops now?"

"I did!" Coleman said. "I don't know what the hell you're even
asking me all this for again. Now Zeke's gone. I'm about to light
out. Then I get a call from goddamn King Rex himself. Chilled
me to the bone. He told me to come here. Told me to tell you all
I know all over again. But all of it. The whole thing. Zeke's part
in it too. I don't know. Now that Zeke's dead I guess he figured
it doesn't matter anymore who knows."

"Again," Jake said. "Why do you keep saying again? Who have
you talked to?"

"Man," Coleman said. "It's like your left and right hand don't
talk. I told all this to that other detective. About Tucker? That
girl? Judge Rand?"

"The other detective," Jake said. "What did he look like?"

Coleman rolled his eyes. "Stocky guy with the gray hair. You should know him. Why are you asking me that?"

Jake felt like an anvil had fallen on his chest. Rex Bardo's words replayed in his mind. There was someone in his building he couldn't trust.

Stocky guy with the gray hair. Coleman just described Ed Zender. Ed meant to bungle Sam Rand's crime scene. Was it on purpose? It didn't make sense. Ed was alone with Mandy Lovett when she fingered Zeke Bardo out of the photo array. Why let her do it if he was trying to cover this all up?

"Ed Zender? Detective Ed Zender?" Jake said. "You talked to him?"

Coleman let out an exasperated sigh. "No, man. The *detective*. The one who handled that Papatonis girl's case. Borowski. Frank Borowski."

And just like that, it was like a hole opened up in the world, threatening to suck Jake through.

THIRTY-SIX

E d was still in the office, greeting Jake with a wide smile as he walked back in. Jake felt like he had tar in his lungs.

"Where've you been?" Ed asked. "Landry was looking for you. She wants a status report. I told her we'd both catch her first thing tomorrow morning."

"Sounds good, Ed," Jake said. He kept his tone even, tried to put himself on autopilot. He had to be sure. Jake couldn't risk having Ed's eyes on him as he looked up the one thing he needed to know now.

"Jake?" Ed said. "Does that work for you?"

Jake snapped out of his own head. "I'm sorry. What?"

Ed laughed. "Have some more coffee, kid. You're in the clouds. I said, I got a couple of things I've got to lock down, but do you want to grab a late lunch? We can go over what we're doing with Doug Lovett. He's getting on a plane as we speak."

"That sounds good," Jake said. "I'll be back in about an hour."

Ed nodded, but his attention was already back on whatever he had on his own computer screen. Jake headed for the stairwell. He didn't think he could handle waiting on the ancient, slow elevator as it creaked its way down to the basement.

He made it down to the bowels of the building. Here, the Sheriff's Department housed its property room, records archive, and storage. Jake's cursed crooked office chair had belched its way upstairs to him from the room at the end of the hall.

He paused before the Records Room door. Blood roared in his ears. Coleman's words. Rex's. He hated to think of them and hoped they were wrong. But every instinct Jake had told him the files in this very building held the key to Sampson Rand's fate.

In Jake's experience, his instincts were rarely wrong. He wished now more than ever that they were. Coleman had to be lying about Frank. Had to. He as much as admitted that he'd say whatever the Bardos told him to.

Jake opened the door. Rick Reilly sat behind the desk reading a magazine. Rick had the honor of being the oldest deputy in the department at sixty-two. That and his current posting as the Records Clerk earned him the nickname The Crypt-Keeper. It didn't help that Rick looked the part. He had nothing but a few wisps of white hair on his head and a mile-wide smile filled with nicotine-stained teeth and receding gums.

"Jake!" Rick said. Despite his ghoulish appearance, Rick Reilly was one of the most cheerful people Jake had met in the department.

"Hey, Rick," Jake said. "I'm looking for an archived murder file. I'm hoping it's one we still have the physical evidence from."

Rick shrugged. "How old? You got a case number?"

"I had it written down but forgot it upstairs. Can you look it up by name? The victim was Nina Papatonis."

Rick's smile faltered. "I don't need to look that one up, Jake. Worst case to ever come through here, if you ask me. I knew that girl. Everybody did. I can't even stomach going into Papa's Diner anymore. There's a lot of us who feel the same way."

"So I've heard," Jake said. "So do you know if we still have the physical file?"

"We do," Rick said. "It takes up two boxes. Come on back. I'll set you up in the back room. You got a lead?"

Jake hesitated to answer. The one thing he'd heard about Rick, he did more than manage the archived files. The man was a vault unto himself. He wouldn't gossip. That said, he kept a record of every file pulled and who pulled it. Jake just had to pray nobody else came looking before he had a chance to do what he needed.

"Not exactly," Jake said. "There's just something I've got to confirm. I'd appreciate it if you didn't mention it to anyone. Like I said. It's just something I want to cross-check. I don't want people getting the idea this thing is getting churned back up."

"Oh, I hear that," Rick said as he led Jake back to a small room behind his desk. There was a small, flimsy table at the center of it with two folding chairs. Jake took a seat in one.

A few minutes later, Rick came back pulling a hand cart with two banker's boxes on it.

"I could have helped you with that," Jake said.

"All good," Rick said. He heaved the boxes on the table. For a moment, Jake thought the table would collapse under their weight.

"Take your time," Rick said. "I'll be out in front if you need anything."

"Thanks, Rick," Jake said. Rick smiled and quietly closed the door behind him.

Jake stared at the boxes for a moment, then opened the first one. He thumbed through the file tabs, quickly finding one he wanted. He pulled out a stack of glossy crime scene photos and spread them out on the desk.

Freddy Coleman had told the truth. God. He'd told the truth.

The half-charred remains of Nina Papatonis barely looked human anymore. The signs of her brutal end tore at Jake. The left side of her face had been caved in. The worst of the burns covered her legs and torso. She was bound with duct tape around her hands and feet.

Alive, Jake thought. Coleman's words haunted him. Through all of it, she had been alive.

Jake put the photos back and pulled the autopsy report. Tucker Macon had used lighter fluid as an accelerant. Some of that had been found in Nina's throat. Macon had failed to make Nina herself disappear, but his actions had evaporated any DNA that would have linked him to the crime.

Jake read through Coleman's detailed statement. It hadn't changed. Not one word. It was the same, grisly recounting he'd given Jake just a few hours ago.

The friends who had been with Nina that night couldn't give reliable descriptions of the other patrons in the bar. None of them was able to identify either Tucker Macon or Freddy Coleman. They'd all been drinking too much. To them and the world, Nina Papatonis had simply vanished into the night then met her hellish fate.

Jake found Tessa and Spiros's statements. They hadn't realized their daughter was missing until five o'clock the next morning when she was due at the restaurant. By then, Jake knew she was already beyond saving. The Papatonis had gathered their life savings and mortgaged their house to put up a reward.

Seven days went by before she was found.

Jake folded his hand beneath his chin. Until Freddy Coleman came forward, this case likely would never have been solved. No other eyewitnesses. No physical evidence. Tucker Macon even had the wherewithal to scrap his shitty, rusted Suburban. It had never been found. He'd likely had it scrapped and burned at a junkyard far away from town.

Then Freddy Coleman came forward. Came forward, then vanished into thin air.

Jake turned to the last page in the report. He scanned to the bottom, anger and bile rising within him. He knew what he would find. No amount of sheer will or wishing could change the name he read at the bottom of the file.

Freddy Coleman was telling the truth. Nina Papatonis had been Frank Borowski's case.

———

He didn't want to believe it. Couldn't believe it. But there was no doubt. Nina was Frank's case. Coleman's memory wasn't faulty. It was Frank he met with before the judge died. He told Frank it was Sampson Rand who had paid him off and made him disappear. Frank who had been lying to Jake all along.

"You doing okay?" Rick's quiet voice jolted Jake.

"Yeah. Thanks, Rick. I'm just finishing up." Jake closed the files and carefully placed them back in the banker's boxes. He helped Rick put them back on the hand truck.

Jake's stomach churned as he walked back upstairs. Frank. It couldn't be Frank.

Except his gut told him it was.

Like a zombie, he walked outside and across the street. He didn't know where he was going. It was snowing. But the frigid air didn't penetrate him, even though he had only his suit coat on.

Jake sat on the green bench directly across from the courthouse. He pulled out his phone and clicked into his browser. The picture on Frank's den wall blazed into his memory. He could see it as if he were staring at it now. The two of them, standing on the deck of the Sea Hawk as Frank held up his prized barracuda. The same fish was mounted somewhere in Frank's basement right now.

There was one thing left. One chance to make this nightmare into nothing more than a bad dream.

He found the website right away and clicked the number. Maybe he won't answer, Jake thought. But he did. It only took two rings. "Captain Russ speaking," the man said in a gruff voice like one would expect. Suddenly, Jake was fifteen years old again.

"Hi, there," Jake said. He existed outside of himself. As if he were watching a movie. A horror film.

"I'm looking to rent a charter with you. You probably don't remember me. I'm a friend of Frank Borowski's? You did a charter with him a few weeks ago, the first week of November? Said he caught another barracuda."

"Frank?" Captain Russ said. "We love having Frank out. He's a hell of a character. I haven't seen him this year though. First time he hasn't made his yearly trip since the nineties. That old fart's either losing it or he's cheating on me with some other charter captain. I'm booked through May, but for Frank, I could shuffle things if you're planning to come with him."

Jake couldn't breathe. "Wow. I guess I may have misheard him. You're sure you didn't take him out last month?"

"No, sir," Russ said. "Like I said, it's the first year he hasn't come out. I actually gave him a call cuz he's got a standing reservation. He told me his sciatica was acting up and he'd hit me next year. If you talk to him, tell him to try Epsom salt."

"I will, Captain Russ," Jake said. "I'll hook up with him and see if May works. I appreciate it. Thank you."

"What'd you say your name was?" Russ asked. But Jake had already hung up the phone.

THIRTY-SEVEN

The house was quiet when Jake pulled up. Frank's truck was in the driveway but Jake's three phone calls had gone straight to voicemail. He hadn't left a message. He hadn't told Landry or Ed or anyone else he was coming. Whatever happened next had to be between Jake and Frank. Coach.

Jake knocked on the door. "Frank," he called out. "We need to talk. You can't dodge me forever."

Jake peered through the small window next to the front door. The house looked quiet. He could make out dishes in the sink, but little else.

Jake walked around the side of the house and out back. Frank had a slider off the dining room but the blinds were closed. His knock on the window didn't do anything either. He came all the way around and tried to peek into Frank's garage. Frank kept a lawn tractor and a workbench in there. He'd been meaning to add on so he could park the truck inside but never got around to it.

It was empty. He supposed it was possible Frank was napping in the basement, but he doubted it.

Jake leaned against Frank's truck. Snow started to fall. They were calling for three inches by morning.

Jake left. He couldn't go home. Couldn't go back to the office. Couldn't think of going anywhere, really. His blood felt like acid through his veins. What he suspected just could not be true. Except he knew it was.

Jake drove for a while. Aimlessly. Looking for Frank, but knowing he wouldn't find him. Jake hadn't meant to go there, but he found himself in the parking lot of Stanley High School. Wrestling practice was letting out. He saw Ryan walking with a group of his friends, oblivious to his uncle's presence. He looked happy. Strong. Young. Behind him, Coach Purcell brought up the rear, turning around to lock the gym doors and make sure his team made it to their rides.

He was a good man, Brian Purcell. A decent coach. He would mean as much to Ryan someday as Frank did to Jake.

Jake pressed his head against the steering wheel, wanting to punch right through it. He would have. But then his phone rang.

It was Frank.

Jake punched the call button on his dashboard. Frank's voice filled Jake's truck.

"Hey, Jake," he said. He sounded normal.

"Hey, Coach," Jake said, knowing he sounded anything but.

The two men stayed silent for a moment. Finally, Jake found the words.

"Frank," he said. "I talked to Freddy Coleman."

It was all he needed to say. Five simple words. But they held the weight of Frank's guilt, and he knew it.

Frank said nothing. A full minute passed. Jake could just make out Frank's breathing on the other end of the phone.

"Why didn't you tell me?" Jake said.

"What was I supposed to say?"

"The truth!" Jake snapped. "Coleman told me everything. Nina Papatonis was your case. I saw the file. You had nothing. Tucker Macon was going to walk without Freddy's testimony. You couldn't put Macon at the crime scene without him. You couldn't tie him to the girl."

"She wasn't a girl!" Frank boomed. "She was Nina Papatonis. She was family."

"I know."

"You don't know," Frank said. "You don't know shit, Jake."

"She mattered to you," Jake said. "I get it."

"She was something," Frank said. "She worked so hard for her parents. She'd stand on a stool on her tiptoes so she could reach over the counter. They had her running the cash register from the time she was seven. She wanted to learn everything. She redesigned Spiros's menu when she was in junior high. A lot of kids might have resented it. Would have wanted to get as far away from their parents as they could. Not Nina. She knew. She had plans for the restaurant. They were going to open another one in Athens. Would have probably made a killing. Nina was going to business school. Spiros and Tessa poured every extra cent they had into her education."

"I'm sorry, Frank," Jake said.

"Don't," he said. "Don't say that to me. Nina was like a daughter to me. The closest thing I ever had to one. She was my goddaughter."

"I didn't know that, Frank," Jake said. "I wish you'd have told me."

"I failed her," Frank said. "I didn't see what was right in front of my face, Jake."

"You mean Zeke," Jake said. "He was your CI, but he was keeping things from you. Is that it? He didn't tell you Macon and Coleman were on his payroll."

"No," Frank said, crying. "I swear to God I didn't know. Coleman and Macon were junkies. They weren't the kind of people King Rex would have ever had on his payroll. He never would have sanctioned them working for Zeke, either. Zeke burned me, Jake. You of all people know what that feels like. You were burned by your CI too."

"Don't," Jake said, his blood starting to simmer. "Don't pretend this is anything like what happened to me with the Bureau."

"Zeke was smart enough to cover his tracks back then," Frank continued, almost as if Jake wasn't listening. "If I'd known those two were working for him. God. That will eat at me until the day I die. I was too close to it. What they did to her tore me up. I should have seen it. I should have figured out Zeke was involved."

"And Coleman," Jake said. "He was smart enough to keep his mouth shut about his relationship with Zeke back then. And Zeke threatened him to keep it shut. Until now."

Jake knew why. The same man who'd told Coleman to wait for Jake at the truck stop had told him to spill everything he knew and not hold back. King Rex. He'd been pulling strings since the moment Jake first visited him in prison.

"I should have seen it," Frank said. "God. If I could go back."

"What happened?" Jake asked.

Silence.

"Frank," Jake said. "You know I'm going to find out."

"I can't help you, Jake," Frank said.

"You lied." Jake lost his temper. "You've played me from the very beginning. Every conversation we've had in the last few weeks about this case. You were interrogating me. You say Nina was like a daughter to you? Well you've been like a father to me. I know it was you. Do you get that? I know you're the one who put a bullet in Judge Rand's head. It's over, Frank. I talked to Captain Russ. You weren't on that charter boat down in Florida the weekend the judge died. You planned it. You waited for your chance. You cleaned up after yourself. It was premeditated murder. You executed Sam Rand for tanking your case against Tucker Macon and making your star witness disappear."

Frank let out a bitter laugh. "She was right about you. Landry. Why did she have to be so goddamn right?"

Jake closed his eyes. "You figured Ed would bungle his way through Rand's murder investigation. Without a body, you didn't think you'd ever get caught. Jesus, Frank. The thing is, you're probably right. Ed's still out there thinking he's got some coup getting Doug Lovett to fly back to Ohio. Were you gonna let Lovett twist in the wind for you?"

"You were never going to have enough to make probable cause against Lovett. Or anyone else."

"Right," Jake said. "So a few months ago Zeke got greedy again. Decided he'd work a side hustle blackmailing Sam Rand over what he put him up to with Nina's case. How the hell was that going to work? How the hell did he think that wouldn't end up bringing him down too? Macon and Coleman were *his* boys!"

"The thing about Zeke," Frank said. "Rex was always right about him. He was too stupid to handle any real power."

"He trusted Macon and Coleman," Jake said. "A psychopath junkie and a garden variety junkie with a conscience. Then when things went sideways with Nina, and Coleman turned rat, Tucker Macon went to Zeke to clean it up?"

"Hell of a clean-up," Frank said.

"Why wouldn't Zeke have just killed them?"

"Probably because Zeke was too much of a coward to get his hands dirty like that. He would have figured money was all he needed to make everything go away."

Frank let out a breath. "There were always little things I should have picked up on. When Rand was a prosecutor, there were smaller things he'd refuse to pursue. We suspected him of being dirty but nothing ever stuck. We couldn't prove it. But like I said, it was piddly shit. Never in a million years would I have thought he'd tank a murder case. Not when Nina was the victim. He knew her too."

"You expect me to believe you didn't know it was Zeke paying Rand off?" Jake asked.

"I swear to God I didn't," Frank said. "Zeke burned me. Coleman wouldn't tell me who was paying the judge off. But it wasn't hard to figure out."

"By using me," Jake said, bile rising in his throat. "I'm the one who told you Zeke was meeting with the judge this fall. I'm the one who took you to his doorstep. Was that a hit too, Frank?"

"No! God. No. You think I didn't want to talk to him as badly as you did? He knew that though."

"Of course he did," Jake said. "Dammit, Frank. Rex warned him. I played into his goddamn hands. The minute Zeke saw us coming, he knew you killed Rand already, didn't he? He probably figured you were there to finish the job with him. Or his Uncle Rex told him so he'd come out shooting and we'd take him out so Rex wouldn't have to."

"I don't know," Frank said. "Maybe. Probably. But it was a good shoot. You were there. I didn't have a choice."

"You've always had a choice, Frank," Jake said.

Something broke in Frank Borowski then. The words poured out of him.

"I didn't know Zeke had anything to do with Coleman or Macon back then. You have to believe that. That's what I'll take to my grave. He was my CI. I should have seen he was lying to me. But then a few months ago, like you said, Zeke must have got greedy. He knew Uncle Rex was never going to trust him with anything real. So he goes to Rand and tries to shake that money tree. Tells him he's gonna let the word out that Rand was on the take back when Nina got killed. Maybe it worked for a while. But Sam Rand wasn't stupid. He knew Zeke would only be shooting himself in the foot if he told the world Sam made Freddy Coleman disappear."

"So Rand called his bluff," Jake said. "When Zeke realized Rand wouldn't be an easy payday, Zeke took Coleman's muzzle off and told him to reach out to you but keep Zeke's name out of it. And Coleman was only too willing to come back out of the woodwork. He's been carrying the guilt of that night with him."

"He's found God," Frank said, his anger rising.

"Zeke had to have put it together that you're the one who killed Rand. That's why he went to ground. He was scared for his life. He figured he'd be next if you ever found out his part in all of this. You hadn't though, had you? Not until I brought you into this."

"Jake ..."

"Zeke didn't know Mandy Lovett saw him meeting with Rand. And neither did you. Until I told you," Jake said, bitter bile almost choking him.

"I did what I had to do," Frank said. "Tucker Macon is probably already dead. He's a ghost. I can't find him. You have to believe me that I've tried."

"It doesn't matter!" Jake roared. "None of that matters! You could have come to me. You could have come to Landry. We could have exposed Sam Rand for what he was."

"Are you kidding me!" Frank yelled. "I had nothing but Freddy Coleman's word. Rand would have found the best lawyers in the country. The trial would have dragged on for years, Jake. Years. And there was no guarantee we'd get justice for Nina at the end of it."

"So you decided revenge would have to do," Jake said.

"Spiros Papatonis doesn't have years," Frank said. "He's had two heart attacks in the last five years. I promised him I'd never let

Nina's case be forgotten. I swore an oath I'd get justice for her one way or another."

"You swore an oath to uphold the law when they pinned that badge on you, Frank," Jake said. "And you swore an oath to me."

"You just don't understand," Frank said. "Someday, some way, there's going to be a case like Nina's for you. The one that blackens your soul and takes someone from you that you care about. And there won't be anything you can do about it. Until the one day you can. Then you come talk to me about the difference between justice and vengeance."

"Where is he, Frank?" Jake said. "Where's Rand's body?"

Frank let out a bitter laugh. "I sent him down to the devil. You'll never find him."

Jake was done. He'd heard all he needed to hear and Frank had said all he could say. There was nothing left.

"It's over, Frank," Jake said. "You know that. You know what I have to do. You know how this has to happen."

He could hear Frank's soft sob on the other end of the phone and it gutted him. "I want it to be you," Frank said. "Can you promise me at least that? Just you."

"Yes," Jake said. "You'll turn yourself in. I'll be there."

"I don't want a whole circus. No media. No perp parade. If I catch wind of that, you'll never see me again."

"Just you and me," Jake said. "Where are you, Frank?"

"I'll meet you on the bridge at Devil's Eye," Frank said. "You know the place? Right when the sun comes up. You have my word. I just need the night."

"Frank ..."

"I promise," he said. "Just the night. I have nowhere else to go, Jake."

"I know," Jake said.

"I loved her," Frank said. "Tucker Macon is gone. Even with Freddy's testimony ..."

"I know that too," Jake said. That's when Jake's own tears started to flow. The two men cried together. They'd only done that once before. The day Frank pulled him off the top of the podium after his win at the state tournament on the tenth anniversary of the day his mother died.

Thirty-Eight

Sheriff Meg Landry lived in a two-story, hundred-year-old brick house on the last plot of land sold off from the Baker farm off County Road 10 in Lublin Township just south of Ardenville. The rest of the land turned into a subdivision so the Landrys' hundred-year-old brick house stood out like a sore thumb. It was a work in progress. Phil Landry was an engineer with South Central Power Company. He wasn't handy, but he tried.

It was just after eleven at night when Jake pulled into their driveway and questioned his decision to come here for about the hundredth time. A motion sensor light went on above the detached garage. A minute later, Phil Landry stepped out onto their wraparound porch. Jake had never met him, but being married to Meg for twenty-five years, the guy likely knew a cop when he saw one, no matter what he drove up in.

Phil held the storm door open and called out over his shoulder. "Meggie," he said. "It's for you."

Jake had never seen Meg Landry without her sheriff browns. Tonight, she had on a pair of pajama pants with blue and green reindeer on them. She pulled her white cardigan tighter around her waist and stepped out onto the porch. She regarded him for a moment, cocking her head to the side. She didn't ask him what he was doing in her driveway this late at night. She wasn't angry. She just opened the door wider and said, "Jake. You're going to freeze to death. Come on inside."

He followed her in. She had a large foyer with cathedral ceilings and what had to be the original Art Deco chandelier. There was a dining room off to the side built-in leaded glass China hutches. Meg was using it as her office. She had a desk in one corner with stacks of papers and files all over the floor.

"We can talk in here," she said. "Phil, can you make us a pot of coffee? Jake looks like he could use it."

"I'm sorry," Jake said. "I didn't mean to barge in unannounced. I …"

"It's all right," Phil Landry said. "I'll have the coffee out in a sec."

There was movement in the living room. Meg's teenage daughter appeared on the stairs. She was Meg's mini-me with tightly curled dark-brown hair and a scowl that could cut glass.

"Your mom's working, Paige," Phil said. "Let's leave her be."

Jake walked into the dining room office with Meg. She shut the French doors and showed him to a plush purple couch. Jake didn't want to sit. Meg did. She took a chair at her desk and swiveled it around so she faced him.

"Sit," she commanded. "Or you look like you're going to fall over. What is it?"

She wasn't wrong. The whole ride over, Jake wanted to be anywhere else. Be doing anything else. But here he was.

"It's Frank," he said simply.

Meg's expression never changed. Jake let his words hang in the air for a moment. It took everything he had just to utter that much. Then slowly, as the seconds ticked by, Meg's face changed.

"Jake."

"It's Frank," he whispered. "He killed Sam Rand. Rand was dirty. He got to the eyewitness in the Nina Papatonis murder when he was a prosecutor. Guy named Freddy Coleman. I spoke with him. He laid it all out. Reached out to Frank a few months ago. Told him Rand was who made him disappear. Frank lied about where he was the weekend Rand was murdered."

Meg rested her elbows on her knees and her nose on her folded hands.

"You're sure," she asked.

"He confessed, Meg," Jake said. "I confronted him. Frank admitted to everything."

Slowly, Meg Landry closed her eyes. A moment later, "Where's Sam's body now?"

Jake shook his head. "Probably somewhere we'll never find him. Tell me there's not a single cop out there who doesn't have a fantasy plan about where to hide a body. He was careful."

"He thought Ed would be the one to investigate this case," Landry said. Jake could see her wheels turning, putting all the pieces in place for herself. "If he had ..."

"Then I'd still be trying to make probable cause against Doug Lovett, or Dickie Gerald."

Then the rest poured out of him. He told her how Freddy Coleman and Tucker Macon had worked for Zeke Bardo. How Tucker had stalked Nina Papatonis out at Digby's Bar. How it went sideways. Coleman's crisis of conscience. Then finally, how Zeke muscled Rand into making it all go away. Cut to now. Zeke using it all to try and shake Rand down and Rand calling his bluff.

"Zeke got greedy," Meg said. "And stupid. Those are always the things King Rex has been afraid of. He thought he could keep the stink off himself if he threatened to expose Rand for what they *both* did all those years ago?"

"It's why Zeke's never had any real power with the Hilltop Boys other than his last name."

"And even that's borrowed," Meg said. "My God, Jake. Where is he? Where's Frank now?"

"I'm not sure," Jake said. "But he's going to turn himself into me. He gave me his word."

She sat up. "Please tell me you didn't take it. Jake!"

"He gave me his word," Jake said. "I know Frank. You have to trust me on this. This has to go down his way. Him and me. I'll bring him in first thing in the morning."

"He can be halfway to Mexico by the morning," she said. "Jake, we need to wake up Judge Cardwell and get an arrest warrant issued. We need to get an APB out on Frank right now."

"You do that," Jake said. "Somebody's going to get hurt. Frank's got nothing to lose right now. The only thing he's got left is his dignity. And mine. We've made arrangements. I'll bring him in myself."

"Where," she said. "How? Jake, you just said Frank's got nothing left to lose. I'm not going to send you out somewhere without backup."

"No," Jake said. "This is going to go down my way or not at all. You're going to have to trust me."

"Trust you?" she said. "Like you trusted Frank? My God. He executed Zeke Bardo, didn't he? If King Rex had known what Zeke was up to, he would have just killed him outright."

"It was a clean shoot," Jake said. "On my life, Zeke Bardo was a clean shoot."

"It was convenient," she said. "God. Jake. This is bigger than you now. I understand your loyalty to Frank ..."

"Loyalty?" Jake said. "Landry, if I wanted to cover for Frank, why the hell would I come to you now? Freddy Coleman, once again, is probably the only person who can put this all together. I could have just kept my mouth shut. Let this whole thing go cold. But I'm here. I know what my duty is."

"Do you?" Meg said.

"You made a promise," Jake said. "When you pinned that badge on me, you gave me your word. You said you'd stay out of my way. That I could handle this case the way I saw fit. Well, this is how I see fit to handle it. If Frank gets even a whiff of some dog and pony show, he's going to go to ground for good. You think he doesn't have some bug-out plan in place?"

She turned stone-faced.

"Don't you?" Jake asked. Her silence was all the affirmation he needed.

"Jake, if this goes south ..."

"It won't," he said. "Not as long as you play it my way. I'll have Frank in custody by tomorrow afternoon. After that, it's your show. I swear it. If not, you can have my badge. You can throw me to the county commissioner wolves, my uncle Rob Arden, the Bureau, and anyone else looking to feast on my carcass."

"All right," she said. "All right. But God. Jake. I'm sorry. Are you okay?"

Jake rose. He needed to be alone. He needed air. He needed something stronger than coffee.

"I will be," Jake said. He'd said all he could stomach to say. He left Meg Landry sitting in her den and headed back out into the snow.

THIRTY-NINE

Jake rose just before dawn. The truth was, he hadn't slept at all. He'd been waiting. Dreading. Wishing there was some way he could restart the last few months. Maybe if he'd come back to Stanley sooner. Maybe if he'd have kept in touch with Frank throughout the years. Would it have made a difference?

He didn't know what made the old man do it, but maybe his grandfather had a sixth sense. He banged on Jake's door just after five in the morning.

Jake was just pulling his shirt on. "Gramps, you shouldn't be down here. I haven't had a chance to run the plow."

"I'm fine," Max said. "It's not cold."

"Get on in here," Jake said. His grandfather knocked the snow off his boots and came into the tiny cabin. Grandpa Max's father had built this cabin by hand almost a hundred years ago.

"Here," Jake said. He had one of Grandma Rose's Afghans on the back of the couch. He wrapped it around Max and made him take a seat.

"Coffee's on," Jake said. He poured them each a cup, black, then set Max's on the table directly in front of them.

"They're saying six more inches by tomorrow," Max said.

"I know, Gramps. Don't worry. I'll plow. There's just something I've gotta do this morning. It shouldn't take too long."

Max sipped his coffee. He stared off, his clouded eyes not really focusing on anything in particular. Jake should have noticed before. It shouldn't have taken Gemma or being shot at to wake him up to what was going on right in front of him. It seemed Grandpa Max wasn't the only one who had trouble seeing.

"I can handle a snow shovel myself," Grandpa said.

Jake set his mug down. It would have been like him to just let the comment go by. Leave the old man to his stubbornness. He would bluster, sure, but in the end he'd sit on the porch and talk to Jake as he shoveled off Grandpa's walk.

"No, Gramps," Jake said. "You can't. And you shouldn't be. You could hurt yourself. Besides all that, you don't have to. I'm here to do it."

Max turned and looked at his grandson. "Are ya?"

Jake knew what he was asking. It was the same thing Gemma had. Was he all in? Was he staying in Worthington County for good? He thought he knew. He definitely knew what Max and Gemma wanted. But what did he want? He'd meant to just find some temporary quiet here. A place to lick his wounds and draw whatever strength he could from the Blackhand Hills themselves. The woods. The land. The place where he grew up. It was supposed to be simple.

"I have to do a thing today," Jake said. "Something that's going to change everything. Something I can't ever take back."

Max chewed his lip. He didn't say anything for a good long while. He finished his coffee. He set it down and folded Grandma's blanket across his lap.

"Is it the right thing?" Max finally said.

"I don't have a choice," Jake answered.

"That's not what I asked you," Grandpa said.

Jake closed his eyes and leaned his head on the back of the couch. "Yes," he said. "It's the right thing. But I don't think that will matter. People will hate me for it. I'll hate me for it."

"Then let them hate you," Max said. "It's you you've gotta live with."

Jake's throat felt thick. "That's the thing," he said. "I don't know if I can after this."

Max put a hand on his grandson's knee. Just that simple touch was almost the thing that sent Jake over the edge and broke him.

"Well, you don't gotta do it alone," Grandpa said.

"Neither do you," Jake said. "You need help. You have to let me. You have to let Gemma. It's going to get harder from here on out. All of it. For me. For you. Your eyes aren't going to get better."

Max was quiet, then dropped his head. "No," he said. "Guess I gotta do a hard thing, too."

Jake slipped his hand inside of his grandfather's. The old man's grip was still oak strong, his fingers still calloused. Blue veins webbed over his knuckles.

"Go on," Max said. "It's time."

Though Max Cashen couldn't know what Jake was about to do, Jake realized it didn't matter. He leaned over and hugged Grandpa Max, drawing what strength from him he could.

FORTY

J ake went to the Shepherd's Hollow bridge just as the sun peeked over the ridge. It cast the river below in shimmering gold, cutting through the rocky shore, and falling snow. Here, just past the largest outcropping of sandstone, was Devil's Eye. The deep, bottomless cavern where the legends of treasure and ghosts intertwined.

Jake waited. Minutes ticked by. From here, he could see both roads leading up to the ridge. Snow covered them. Not a single tire track could be seen. No human footprints either. Most likely, no one had been up here for days. Maybe more.

As the sun rose higher in the sky, Jake knew. Coach Frank wasn't coming. As dread pooled in his gut, Jake knew something was wrong. Something had happened. There was only one other person besides Frank who knew what he'd come to do today.

Jake punched in Frank's number. It went straight to voicemail. Jake drove up and down the road. No plows or salt trucks had come through. Neither had anyone else.

"Son of a bitch," Jake said. "What are you up to?"

He picked up his phone to try Frank once more. Before he could dial, he got an incoming call. Sheriff Landry. Taking a steeling breath, Jake answered.

"I'll tell you something when I have something," Jake said. "You need to trust me."

"Jake," she said. "I need you to come out here."

"Out where?"

"Frank's house," she said. "I'm sorry. This is too big. Too much is at risk."

Jake's heart hammered behind his rib cage. "Landry, what have you done?" He remembered Frank's words. If they brought the dog and pony show, he'd disappear into the wind.

"I've covered my bases," she said. "You know I didn't have a choice."

Jake threw down the phone. He jammed his truck in reverse and sped toward Frank's house as fast as the slick roads would allow.

T he whole street was blocked off. Two deputy cruisers sat at the end of it, their lights flashing. They recognized Jake and waved him on through.

"Son of a bitch," Jake muttered. Landry had the whole SWAT team assembled. Two vans. Half a dozen cruisers. Sharpshooters across the street. Landry herself sat in a cruiser behind the barricade.

"His truck is parked around back," she said.

"How is this you letting me handle this?" Jake yelled.

"It's nine o'clock," she said. "You had until dawn, Jake. I waited as long as I could. The neighbor said he saw Frank pull in last night. I've had someone watching the house."

Jake wanted to punch something. He settled for the nearest tree. Bark splintered. He tore off a layer of skin across his knuckles.

"He made your guy," Jake said. "Frank saw him watching the house. He ran!"

"He didn't make my guy," Landry said. "Officer Denning knows what he's doing."

"You had him sitting down the block in an unmarked car. Frank knows his own neighborhood, Landry. I told you. He'd know if something was up. He'd know if I reneged on our deal."

"He's in there, Jake," Landry said. "The car hasn't left."

"Where's Denning?" Jake said.

Landry called for the deputy. Denning appeared, walking with purpose.

"Tell him what you told me," Landry said.

"I've had eyes on the place for the last six hours," Denning said. "Next-door neighbor saw Borowski pull in about two a.m. I've been here since three. No one's gone in or out."

"Frank," a voice called over the bullhorn. Jake recognized him as one of the Sheriff Department's chief hostage negotiators. "Nobody wants to take this to the next step. Just come on out. This is Bud Messer talking. Come on, Frank."

"You're wasting your breath," Jake said. He walked over to Messer and pushed the bull horn down.

"Jake," Landry said.

"He's gone!" Jake shouted. "Or he's already put a bullet in his head."

Messer and Landry exchanged a look.

"Well," Jake said. "You're here. This is what you do. Go ahead and do it. Let them in."

Meg Landry at least had the decency to look like she was going to be sick. She gave the order. The SWAT team moved in, taking tactical positions at the front and back of Frank Borowski's house.

The first team came out in front, taking their stacked positions. The lead man held a battering ram, the second had his shotgun ready at hand, six deputies brought up the rear with their weapons drawn. They threw a flashbang through the front window. Whitish gray smoke billowed out. Next, the team rammed through the door and made their entry.

Pulse racing, Jake waited behind the barricade with Landry. It took seconds. It seemed to take hours. It was five minutes. The team leader's "all clear" shout cut through Jake.

Jake didn't wait for the next order to come. He ran ahead of Landry and everyone else. Stepping over the wreckage of Frank Borowski's front door, he walked inside the house. A thousand memories flooded into his mind.

Jake at sixteen, puking his guts out in Frank's bathroom because he needed to make weight. Frank sitting quietly with him at the kitchen table after Jake had broken the nose of a teammate who'd said something unforgivable about Jake's father.

Frank. Just ... Frank.

"The house is empty," one of the members of the SWAT team said. He was talking to Jake. He was talking to Landry.

"He's gone," Jake whispered.

"He can't be gone," Landry said. "We've been watching the house."

"He's gone," Jake said. He walked over to the kitchen table. The answer was there in a rocks glass engraved with the Worthington County Sheriff's patch and Frank's name beneath it. It was there in the open bottle of twenty-three-year-old Pappy Van Winkle with just two shots poured out. It was there in Frank's badge and pocketknife he'd laid carefully next to the bourbon. And it was there in the empty space on the wall, where the picture of Jake and Frank on Captain Ron's boat had hung.

Jake picked up the badge, running his thumb over the raised metal. He tossed the badge to Landry.

"He's gone," Jake said. "And he's never coming back."

FORTY-ONE

Five days later, and all efforts to find Frank Borowski had failed, just like Jake knew they would. It was Tuesday morning.

Jake walked into Papa's Diner. When Tessa poured him a cup of coffee, he met her sad eyes. The news had hit the media the night before. Judge Cardwell had signed an arrest warrant for Frank Borowski for the murder of Judge Sampson Rand. Frank's picture was tacked up at every bus and train station in the state and beyond. It was futile though, Jake knew.

"I think they figured you'd be in today," Tessa said. Jake tried not to look at the picture of Nina Papatonis, smiling down at him from behind Tessa's left shoulder. He felt her ghost today. Maybe he would feel her every day. As if Frank had touched him and passed it on. It was his burden to carry now.

He heard the now familiar laughter of the group of men. One fewer than they'd had before. The laughter died down as Jake walked back to the table. The one remaining empty seat seemed to taunt him. Or beckon him, maybe.

"Have a seat, Jake," Bill Nutter said. All traces of the smiles on their faces faded. Jake didn't know what to feel. Sadness? Anger?

Jake gripped the back of the chair but stayed on his feet. "Did you know?" Jake asked.

"Drink your coffee, kid," Virgil Adamski said. "You look like shit."

"Haven't been sleeping much," Jake said.

They let the conversation drift to normal things as Jake stood there. The snow had melted, but a new storm was expected next week, just in time for Christmas.

"We haven't had a real white one in about six years," Chuck Thompson said. "The grandkids like to go sledding up on Lucky Hollow. Did you hear one of the county commissioners is trying to prevent the church from putting the living nativity up in courthouse square?"

"Yeah," Nutter said. "Your Uncle Rob, Jake."

"I don't know," Jake said. "We aren't exactly close."

"Big match is coming up this week," Adamski said. "We're all rooting for your nephew, Ryan, to knock the snot out of that kid from St. Iz. Everyone says he's got a real shot at the state title if he gets past him. He looks good, Jake. Real good. You and Frank have worked wonders."

Jake stared at nothing. Finally, he settled on an emotion. Anger.

"Did you know?" his voice boomed.

The group fell quiet. Nutter's eyes narrowed. "Know what, son?" Vitriol dripped from his words. It was a warning. It might as well have been an admission.

"Goddammit. You knew. He told you Rand was dirty. He told you he was going to take care of it."

"I think you need to calm down," Chuck Thompson said. "Sit, will you?"

Jake leaned over and pounded his fist on the table, sending the nearest silverware jumping. "He could have come to me. You should have made him come to his senses."

"You think that would have worked?" Nutter said.

"I know what she was to you," Jake said, lowering his voice. "To all of you. Did you help him? Do you know where he is? I know Frank. He's not going to come quietly. He's going to get hurt when they catch up with him. Or he's going to hurt someone else. There's been enough of a body count already."

But the Wise Men weren't talking. They all glared at Jake. Seconds passed by. A minute. Then Adamski broke the silence.

"Hey, Jake," he said. "Why don't you sit down?"

Jake took a moment to meet the eyes of each of these men. The Wise Men. They would hold their secrets. They would hold Frank's.

"Maybe some other time," Jake said. He squared his shoulders, turned, and walked out of the restaurant, passing Nina Papatonis's smiling face from her picture on the wall.

Forty-Two

Once again, Jake told the guards not to tell King Rex who'd come to see him that afternoon. And yet, when Rex walked through the door, Jake saw no surprise in his eyes.

Of course, there wouldn't be. Frank Borowski had made national news. A wanted man from coast to coast. Only a handful of people knew why Frank had killed Sam Rand. Jake stared hard into the eyes of one of them.

"Hello, there, Jake," Rex said. "I'm flattered you took the time to come out and see me. You've had a busy couple of days. To what do I owe the pleasure?"

"They buried your nephew today," Jake said. "Did you know that?"

"You'll have to pay my respects on my behalf."

"The governor's planning to announce a replacement for Judge Rand's seat later this month. Did you know that? After everything that's happened, Cardwell's decided he'd rather stay in Muni Court."

"Nature abhors a vacuum," Rex said.

"A betting man might think you'd take an interest in that appointment."

Rex smiled. "And I know I don't have to tell you, my particular brand of troubles sprout from the federal bench, Jake. I truly hope Governor Ramsey finds the right man. Or woman, to serve the needs of justice in little old Worthington County."

"I'm sure you do," Jake said.

"So," Rex said. "Why are you here, Jake? People are going to start to think you and I are friends."

"I wanted to see you in person," Jake said. "I wanted to hear you tell me to my face what you told me the other day."

Rex sat back. There was a hint of a smile on his face, but he held it in check.

"Your friend," Rex said. "Detective Borowski. There are those who seem to think he had a vendetta against my family."

"And I trust you'll make sure those people understand that Frank Borowski is his own man with his own beef. A homegrown war on cops doesn't do you any good, Rex."

"And a war on my family doesn't do you any good, Detective," Rex said.

"So then you understand," Jake said.

"You want to hear me say it?" Rex leaned forward. "My nephew got ideas in his head. A man like Sam Rand is unreliable. Whatever ... arrangement my late nephew had with him had nothing to do with me. Whatever bad deeds his idiot crew got up to ... had nothing to do with me. Your friend Frank? I've got nothing to do with him."

"Good," Jake said. "And the next time you have a problem with your family, I trust you'll take care of it yourself. Not send me or another cop out there to do it for you."

Rex just smiled.

"We're not friends, Rex," Jake said. "We'll never be friends."

"Well now you're just trying to hurt my feelings," Rex said. When Jake kept his gaze, Rex cocked his head to the side. "But to answer your original question ..."

"We're square," Jake said. "You stay on your side of the cage, I'll stay on mine."

"Square," Rex repeated. "No. No, Jake, I don't think we are. I think the crux of it is, you owe me."

"We're done here today," Jake said, starting to rise.

"Don't you wanna know why?" Rex said. He was calm, casual, shooting Jake that knowing half-smile.

"See ya around, Rex," Jake said. He was done with Rex Bardo's games for now.

"You should shake my hand, Detective," Rex said. "That's what gentlemen do. People who don't have beefs with each other."

An odd thing to say. It happened so quickly. But when Rex Bardo shot out his hand, Jake took it. Rex was a bigger man. At least six inches taller than Jake and fifty extra pounds. Jake matched his grip, the two men's hands staying locked for a full second, before Rex pulled away.

When he did, Jake felt a small square of paper in his palm. He closed his fist. When he turned away, Jake slid the paper in his pocket, careful not to let anyone see.

YOU OWE ME.

Rex's words thundered in Jake's ears. He heard it like a mantra, in time with his pulse as he collected his gun from the guards and headed out of the prison and back to his car.

It was only when he got behind the wheel he pulled the paper out. Heart still pounding, he unfolded it. There was a Brown Creek Township address written on it in pencil in a scrawling hand. And a name. Jake blinked twice, making sure he read it right.

Tucker Macon.

FORTY-THREE

The one person Jake knew would have the answers he needed was Frank. Jake took a moment, gripping his steering wheel as he sat parked in the street across from the rundown house on Fayetteville Street. It might have been white once, but now it was a dingy gray with only one black shutter in the front, hanging by a rusted nail and a prayer.

"We're ready when you are," Deputy Malvo said. Landry gave strict orders to Sergeant Hammer. Jake had his pick of field ops for this one. He'd chosen five deputies he trusted.

Jake gave Malvo a nod and stepped out of his vehicle. Malvo and Deputy Fox flanked him as he approached the front door. The car in the driveway was registered to a Christine Pulaski. Same as the name on the deed. She had no tie to the Hilltop Boys as far as Jake could figure.

As they approached, he saw a woman peek through the curtains in the front room. She quickly snapped them back. Jake kept his right hand resting loosely on his holstered weapon. He stepped to the side of the door and knocked.

"Ms. Pulaski," he said. "This is Detective Jake Cashen. We're with the Worthington County Sheriff's Department. Can we talk for a minute?"

Jake gave a silent nod to Malvo and Fox. Malvo signaled to the three other deputies behind him. They took tactical positions around the side of the house.

A neighbor poked her head out next door. An old lady in a yellow house coat. Jake gave her a stern look. She popped back inside.

"Ms. Pulaski?" Jake said.

"Keep your pants on," the woman inside said. Jake heard a series of door chains unlatch. She kept one attached, opening the door to a two-inch crack.

She was in her mid-thirties, maybe, but with an over-tanned, heavily lined face.

"Are you Christine Pulaski?" Jake asked.

"Who's asking?" she said.

Jake held up his badge. "Detective Jake Cashen. You mind stepping outside and having a conversation?"

"It's cold," she said.

"It'll only take a minute," Jake said.

She let out a great sigh, closed the door, and unlatched the final chain. When she opened it again, Christine pulled a terry-cloth robe around her. She stepped out onto the porch, a cigarette dangling in her hand.

"I'm looking for Tucker Macon," Jake said. "I've got information he might be staying with you."

Christine took a drag of her cigarette and flicked the ashes away.

"Says who?" she asked.

Jake pulled out his phone and flipped to a photo of Tucker Macon's mugshot. He held it up to Christine.

"You seen him?" Jake asked.

She took another drag of her cigarette. This time, Christine Pulaski's hands were shaking. She didn't answer.

"You're his girlfriend?" Jake asked.

Still, she didn't answer.

"Christine," Jake said, lowering his voice to a whisper. "If you're in trouble, I can help you. Just tell me, is Tucker here?"

"I haven't seen him," she said; all of a sudden, her voice rose to almost a shout. "But if you see him, you tell that piece of trash he better not ever darken my doorstep again."

When she spoke, she turned her head, making sure her voice carried back inside the house. Beside him, Luke Malvo stiffened. Jake shot him a glance. Something was wrong. Malvo signaled to Deputy Fox. He stepped off the porch and quietly walked to the side of the house.

Jake gestured to Malvo. Malvo moved to his left, casually. There was a large bay window to the side of him. Malvo quietly unsnapped his holster.

Jake locked eyes with Christine. He whispered to her, low, so Malvo wouldn't hear.

"Rex told you I was coming," he said.

Christine's hand trembled so badly, her cigarette barely made it to her lips. She nodded, ever so slightly.

"I told you I haven't seen Tucker," she shouted. Jake put a hand on her arm. He jerked his chin over his shoulder, signaling Christine Pulaski to step away from the door. She locked eyes with Jake. She mouthed two words.

"He's inside."

Jake gave her a subtle nod. Then another to Malvo. The rest of the team moved quietly in position at the back and sides of the house. "Where," Jake mouthed to Christine. "How many?"

She quickly shook her head.

"You mind if we take a look around anyway?" Jake said to her.

"I mind if you don't got a warrant," Christine said, but she was nodding.

Jake pushed her behind him. He drew his weapon but held it low. Malvo did the same. Jake slowly pushed the door open, standing off to the side of it. Malvo took a position on the other side.

Jake counted down with his fingers. One. Two. Three.

"Mr. Macon!" Jake shouted. "We know you're in there. This is Detective Jake Cashen. I'm going to need you to show yourself. Hands where I can see them."

"He's in the back bedroom!" Christine shouted. Another deputy had come around the front. Christine ran toward him, hair flying. He grabbed her and pulled her down the sidewalk then behind the nearest cruiser.

"Tucker?" Jake shouted. The house was dark. They entered into a living room, a small kitchen off to the side. There was just one hallway off the back of it.

Jake brought his weapon up, holding it close to his chest. He scanned the four corners of the kitchen while Malvo cleared the living room. Then the two of them flanked either side of the hallway. Jake saw three doors. Probably a bathroom and two bedrooms. If Christine were telling the truth, he expected to find Tucker Macon hiding in the one farthest down the hall.

"Tucker?" Jake said. "There's no place to go. I've got deputies all around the house. We just want to talk to you."

Deadly silence. Jake and Malvo kept their backs to the wall, and started their slow approach to the first bedroom. Malvo gave a signal, the other deputies kicked in the back door.

"Come on, Tucker," Jake said.

They'd reached the first door. He looked at Malvo. A slight nod. They were both ready.

Jake pushed it open, then dropped low. Malvo went in. It took less than two seconds, but Malvo shouted, "Clear!"

The other deputies went down a basement doorway. Jake held his breath, holding his position. Time seemed to stand still. Finally, he heard an "All clear!" from the basement.

Then something happened. A shuffling sound. Not from the back bedroom, but from the door between him and Malvo.

"Behind you!" Jake shouted.

The door blew open. The shotgun blast nearly deafened Jake. He'd dropped to one knee, aiming toward the sound. Everything seemed to happen in slow motion then.

Malvo turned. Three deputies ran up from the basement when they heard the shots ring out. Jake saw the double barrels emerging through the smoke. He fired, emptying his magazine. Jake's shots hit Tucker Macon square in the chest. He jerked and danced for a moment, still holding on to his shotgun. Malvo and the other deputies fired too. Later, they would recover fourteen rounds out of Tucker Macon's body. There'd be no official determination as to who fired the kill shot.

There wouldn't have to be. Jake knew. When Tucker Macon met Jake Cashen's eyes in that final instant before he pulled the trigger, he knew he was his executioner.

Forty-Four

"Smile," Landry said beside him. Jake wanted to be anywhere else. She stepped in front of him, looked him up and down, then straightened his tie.

"This is your thing, not mine," he said. When she licked her finger and moved to smooth down his hair, Jake stepped out of her reach.

"Quit it," he said.

"Five minutes," she said. "Ten tops. Let Mayor Devlin and the county commissioners get their little photo up, then you can finish the rest of your vacation."

"I don't need this, Landry," he said. "You're the sheriff. I work for you. Take the credit. I don't need a damn plaque."

"Listen to me, Jake," she said. "What you need is to be the public face of this investigation. You solved Judge Rand's murder. You put an end to the Papatonis' nightmare and apprehended Tucker Macon."

"Dead isn't apprehended," Jake said.

"Same thing," she argued. "Nobody else could find him. You did. If it weren't for you, he'd still be at large."

"But Frank still is," Jake said.

"Doesn't matter," she said. "Take the win."

"I hate this."

"Quit your bitching," Landry said. "The bigger the circus, the better I can keep the monkeys busy."

"I don't think that's how that saying goes," Jake said.

"Listen to me," she said. "Right now, you're the Attorney General's favorite cop. So go get your picture taken beside him. Let it be plastered on the front page of the *Columbus Dispatch*. This is how I protect you."

"Protect me?"

"Yes," she said. "Your good old Uncle Rob won't be able to convince the rest of the county commissioners to fire you. Right now, that would look too bad. This will take the heat off you from anyone left at the FBI who wants to mess with you. It'll give you cover. It'll give us both cover. At least for a little while."

"You engineered all of this for that?"

Landry smiled. "You're good at solving murders. I'm good at making sure you still can. I know what this case cost you, Jake. I won't forget it. I promise you. As long as I'm sheriff, you have a job."

Jake was touched. At the same time, he couldn't keep the sly grin from his face. "As long as you're sheriff? The way things are going in this county, I'm not sure that's such a good deal for me."

They both laughed. Landry rolled her eyes.

"We're ready for you." Neil, Landry's media liaison, poked his head into her office.

"I'm not talking," Jake said. "You don't want me answering questions."

"That's my job," Landry said. "Come on. And be nice!"

She walked ahead of him while Neil held the door. Growling to himself, he walked behind her.

"You sound like a bear," Landry said as they made their way downstairs in the elevator. They took the side entrance into the tiny little press room that served both the courthouse and the Sheriff's Department.

Lights flashed as Landry and Jake walked in. A press core of about twenty assembled. Most of them had come down from Columbus at the Attorney General's request.

Landry took her place beside the podium as Mayor Devlin adjusted the mic. Jake stood beside Landry, trying to find a neutral expression. He'd be damned if he'd smile. He would at least try not to frown.

Gemma popped up in the back row. She waved frantically at Jake and blew him a kiss. Smart ass, he thought. His sister knew exactly how he felt about being here for this.

"Thank you for coming," Mayor Devlin started. "I'll be brief."

"That's a first," Jake muttered. Landry elbowed him hard in the side.

"The last two months have been very dark for this county. The loss of Judge Sampson Rand will be felt for years, maybe a generation to come. He can never be replaced. It was through the dedication, and tireless efforts of Sheriff Landry and Detective Deputy Jake Cashen that we have a measure of justice today. And finally, after all these years, one of Worthington County's lost daughters can rest easy. On behalf of the mayor's office, I'd like to turn the microphone over to Attorney General Matt Stacy."

Stacy smiled and leaned down. "Thank you," he said. "I'll echo Mayor Devlin's words. Sheriff Landry, Detective Cashen, it's my honor to present you with this Award for Outstanding Service in the field."

He handed the plaque to Landry. She gave it to Jake. The two of them stood side by side holding it as the photographers took their pictures.

Jake found it excruciating. There was one with Attorney General Stacy, one with the mayor. Then, all eight county commissioners lined up on either side of Jake. Rob Arden conveniently chose the farthest spot away from him. That was fine with Jake.

It was not fine with Gemma.

After the official bit was over, she made a beeline for Arden and threw her arms out. "Thank you so much for coming, Uncle Rob," she said, loud enough for a few reporters to hear. Gemma wrangled a befuddled Rob Arden into a new group of photos with Jake, holding the cursed plaque.

Jake turned to leave then stopped cold. He hadn't seen them in the back of the room. They'd stayed quiet, eschewing the chance to be part of the photo ops. It wasn't their style.

"Jake," Tessa Papatonis said. She had tears in her eyes. She held a framed picture in her arms. It was Nina. Her high school senior picture. Spiros held out his hand.

"Spiros," Jake said. "I ..."

"Thank you," Spiros whispered. Then he crumpled into himself. Jake caught him, pulling the man against him into a hug.

"Thank you," Spiros whispered again, his voice ragged, grief worn.

Jake didn't know what to say. What can you say? When Tessa reached for him, Jake held her hand.

"You're welcome," Jake said. Then Spiros let him go. He put his arm around his wife, then the two of them quietly left through the back door, away from all the reporters.

Gemma put her hand on her brother's back. She blinked back tears of her own.

Finally, Landry found him again. She leaned over and whispered to him, "You can escape now. I'll handle the rest of this."

Jake didn't have to be told twice. He held the plaque under his arm and grabbed his sister. If he left her alone too long, she'd start passing out business cards.

"Let's go," he said through gritted teeth.

Heels clacking, she finally let him lead her out of the building.

"I'm proud of you, baby brother," she said. He knew she meant it. Before Jake could slide away, she planted a sloppy kiss on his cheek.

"I love you," she said.

"I love you too."

"Now go change," she said. "Ryan's driving me crazy. This match tonight might very well be the death of me."

"Oh," Jake teased. "We're not going to be that lucky."

"Is he ready?" Gemma asked. She looked nervous. Terrified, actually. "Jake, that St. Iz kid is a monster. I'm scared for Ryan."

"Don't be," Jake said. "He's ready. And I'll be in his corner. Promise."

Gemma nodded. They were already at her car. He hugged her again and handed her the plaque.

"Here," he said. "You keep it. I don't need it."

She ran her fingers over his name then held it to her breast. "I'll put it somewhere safe."

He would have made a suggestion as to where she should keep it. His phone rang. When he pulled it out, he didn't recognize the number, but something told him it was more than spam. He promised Gemma one more time he'd meet her at the gym in a couple of hours. Then, he ducked into the alley and took the call.

"Hey, Jake," Frank Borowski said in that unmistakable gruff voice.

Jake said nothing. He held the phone so tightly against his ear his fingers soon went numb.

"Congratulations," Frank said. "Landry's smart. That little ceremony should give you some job security for a while. If you want it."

Still, Jake said nothing. He could hear Borowski breathing. In the distance, he heard seagulls.

"Jake," Borowski said. "I'm sorry. I really am."

"For which part, Frank?"

"The part where I let you down," Frank said. "I never wanted to lie to you. You're like a son to me."

Jake bit his tongue past the obvious comparison. His own father had been a murderer too.

"You need to come home, Frank," Jake said. "Get a good lawyer. This doesn't have to be the end of your life."

Frank quietly laughed.

"Why are you calling me, Frank?"

"To say goodbye," Frank answered. "And to tell you ... I'm proud of you."

There was a time those words meant everything to Jake. He realized the bitterest truth. They still did.

Frank didn't answer for a moment. "Tell Ryan I'm sorry too. He can win tonight. I'm rooting for him. Make sure he watches for that ankle pick."

"I will," Jake said.

"And make sure he explodes off bottom. That St. Iz kid is tough on top. You were the same way. Nobody could beat you when you exploded."

"I know, Frank," Jake said. "I know."

The line went silent. If it weren't for the seagulls, Jake might have thought Frank was gone.

"Frank," Jake finally said. "You have to know. I won't stop looking for you. And when I do, I'm going to have to bring you in."

Frank let out a breath. "And I'd expect nothing less."

Jake closed his eyes. His voice dropped to a whisper. "Just promise me you'll be hard to find."

FORTY-FIVE

Three hours later, Jake pressed his forehead against Ryan's as the ref waited for him in the center of the mat.

"You know what to do," Jake told his nephew. "You're ready for him. This is your match to win or lose."

Ryan nodded. His chest heaved. He slapped his arms, pumped his fists. When Jake let him go, Ryan bobbed on one heel, then the next.

"Go get him," Jake told him. He took his seat on the folding chair at the corner of the mat next to Coach Purcell.

Ryan wrestled smart. Clean.

At the start of the third period, the score was tied 3–3. Jake knew all Ryan had to do was ride McManus out and send the match into overtime.

Stay on him, Jake thought. *Stay on him!*

Jake flinched as Ryan got too high on the kid. Jake saw it before Ryan did. McManus got the reversal. The ref held up two fingers, putting Jake down 5–3 with fifteen seconds to go.

Fear streaked across Ryan's face as he searched for his uncle on the side of the mat. Jake slapped his hands together. It was his voice, but he heard Coach Frank's words coming out of him. "Ryan!" Jake yelled. "There is time on the clock. You hear me? You have to *explode* off the bottom. Hand control!"

Ryan got into position as McManus curled his arm around Ryan's torso. Jake held tension in his own legs. Ryan shot straight up off the whistle. His hands were a blur of motion, gripping McManus's, immobilizing him. Ryan spun around. The ref shot one finger up. 5–4.

Across the gym, Jake spotted Gemma pacing under the bleachers. She couldn't watch. Jake barely could.

McManus lumbered to the side, sluggish. Stalling. That's when it happened. With Jake shouting for all he was worth, Ryan shot forward as if his legs were on springs. He carved his arm through McManus's legs and lifted him in the perfect arc of a fireman's carry. McManus hit the mat on his back. Ryan curled his body tight as a boa constrictor.

"Squeeze!" Jake shouted. "Squeeze!"

The ref lifted his arm, then brought it down with the force of thunder, calling the pin with two seconds left on the clock.

Jake didn't jump. He didn't cheer. He just hugged his nephew when he came back to the corner.

"Good job," he said. "It's a good start."

Ryan sobbed against him. He held on to his uncle as if he might vanish if he didn't. "I love you. Thank you for being here." Ryan whispered it so low, Jake almost didn't hear it. But he did.

"I love you too," Jake said back.

And then his teammate took the mat, squaring off with the next opponent.

Later, as Jake made his way out of the gym at the end of the match, Gemma found him. For the second time today, she tackled him and laid a kiss on his cheek. They walked out into the parking lot together.

"Ryan will be out in a second," Gemma said. "My friend taped the match."

"Good," Jake laughed. "Maybe you can actually watch it."

"We'll hook it up to Grandpa's television," she said. "He can see it that way if he sits real close."

"He'd like that," Jake said.

Ben Wayne caught up to them. He had a hearty handshake for Jake and tears in his eyes. "He was a beast," Ben said. "Man, it's good having you around."

"It's not so bad being around," Jake said.

Ben narrated a replay of the match as if they all hadn't just been there. It was good. Ben's excitement made Jake happy for a moment.

Ryan walked out beside Coach Purcell. Gemma ran to her son and tackled him, too.

"It was great having you there," Purcell said. "You're a born coach."

"Thanks," Jake said. "But that was all Ryan out there."

"I mean it, Jake," Purcell said. "My offer still stands. We could use you on a permanent basis. The assistant coaching job is yours if you're planning on sticking around and if you want it."

Gemma, Ryan, and Ben all froze, waiting for Jake's answer. He pursed his lips into a smile.

"I think that'd be good for me. I'd be honored for the chance. And yes," he said, directing his words to his sister and nephew. "It looks like I'm sticking around."

Gemma took his hand. She kept holding it as they walked to the truck. He knew she had no plans to let go. Up ahead, Aiden was jumping up and down, hanging out with four other little boys his size.

"He was two hundred and fifty pounds!" Aiden shouted. "They called him the Oak Tree! That's him! The one I was telling you about! That's my uncle over there. Right there with my big brother! His name his Jake Cashen. That makes me famous!"

"Oh boy." Gemma sighed. "Last chance to run for it, baby brother."

He squeezed her hand. "I keep my promises," he said. "And I'm here for good."

"Excellent!" she said. "Grandpa's house needs a new roof. My furnace is on the fritz. Oh ... and you need to teach your nephew how to parallel park. I'm not getting into a car with him again ... he's failed his driving test twice already ..."

Ryan stepped forward, arguing with his mother. There was a party he wanted to go to. She didn't know the parents. Aiden ran up, asking Jake to regale his friends with the epic story of the final seconds of his state championship match for the millionth time. This time, Jake's opponent somehow reached the mythic height of seven feet tall and four hundred pounds of solid muscle. Gemma gave Jake a look, telling him it was pointless to try and reign Aiden in. Behind him, Ben and Brian Purcell were already strategizing for this week's tournament. Travis, Ben's son would have his toughest match of the year.

Jake smiled, listening to all of them, his family, his friends...his people. For the first time in a very long time, Jake welcomed the chaos of home.

One-Click Kill Season - Jake Cashen Book 2 so you don't miss out!

Keep reading for a special preview...

Interested in an exclusive extended prologue to Murder in the Hollows?

Join Declan James's Roll Call Newsletter for a free download.

SPECIAL PREVIEW

KILL SEASON
JAKE CASHEN - BOOK 2

The Following November
Opening Day—Gun Season

A fat red-tail hawk sat in quiet judgment of Ben Wayne as he adjusted his camp chair. It made a small squeak that echoed through the woods. Any movement and the unsuspecting squirrels beneath the hawk's perch on the hickory branch above would spoil the bird's kill. It was bad form on his part, Ben knew. On this crisp November morning, he and the hawk were fellow hunters.

"Sorry," Ben silently mouthed to the bird. He got no more than a slow, unamused blink from the bird's great yellow eye.

Ben refocused his attention on the ravine in front of him. A light northwest wind blew in his face, carrying the scent of wet leaves as the rising sun began to melt the frost from the woods.

In the distance, Ben heard the first shot crack. It came from maybe a half a mile to the east.

"Come on, boy," Ben whispered to himself. His son Travis sat perched in a blind up that way. Ben reached down to make sure his phone was silenced. If the shot was Travis's, and he'd bagged his deer already, the kid would blow up Ben's phone and ruin any chance he had of bagging his own buck before lunch.

Travis had been antsier than usual this morning. He'd had bad luck last year and hadn't shot a buck since he was fourteen. Travis was also at the age where he knew everything and to him, his father had suddenly become an idiot.

Ben smiled to himself. Travis had a growth spurt this summer. He was all gangly muscle and headstrong attitude. But he was becoming a beast. He'd have his first varsity wrestling match against a state contender next week. Ben knew Travis would give the kid something to be scared of. He couldn't wait to see it.

The hawk went airborne as Ben heard a crash of leaves. Something was moving. He kept his twelve-gauge ready at hand. Through the trees, a young, six-point buck ran directly toward him. The deer skidded to a stop in front of Ben, aware of him. His ears pricked as Ben and the deer made eye contact.

He was beautiful with a perfectly symmetrical rack that would be a shooter in another year. Ben eased up on his gun. The deer lowered his head as if in understanding and gratitude. Then he vaulted out of view.

Behind him, the leaves crunched and scattered. With the hawk gone, the squirrels got even braver. Ben looked over his left shoulder, ready to watch them for a moment.

He never heard the next shot. It entered his right temple, carving its fatal path through his brain and out the other side.

Ben felt nothing before he died. He saw only a flash of lightning behind his eyes before slumping slowly to the ground for the last time. High above Ben's lifeless body, the hawk's piercing screech cut through the air.

There's a killer on the loose deep in the back woods of Blackhand Hills. When someone close to Jake falls prey, the line between justice and vengeance becomes razor thin. Don't miss Kill Season, Book 2 in the Jake Cashen Crime Thriller Series. To learn more, click the book's cover or here: https://declanjamesbooks.com/KS

CLICK TO LEARN MORE

Acknowledgments

I have a long list of people to thank for their help and support in the writing of this book. First and foremost, to my wife, kids and family. To my brothers and sisters in blue. Most especially, the Coffee Club members. To Dave, Chip, George, Greg, Duane, Rick, and Janet. And to those who have gone before me and to those who have fallen. We've got the watch from here.

About the Author

Before putting pen to paper, Declan James's career in law enforcement spanned twenty-six years. Declan's work as a digital forensics detective has earned him the highest honors from the U.S. Secret Service and F.B.I. For the last sixteen years of his career, Declan served on a nationally recognized task force aimed at protecting children from online predators. Prior to that, Declan spent six years undercover working Vice-Narcotics.

An avid outdoorsman and conservationist, Declan enjoys hunting, fishing, grilling, smoking meats, and his quest for the perfect bottle of bourbon. He lives on a lake in Southern Michigan along with his wife and kids. Declan James is a pseudonym.

For more information follow Declan at one of the links below. If you'd like to receive new release alerts, author news, and a FREE digital bonus prologue to Murder in the Hollows, sign up for Declan's Roll Call Newsletter here: https://declanjamesbooks.com/rollcall/

Also by Declan James

Murder in the Hollows

Kill Season

With more to come...

Stay in Touch with Declan James

For more information, visit

https://declanjamesbooks.com

If you'd like to receive a free digital copy of the extended prologue to Murder in the Hollows, sign up for Declan James's Roll Call Newsletter here: https://declanjamesbooks.com/rollcall/

Made in the USA
Middletown, DE
04 January 2024

47188891R00227